BLACKFLEET BROAD

A DCI Tanner Mystery
- Book Fourteen -

DAVID BLAKE

www.david-blake.co.uk

Proofread by Jay G Arscott

Special thanks to Kath Middleton, Ann Studd, John Harrison, Anna Burke, Emma Stubbs, and Jan Edge

Published by Black Oak Publishing Ltd, Design House, 40 Walmington Fold, London, N12 7LL, in Great Britain, 2025

Disclaimer:
These are works of fiction. Names, characters, businesses, places, events and incidents are either the products of the author's imagination or used in a fictitious manner. Any resemblance to actual persons, living or dead, or actual events is purely coincidental.

Copyright © David Blake 2025

The right of David Blake to be identified as the Author of the Work has been asserted by him in accordance with the Copyright, Designs and Patents Act 1998. All rights reserved. This book is for your enjoyment only. No part of this publication may be reproduced, distributed, or transmitted in any form or by any means, including photocopying, recording, or other electronic or mechanical methods, without the prior written permission of the copyright owner except in the case of brief quotations embodied in critical reviews and certain other non-commercial uses permitted by copyright law.

All rights reserved.

Cover Photograph ID 151139030 © Gary Rayner | Dreamstime.com

ISBN: 978-1-7385418-3-6

DEDICATION

For Akiko, Akira and Kai.

THE DCI TANNER SERIES

Broadland
St. Benet's
Moorings
Three Rivers
Horsey Mere
The Wherryman
Storm Force
Long Gore Hall
Weavers' Way
Bluebell Wood
Swanton Morley
Stokesby Grave
The Bastwick Testament
Blackfleet Broad

"Thou scarest me with dreams, and terrifiest me through visions."
Job 7:14

- PROLOGUE -

Monday, 15th June

DEREK EDWARDS CLIMBED wearily out of his car to gaze about. 'Where the hell is he?' he muttered quietly to himself, glancing down at his watch. 'We were supposed to meet at five, not at what is now nearly twenty bloody past.'

Seeing a pair of dull yellow headlights swing into Blackfleet Broad's otherwise deserted car park, he ground his teeth. 'About bloody time,' he muttered, stomping around to the back of his car.

Opening the boot as the car pulled up beside his, he called out to the driver, 'What sort of time do you call this?'

'Sorry I'm late,' said a slim, handsome middle-aged man, climbing out to present Edwards with a guilty frown.

'We said five – at the latest!' Derek continued, heaving a holdall out from the back of the car.

'I had to stop for petrol,' the man replied, closing the door behind him.

'Couldn't you have filled up last night?'

'I didn't have a chance. Besides, it's only just gone ten past.'

'No, it's nearly twenty past,' Derek said, staring

again at his watch. 'Actually, it *is* twenty past! I've been waiting here for over twenty minutes!'

'No offence, Derek, but you're the one who always wants to meet up so early. I'd be quite happy going in the afternoon.'

'No offence, Mark, but you don't go fishing in the afternoon, not if you expect to catch an actual fish.'

'I think you'll find plenty of people do,' Mark countered, pulling a similar-sized bag from the back seat of his car.

'I'm sure they do, but that doesn't mean they catch anything, though, does it!'

'Do you want to go or not?' Mark demanded. 'I can go home, if you like?'

'You're here now, so we may as well. Besides, I didn't only want to go fishing,' Derek added, hoisting his holdall onto his shoulder.

'I'm not sure what else we'll be doing in a boat in the middle of a broad – unless you fancy a spot of birdwatching?'

'There's something I want to talk to you about.'

'That sounds ominous.'

When Derek didn't reply, Mark added, 'It's not another one of your so-called business ideas, I hope. Because, if it is, I can't afford it.'

'Are you coming, or not?' asked Derek, locking his car to glare back at the man who'd been his best mate since college.

'Alright, alright. I'd hate to keep the fish waiting,' Mark muttered, trudging after him as Derek began marching away.

It wasn't until they'd reached the end of a creaking jetty to start climbing aboard an old wooden rowing boat tied at the end that Mark spoke again.

'Any idea where we should go?'

'I'm not sure it matters,' Derek grumbled, glancing over his shoulder to see a band of orange light stretching across the horizon. 'By the time we get there, the sun will be up.'

'Honestly, Derek, does it really matter?'

'The fish will be able to see us, so yes, of course it bloody matters!'

'Why's that? Are you worried they'll recognise you?'

'Don't be stupid,' Derek muttered, untying the painter to push the boat out.

'Perhaps they've got posters up of you,' Mark continued, gesturing down at the water, 'warning their fellow fishy friends to be on the lookout for a fat, bald-headed man with a fishing rod.'

'Isn't it your turn to row?' asked Derek, deliberately ignoring him.

'I thought I'd let you, given you're the one who's supposed to be losing weight.'

'Then you can bait the hooks. I've brought some deliciously enticing maggots for us.'

Mark turned his nose up at the contents of a small round tin that Derek was holding out for him. 'You know I hate doing that.'

'Then I suggest you start rowing.'

'I'm still waiting for you to tell me where to go.'

'Tell you what, how about we try the middle? I'm fairly sure that's where all the fish will be.'

'Probably queuing up, wondering why we're so late,' Mark chuckled, heaving the boat around with the oars.

'And whose fault's that?'

'My car's, for not having a bigger fuel tank.'

'Nothing's ever your fault, is it?' said Derek, fixing

him with an accusatory glare.

'That's probably because I've never done anything wrong,' Mark replied, flashing a sardonic grin as he pulled easily on the oars.

'Which reminds me of what I wanted to talk to you about.'

'Oh God. What have I done now?'

'I thought I saw you the other day.'

'Well done.'

'Coming out of that new restaurant, in Wroxham.'

Derek's remark left Mark unusually silent as he continued rowing them towards the middle of the broad.

'I wasn't sure it was you,' Derek continued, 'but there was someone with you I *did* recognise. My wife!'

'Then you must have mistaken me for someone else.'

'So it wasn't you, then?'

'I've never been to that restaurant, so it couldn't have been.'

'Oh, right,' Derek said, reaching inside his holdall to pull out a digital SLR camera. 'So you didn't go there the day before either, around lunchtime?'

'As I said, I've never been. Certainly not at lunchtime.'

'Because I could've sworn I saw you then as well, once again with my wife,' Derek continued, his eyes gazing down at the camera. 'You were walking together, holding hands, to a car that looked remarkably like yours. It even had the same number plate. You then stopped to start kissing each other before climbing in. Then I called your mobile, which you pulled out to stare at, before declining to answer. I then had the pleasure of watching you drive off to a Travelodge, not to come out again until gone five. I even took some pictures,' he added, glancing up. 'Would you like to see them?'

Mark stopped rowing to rest the oars on his knees. As the boat glided gently through the still water, he lifted his eyes to meet his friend's antagonistic glare. 'Listen, Derek, I'm sorry – but – it wasn't my fault.'

'Yes, I know,' Derek replied, tears pooling at the corners of his eyes. 'It never is.'

'She came on to me at an office party and – well – we were both a bit drunk, I suppose.'

'So you decided to have sex?'

'We didn't decide to. It just sort of happened.'

'Were you drunk when I saw you on Friday. The day before that, as well?'

Derek's question left Mark staring down at his hands as the boat rocked gently beneath them.

'Are you going to answer?' Derek demanded, his voice breaking with emotion.

'No, Derek, we weren't drunk. Not then.'

'Dare I ask how long it's been going on for?'

'Not long.'

'Not long – as in a few days?'

'Does it matter?'

As an unsettling silence fell over the boat, Derek wiped angrily at an escaping tear. 'Do you love her?'

'Honestly, Derek, it's nothing like that.'

'What is it, then?'

'You know – it's just...'

'What – sex?'

'Well, yes, I suppose it is.'

'You still haven't answered my question.'

'I'm sorry, Derek. Which question was that?'

'How long have you been having sex with my wife?'

'I thought I said.'

'You said it doesn't matter, when I can assure you it most definitely does.'

'I really can't remember.'

'You mentioned an office party?'

'Well, yes, but...'

'But what?'

Mark stared out over the water as the sun broke free of the horizon, setting fire to the sky above with a blazing red. 'As I said, it doesn't matter.'

Derek narrowed his tear-stained eyes. 'That night of our engagement party – when I saw the two of you coming out of that hotel room. You weren't...?'

Mark's eyes dropped to the water.

'You fucking bastard!'

'I'm sorry, Derek. I never meant to hurt you.'

'You're seriously telling me that you've been screwing my wife since before we were married – but that you're sorry – and you never meant to hurt me?'

'You weren't married then. She was fair game.'

Derek's breathing grew heavier, his knuckles whitening as he gripped the edge of the boat. 'Fair game?' he repeated, his voice becoming an ominous whisper. 'She was my fiancée. The woman I was about to commit my life to. How the hell does that make her "fair game"?'

'I didn't mean it like that. I...' Mark's words caught in his throat. 'Look, I know I screwed up,' he went on, daring to meet Derek's furious gaze. 'I didn't exactly plan for this to happen.'

'You didn't plan?' Derek spat, clenching his fists as he rose to his feet. 'You've spent five years screwing her behind my back. How could that not have been planned?'

As the boat rocked sharply, Mark grabbed the

gunnels. 'Derek, sit down! You're going to tip us over.'

'What do I care? I've lost everything because of you!'

'Look, I understand that you're angry –'

'Angry?' Derek shouted, his voice echoing over the water. 'Do you have any idea what it feels like to find out your best mate – the one person you thought you could trust – has been screwing his wife behind his back since before they even got married?'

'What do you want me to say, Derek? That I'm a terrible person? Fine. I've been selfish and stupid. But I meant what I said – I never wanted to hurt you. Neither of us did.'

Derek threw his head back to laugh at the burning sky above. 'You didn't want to hurt me? Well, you fucked that up,' he growled, glaring back. 'You haven't only hurt me – you've fucking destroyed me!'

As the boat rocked violently beneath them, Mark lifted himself off the seat, desperate to steady it – only to see Derek's fist come flying towards him.

Ducking just in time, Mark watched as Derek's wayward punch spun him all the way around, knocking him off balance to send him spiralling overboard.

'Derek!' Mark bellowed, scrambling to the edge, only to see his friend's head vanish beneath the turbulent water.

'Jesus Christ – DEREK!' he screamed, his heart pounding as he frantically searched the surface.

Remembering his best friend couldn't swim, he tore off his coat, ready to throw himself in. But as he leaned over the edge, he froze. Through the murky troubled depths he saw a face – but it wasn't Derek's, gasping for air. It was a pale, beautiful young woman, staring up at him with an unsettling awe.

Certain he must be imagining it, he shook his head

and closed his eyes. But when he dared to look again, she was still there, gazing up at him with an enticing smile.

As he watched her lips move, shaping his name like an unspoken whisper, he stumbled back. Catching a foot against one of the oars, his head struck the side of the boat with a sickening crack, leaving the world spinning into darkness around him.

- CHAPTER ONE -

WITH HIS ELBOWS resting on his kitchen's breakfast bar, John Tanner took a series of tentative sips from his first coffee of the day whilst staring bleary-eyed at his laptop's login screen.

Hearing something move near the door, he glanced around to see Christine creeping slowly up behind him, looking every bit like a pregnant zombie.

As she leaned over his shoulder to kiss him lightly on the cheek, she continued on to the kitchen before eventually saying, 'You're up early.'

'I didn't sleep well,' Tanner muttered, tapping in his laptop's four-digit login code to be immediately presented with his burgeoning email inbox.

'You didn't have that dream again?' Christine asked, washing her hands in the sink.

'Uh-huh,' came Tanner's monosyllabic response.

'Isn't that the third night in a row?'

'I haven't been counting.'

'Was it exactly the same?'

'Pretty much.'

'Then don't you think it's time you told me what happens?'

'For you to psychoanalyse me, before calling Forrester to let him know I'm in urgent need of counselling? Er... no thanks.'

'Don't be silly, John. I'm hardly going to tell your boss that you're suffering from Post-Traumatic Stress

Disorder just because you've had a few bad dreams. Besides, I don't know his phone number.'

'Anyway,' said Tanner, taking another sip from his coffee as he scrolled through his seemingly endless unopened emails with a distinct lack of interest in what any of them were about, 'I can barely remember it now.'

'What *can* you remember?' she asked, drying her hands whilst leaning back against the kitchen counter to stare at him.

Faced with the prospect of either opening some of the more urgent-looking emails, putting on his tie to leave for work, or spending ten minutes telling his wife about his dreams, he let out a reluctant sigh. 'Just between you and me?' he asked, glancing up to meet her penetrating gaze.

'Does that mean I can't film our conversation to post on YouTube?'

'Seriously, Christine. I don't need HQ on my back just because I've been having a few bad dreams.'

'Of course it'll be between you and me. You don't really think I'm going to derail your career two months before I'm due to give birth to our second child?'

'You're going to give birth to our second child?' Tanner asked, staring at Christine's bulging abdomen with a look of perplexed apprehension.

'Sorry, I thought I'd mentioned it.'
'But – that was months ago!'
'These things do take time.'
'What about the other one?'
'The other what?'
'The other baby?'
'I think the idea is that we'll have two.'
'Two!' Tanner exclaimed. 'What do we want two

for?'

'I told you before – so they can keep each other company.'

'You still haven't answered my question.'

'Which was?'

'Where are we going to keep two babies?'

'Don't worry. I've already made space for them in the cupboard.'

'That's a relief. For a minute there I thought I was going to have to put up with two of them crawling around on the floor. One's been bad enough. I keep having to check behind me every time I turn around, just in case I tread on it.'

'OK, enough of the baby talk. Can we move the conversation back to your dream?'

'And there was me trying to steer the conversation away from it.'

'Just tell me what happened, John. I promise you'll feel better for it.'

'I will?'

'Well, probably not, but at least I'll know what's on your mind the next time you wake up screaming.'

With Tanner's attention returning to his emails, he heard Christine ask, 'Why don't you tell me how they start?'

Seeing an email arrive from Forrester entitled "URGENT", he closed the lid of his laptop to let out a heavy sigh. 'By me walking into someone's bedroom,' he began, 'only it isn't me – at least it doesn't feel like it is. It feels more like I'm seeing the room through someone else's eyes.'

He stopped to take a sip from his coffee.

'What happens then?' Christine prompted.

'There's a girl on a bed.'

'You didn't say it's one of *those* dreams,' she said, shaking her head as she filled the kettle.

'I know her,' Tanner continued, 'but I don't – if that makes any sense.'

'Not really, but go on.'

'I start shouting at her, saying horrible things. Then she starts crying, only I don't care. It's almost as if I want her to. Then I step inside and – well – I'm not sure I want to tell you the rest.'

'You've started now,' said Christine, switching the kettle on, 'so you may as well finish.'

Tanner took another sip before continuing. 'As I close the door behind me, she jumps up, her eyes smudged with mascara, and starts screaming at me. That's when I hit her, and I don't stop until she's lying on the floor, her face covered in blood.'

As the kettle began to boil, Christine leaned back against the counter. 'And then you wake up?'

Tanner shook his head. 'The next thing I know, her head's underwater and I'm holding it there, watching her plead for me to let her come up. But I don't. I keep her there as her body starts convulsing, her eyes never leaving mine. I hold her down until she becomes completely still, her body floating just beneath the surface, her lifeless eyes still staring into mine. Then I wake up – only to find she's lying beside me, the skin of her rotting face hanging from her jaws while her translucent green eyes keep boring into mine.

'It's only when she blinks that I wake up screaming.'

As the kettle clicked off, the room fell into an uneasy silence.

'Having heard all that,' Christine breathed, 'I can see why you do.'

'Am I mad, Doc?' Tanner asked. 'Have I finally lost my marbles?'

'No, dear. It's just a particularly nasty dream.

To be honest, with your job, I'm surprised you don't have more.'

'But it feels so real.'

'Don't they always?'

'Never anything like this. And it's always the same. Even the girl. And when I'm having it, I know her, but the moment I wake up – properly wake up – I can never remember who she is.'

'Would you like my advice?' asked Christine, pulling a mug from a cupboard.

'Not really.'

'That you ask to see a psychologist.'

'No surprises there.'

'I'm not just saying that because I used to be one,' Christine shot back. 'It's quite normal these days, especially in your line of work.'

'I'm fine. As you said, it's just a dream.'

'Er, no, John, it's a recurring nightmare. The fact that it's so vivid and feels so real points to the possibility that it's related to Post-Traumatic Stress Disorder.'

'I thought people with PTSD dreamt about whatever had traumatised them. I can assure you I've never beaten up a girl. I've certainly never drowned one!'

'PTSD takes different forms. I'm not saying you have it, but I wouldn't be surprised if you do – even in a mild form. Either way, talking about some of the more troubling experiences you've had wouldn't do you any harm. Seeking help isn't a sign of weakness. You do know that, don't you?'

'I never said it was!'

'Then why are you always so against it?'

'Because I honestly don't think I need it.'

'Which is why you're having a recurring nightmare about beating a girl half to death before drowning her?'

Tanner opened his mouth to respond, only to close it again. She was right, of course. He couldn't remember the last time he'd had a proper night's sleep, and while this series of recurring nightmares might have been the first of their kind, it wasn't as if he hadn't had them before. Over the years he'd been plagued by them. They'd just never been bad enough to wake him up screaming – or to make him question his sanity.

'I'll think about it,' he said at last, taking another sip just as his phone began to ring.

'This better not be bloody work,' he moaned, picking it up.

Seeing it was Vicky, he raised an eyebrow to answer. 'Morning, Vicky! Let me guess – you've broken down and need a lift into work?'

'Sorry, boss, I've just had a call from the office. There's been a report of a boating accident.'

'Whereabouts?' asked Tanner, draining his cup.

'Blackfleet Broad. Sounds like someone fell out of a fishing boat and drowned.'

Her words sent a jolt running along his spine.

As his dream came surging back into life, his mind spun to the point where he had to grab hold of the breakfast bar to steady himself.

Struggling to separate his dream from reality, he took a moment to stare breathlessly down at the floor.

'Are you still there?' came Vicky's voice through the tiny speaker.

Relieved to see Christine preoccupied at the counter, he drew in a calming breath. 'Yes, sorry Vicky. I'm still here.'

'I was just wondering if I should meet you there?'

'Where was it again?'

'Blackfleet Broad. Do you know it?'

'Never heard of it, but I can look it up on my satnav.'

'You're sure? You're on my way – I can pick you up if it's easier?'

'Don't worry, I'll be fine.'

'Then I'll see you there?'

'OK, but I might be a few minutes late.'

About to hang up, he stopped where he was. 'Vicky – sorry – before you go – the person who drowned – was it a man or a woman?'

'It's a man,' she replied. 'Why?'

'No reason,' Tanner said, ending the call.

Placing the phone back on the counter, he closed his eyes to steady himself – only to see the woman's face from his dream, still gazing up at him from some murky depth.

- CHAPTER TWO -

HALF AN HOUR later, Tanner turned into a car park signposted Blackfleet Broad, only to be brought to a halt by a vaguely familiar young police officer, who stepped in front of his car before circling round to the window.

'Bloody idiot,' Tanner muttered quietly to himself whilst winding it down.

'I'm sorry, sir,' the young man began, not even bothering to look at Tanner's face, 'but I can't let you through.'

'What are you talking about?'

'There's been an incident, I'm afraid,' he continued, staring vacantly about, 'which means we're unable to allow members of the public into the car park.'

'But I'm not a member of the public, though, am I!'

Turning to look at Tanner for the first time, the constable's mouth fell open as his face turned bright red.

'I'm sorry, b-b-boss,' he stuttered, as Tanner continued to glare at him as if he were a complete imbecile. 'It's your car – you see – I didn't recognise it.'

'Then perhaps it might be an idea to look to see who's behind the wheel before making a judgement as to who can and who cannot enter a crime scene!'

'Yes, of course, boss,' he said, standing to attention. 'It won't happen again.'

'I should hope not,' Tanner muttered quietly to himself, winding up his window to continue on.

Seeing Vicky's car parked between an ambulance and a group of New Age Traveller types, with no sign of her, he pulled up beside it to climb wearily out – only to find her still inside, using her rear-view mirror to apply some lipstick.

Rapping his knuckles on the glass, he watched her glance up at him with surprise before quickly climbing out.

'Sorry, boss,' she said, reaching back inside to grab her handbag. 'I didn't see you arrive.'

'Neither did that idiot at the entrance,' he muttered, gesturing over at him with his chin – only to find Vicky staring at his car.

'What on earth is that?' she demanded, staring at the vehicle beside him with her mouth hanging open.

'It's my new car!' he announced, turning to cast a proud eye over it.

'Not seriously?'

'Yes, seriously. Why, what's wrong with it?'

'But – it's even older than your other one.'

'Only by a few years.'

'What is it, anyway?'

'Don't you know?'

'Well, no, but only because it must have rolled out of the factory before factories had even been invented. Was it built before the First World War, or back when Sir Francis Drake saw the Spanish Armada drifting over the horizon?'

'It's a Triumph Stag!'

'And that's a thing, is it?'
'Of course it's a thing!'
'Does it work?
'Most of the time.'
'What happened to your XJS? I used to love that car!'
'No you didn't.'
'OK, maybe I didn't – but it's got to be better than that. Actually, that's not true. *Anything's* got to be better than that.'
'I'll have you know the Triumph Stag is a much-admired classic British sports car.'
'But – it's yellow!'
Tanner turned to look at it. 'I'll admit, the colour wasn't my first choice, but it was all I could find at short notice.'
'You still haven't told me what happened to your other one.'
'Unfortunately, the sills went.'
'You mean the windowsills?'
'The ones under the car. They'd been on their last legs for ages. With those, and the wheel bearings, the brakes, the electrics, and just about everything else, it was time to move on.'
'So you thought it would be a good idea to buy a Triumph Antelope instead?'
'It's called a Stag, young Vicky.'
'I'm not sure it makes much difference. I'm still going to have to put up with everyone in Norfolk watching me being driven around in something that looks like an old man's prehistoric wet dream – probably while thinking I'm your girlfriend.'
'If it's any consolation, it has a satnav, so at least you won't have to give me directions anymore.'
'It actually has a built-in satnav?'
'Well – no. It's the one I kept in the XJS's

glovebox.'

'I thought Christine didn't like you using it?'

'Only when she's in the car. But when she saw what I'd bought, I thought I might as well dig it out.'

'I assume that's because she said she wouldn't be seen dead being driven around in it.'

'Something like that.'

'I know how she feels,' Vicky lamented, staring at it as if taking in a piece at a modern art exhibition, wondering if it was part of the collection or if it had been left there by accident. 'I like the wheels,' she added eventually.

'Really?' asked Tanner.

'No – they're hideous, just like the rest of it.'

'Don't worry, it'll grow on you.'

'You mean like chlamydia?'

'In a good way,' Tanner clarified.

'Chlamydia grows on you in a good way – at least it does when you first get it.'

'Perhaps we should move the subject along to why we're here?'

'Sounds good to me,' Vicky replied, turning away from the car with a relieved grimace.

'Which leads to my first question,' Tanner continued.

'I suppose you're wondering how long it'll be until you break down.'

'I was actually wondering who the New Age Travellers were,' he said, gesturing towards them. 'For some reason, they look familiar.'

'They were here when we arrived. They were about to start some sort of protest, but now that we're here, they've decided to wait for their illustrious leader before deciding if it's worth continuing.'

'Dare I ask what they'd be protesting about?'

'The broad's due to be drained.'

'Not another bloody housing development?'

'Apparently, it's part of an archaeological dig. Something about a Viking burial ground.'

'And where's the more recent body?'

'Still in the water. A dive team arrived at the same time I did. I'll take you through to where they're setting up.'

- CHAPTER THREE -

FOLLOWING A LITTLE-USED path through a small clump of trees, they emerged to find Blackfleet Broad stretching out before them, its tranquil surface broken only by a single orange inflatable dinghy, buzzing away from a lopsided jetty with two divers perched on either side.

'Are you Detective Chief Inspector Tanner?' called a tall, thin man with closely cropped grey hair and a military bearing, standing amid half a dozen half-open carryalls filled with diving equipment.

'On a good day,' Tanner replied, leading Vicky towards him.

'I'm Sergeant Woodruff. My boys have just gone to see if they can find the poor chap who drowned.'

'So I saw,' Tanner replied, gazing after them as the dinghy glided to a halt. 'Do they have any idea where to look?'

'The person who reported the incident said he thought they were somewhere near the middle, so we thought we'd start there.'

'And where is he?' Tanner asked, glancing about.

'Probably still in the back of the ambulance.'

'Did he tell you what happened?'

'He said he was knocked unconscious when he fell back inside the boat, just after his mate went over the side – which is why he couldn't save him.'

A distant splash had them all turn to see one of the

divers' heads break the surface, glance briefly about, then duck back under.

'I don't suppose you've any idea how long it'll take to find the body?'

'Not a clue, I'm afraid. Sometimes it takes hours; other times we find them pretty much straight away. It generally depends on how clear the water is, and how accurate the information was about their whereabouts.'

Wondering if it was worth speaking to the witness while they waited, Tanner was about to suggest the idea to Vicky when the sergeant's two-way radio crackled into life.

'Sarge, are you there, over?'

Lifting the radio in his hand, Woodruff looked across the broad at his men to see the one still in the dinghy gazing back.

'Go ahead, Gates.'

'We think we've found him.'

Nodding with satisfaction, Woodruff replied, 'Do you think you'll need help bringing him in?'

'We should be alright, but there's a slight complication.'

Woodruff raised an intrigued eyebrow at Tanner before repressing the button. 'Go on.'

'There's another body,' came the man's voice, crackling with heavy static.

'Sorry, Gates. Can you repeat that?'

'We've found another body,' Gates said once again, 'and it looks like one's managed to get itself tangled up with the other.'

'OK, hold on,' said Woodruff, turning to present Tanner with a questioning frown. 'Sounds like we've found two people for you to take a look at. Do you want us to bring them both in, or would you rather see them for yourself first?'

A quick glance at Vicky had Tanner turning back. 'Under the circumstances, it may be better if we take a quick look before you do.'

- CHAPTER FOUR -

AS THE INFLATABLE dinghy was spun around to begin skipping over the water towards them, Tanner and Vicky each donned a buoyancy aid whilst making their way to the end of the jetty.

Meeting the dinghy there, they were soon being blasted over the surface towards where the diver's head could be seen, marking the spot where the bodies had been found.

As the driver eased off the throttle, they approached the submerged diver at a more leisurely pace, until Tanner eventually called out, 'DCI Tanner and my colleague, DI Gilbert. You say you've found two bodies?'

'A man and a woman,' the diver nodded. 'The woman's body is being held underneath by a length of rope attached to a mud weight at the bottom. It looks like the other one got his foot caught around it when he went in.'

'Is the woman young or old?' Tanner cautiously enquired, as they inched ever closer.

'You can take a look for yourself,' the diver replied, taking hold of the dinghy as it came drifting towards him.

Taking a nervous breath, Tanner stared cautiously over the side to find himself gazing into the mesmerising eyes of a serenely beautiful young woman – just as she had been during his so recent dreams.

As the nightmare began to unravel itself inside his mind once more, he closed his eyes to feel himself spin around and around, before spiralling down into a never-ending chasm, until he was surrounded by the static silence of all-consuming blackness.

- CHAPTER FIVE -

BLINKING HIS EYES open, Tanner found himself lying on a grassy bank with one of the boat's divers staring down at him with a concerned frown.

'Are you alright, mate?' the man enquired, as Tanner glanced vacantly about. 'You gave us quite a scare.'

Seeing Vicky talking to the grey-haired sergeant at the end of the jetty, he tried pushing himself up, only for his head to spin once again.

'If I were you, mate,' the diver continued, 'I'd stay where you are – at least until a paramedic can check you over.'

'I'm fine,' Tanner replied, waiting a moment for the dizziness to pass. 'Did anything happen with those bodies?' he added, in a deliberate attempt to take the focus off himself while pushing himself up.

'Don't worry, they're not going anywhere. We thought we'd better carry you back to shore before bringing them in. Are you sure you're OK?'

'I'm fine!' Tanner repeated, his tone tinged with embarrassed irritation. 'Seeing that woman's face under the water was just a bit of a shock, that's all.'

'If you say so,' the diver said, helping Tanner to his feet.

'How long will it take for you to bring them in?'

'I assume you're happy for us to do so?'

'There's not much we can do with them out there,' came Tanner's terse response.

'Fair enough,' he shrugged. 'If we head out now, we should have them both in within a few minutes.'

'Then if you could push on, I'd be grateful.'

Watching him turn to make his way along the jetty to the dinghy moored at the end, Tanner saw Vicky heading towards him from the other direction.

'I've spoken to forensics,' she called out. 'Dr Johnstone, as well.'

'Aren't you going to ask if I'm OK?'

'I didn't think there was much point,' she replied, offering him a stoic frown. 'You'd have only said, "I'm fine", while glaring at me with unappreciative dispassion.'

'I might have said something else.'

'Like what?'

'Like... I'm feeling much better, thank you for asking.'

'That would've been a first,' she laughed.

'Actually, you're right. When the diver asked me, I said exactly what you said I would. How long was I out for?' he continued, glancing down at his watch.

'Only as long as it took to drive the boat back to the jetty and then carry you here,' Vicky replied, looking around to see the boat in question making its way back out into the middle of the broad.

'That's not so bad.'

'Really?' she replied, staring back. 'So, how long do you normally pass out for?'

'That depends on how much I've had to drink.'

'But you're not drunk, though, are you.'

'Well, no, but I will be when I get home tonight. I think my body was just anticipating it.'

'Are you going to tell me what happened, or are

you just going to stand there pretending there's nothing wrong with you?'

'I told you – I'm...'

'...fine,' Vicky said, rolling her eyes. 'Only you're not, though, are you?'

'I just felt a bit dizzy when I saw that woman's face,' Tanner continued.

'OK, but it's hardly the first time you've seen a dead body, though, is it?'

'Well, no, but...'

'Well, no, but what?'

Unsure if it was sensible to tell her about his recurring dream, he eventually said, 'I had the feeling I'd seen her before, that was all.'

'I hope you're not about to tell me that you know her?'

'No,' Tanner replied, shaking his head, 'at least, I don't think I do.'

'Then perhaps you can remember how you think you might?'

'I'm not sure,' came his hesitant response, 'but it doesn't matter – at least not until we find out who she is. If it turns out that I do, then we'll probably have to have this discussion again. Between now and then,' Tanner continued, gazing about, 'I suggest we talk to the guy who called in the initial boating accident. Hopefully he'll be able to shed some light on the situation.'

- CHAPTER SIX -

LEADING VICKY BACK to the car park – and the ambulance they'd seen when they'd first arrived – they found a dishevelled man sitting in the back, being looked after by a male paramedic.

'DCI Tanner and DI Gilbert,' Tanner announced, peering inside to catch the paramedic's eye. 'May we have a word with your patient?'

'By all means,' the young man replied, climbing out. 'He's sustained a head injury. It's nothing serious, but he'll need to be taken to hospital to be checked over – just so you know.'

'Understood,' said Tanner, standing to one side to let the paramedic out before climbing in.

'Perhaps we can start with your name?' he began, offering the witness an amiable smile.

'Mark Harris,' the man replied, staring down at the floor while tugging nervously at the ends of the NHS blanket that had been draped over his shoulders.

'And the name of your friend, Mr Harris?'

'Derek. Derek Edwards,' he continued, glancing up. 'Have you found him?'

'I'm afraid we have.'

'Is he – is he...?'

'It would appear that his leg got caught around a rope, which would explain why he was unable to make it to the surface.'

Seeing Harris return to staring at the floor, Tanner

continued, 'I don't suppose you'd like to tell us what happened?'

'We were fishing – or at least, we were about to.'

'Go on,' Tanner prompted.

'Then we had an argument. I was late, you see.'

'You had an argument because you were late?'

'Not exactly.'

'Then what – exactly?'

The man wiped away an escaping tear. 'He'd found out that I'd been having an affair with his wife.'

Shaking his head, Tanner glanced briefly back at Vicky.

'I was trying to explain to him that it didn't mean I loved her – nor that she loved me – but he didn't want to listen.'

'How did he end up falling overboard?'

'He stood up. I'm not sure, but I think he may have been trying to tip the boat over. When I tried to stop him, he threw a punch at me.'

'Did you hit him back?'

Harris quietly shook his head.

'If you didn't hit him, then how did he end up going over?'

'I saw it coming. He must have lost his balance when he missed – and what with the boat already tipping over – he just went straight in. I didn't even see him go under. And when I went to look for him, all I saw was – all I saw was a girl, staring back at me.'

'What happened then?'

'I must have passed out. The next thing I knew, I was lying on my back with blood coming out of my head.'

'Are you *sure* that's what happened?' Tanner demanded. 'Our forensics department will be able to tell us if you've missed something out – like you hitting him, for example.'

'I swear to God,' he began, looking up to stare imploringly into Tanner's eyes. 'It was just like I said. The only thing I'm not sure about is the girl. Was someone else down there with him, or did I just imagine her?'

'Don't worry,' Tanner replied, 'she was there, alright.'

'That's a relief,' he sighed. 'For a minute there I thought I was losing my mind.'

'Which leads me to my next question,' Tanner continued. 'Did you see anyone else there when you arrived?'

'Not a soul.'

'There wasn't anyone else in the car park?'

'Well, it was still dark, but I don't think there was anyone else there – at least, I didn't see anyone.'

'There were no other cars?'

'Just Derek's, and mine, of course.'

'And what time was this?'

'About twenty past five – just before sunrise.'

- CHAPTER SEVEN -

AFTER TAKING THE man's contact details, and instructing the paramedic that they'd need his fingerprints and DNA before he could be released, Tanner stepped out of the ambulance to see Dr Johnstone's boxy old Volvo parked alongside.

Unable to see the man himself, Tanner said to Vicky, 'Did you see our illustrious medical examiner?'

'As I said before – I've already spoken to him.'

'Did you tell him we had two bodies instead of one?'

'When you were passed out,' she nodded.

'Yes, of course. I hope you didn't mention anything about that?'

'I actually forgot, but now that you've reminded me...' she continued, glancing around as if looking for him.

'Listen, Vicky,' began Tanner, lowering his voice to lean his head towards her, 'I don't suppose there's any chance we can keep it between ourselves, for a change?'

'You mean, you don't want me to tell Sally?'

'I'd rather you didn't. If Forrester finds out, he'll only line me up for a series of tiresome psychological examinations.'

'Because you passed out?'
'More because of what I told you earlier.'
'Which was...?'
'That I thought I'd seen the woman somewhere before.'
'So you had, then?'
'Well, yes, but not in the here and now.'
'I'm sorry, boss, you've lost me.'
'You're going to think I'm losing my mind.'
'Don't worry, I thought that when I saw your new car.'
'But I've been having a series of recurring dreams,' Tanner continued. 'Actually, they're more like nightmares.'
'Presumably about your car?'
'About me beating a woman to death before drowning her.'
'Was your new car involved at all?'
'I don't suppose there's any chance you can stop going on about my car?'
'No chance, I'm afraid – unless you're somehow able to sell it, of course.'
'Don't you want to hear about my dream?'
'You just told me: you beat up some girl before drowning her.'
'Doesn't that worry you?'
'Not as much as that new car of yours.'
'Vicky, please!'
'I'm sorry, boss,' she shrugged, 'but it's just a dream. I have them all the time. OK, perhaps they don't involve going around beating people up before drowning them, but some of them could certainly be considered a little harrowing. I've always put it down to the job. After all, dreams are nature's way of helping us to process life's experiences. With some of the things we've seen, it's hardly surprising that ours

tend to be a little darker than most.'

'I completely agree, but you're forgetting what I said before.'

'Which was?'

'That the woman we found – she's the girl from my dream.'

'I'm sure she may have looked like her...'

'No, Vicky, she *is* the girl from my dream!' Tanner insisted, stopping to stare at her. 'And I've seen her before – in real life. I just can't remember from where.'

'OK,' Vicky replied, trying to hide a look of concern, 'how about we see what Johnstone says? It's possible she may have some ID on her, which would at least tell us who she is. If you do know her, then perhaps hearing her name will remind you where you know her from.'

'Or perhaps I've just imagined the whole thing,' muttered Tanner, looking fitfully away, 'and somewhere along the line I've managed to completely lose my mind.'

'It's always possible,' Vicky shrugged, her eyes searching the ground. 'But don't worry, if you have, no doubt it'll turn up somewhere. These things normally do.'

- CHAPTER EIGHT -

MAKING THEIR WAY back through the trees towards the broad, they saw the two divers laying the body of the young woman respectfully down on the jetty beside that of the man.

As they watched Johnstone crouch quietly beside her, Tanner led Vicky over until they were standing behind him.

'Ah, Tanner!' Johnstone eventually said, glancing around. 'When did you get here?'

'I've actually been here a while.'

'Oh, right! I didn't see your car.'

'That's probably because I've got a new one,' he replied, with just the hint of a smile.

'Don't tell me it's that Triumph Stag?'

'What's wrong with that?'

'Apart from the colour?'

'I admit, it wasn't my first choice.'

'What happened to your XJS?'

'The MOT happened.'

'So you decided to buy a bright yellow Triumph Stag instead?'

'Would it help if it was a different colour?'

'Marginally.'

'Anyway, moving the subject away from my taste in classic cars, what do you think?' Tanner asked, bringing Johnstone's attention to the young woman's discoloured face.

'I'd say she'd been beaten up pretty badly.'

'Enough to have killed her?'

Johnstone levered her mouth open before leaning forward to peer inside. 'The facial bruising occurred at least an hour before she died. I'd need to confirm it, but judging by the purple discolouration around her nose and mouth, I'd say the cause of death was most likely asphyxia due to her inability to breathe while being submerged in water.'

'In other words, she drowned?'

'I'd say so. The divers mentioned that her body was held under by a mud weight tied to a rope around her ankles. The marks on the skin confirm that. Whether the person who left her there knew she was dead, I can't say, but with the extent of her facial injuries, the fact that her hands weren't tied together, and the lack of lacerations where the rope was tied, I'd say there's a good chance she was unconscious at the time. That could either mean that whoever left her there thought she was already dead and was hoping to hide the body, or they knew she wasn't and were keen to rectify that. Either way, it's a horrific way for someone to go – especially when they're so young, and dare I say, so beautiful.'

'Quite,' agreed Tanner. 'I don't suppose you've found any ID?'

'I've had a quick look through her pockets, but there's nothing there. I've asked the divers to go back to where she was found, just in case something fell out, or if she had a bag with her.'

'Any ideas about her age?'

'Late teens – early twenties? Something like that.'

'And can you give me some idea as to how long

she'd been down there for?'

'At a guess, I'd say about two days – maybe three.'

'Are you sure?' Tanner queried, recalling his conversation with Christine that morning, and the fact that his recurring nightmare featuring the very woman lying on the jetty before him had started exactly three nights earlier.

'It's going to be something like that,' Johnstone continued, 'but I'll be able to give you a more accurate time when I get her back to the lab.'

Stepping carefully over to the much larger body of the man, Tanner drew in a breath. 'I don't suppose you have any thoughts about this one?'

'That would appear to be a straightforward case of drowning,' Johnstone replied, pushing himself up, 'most likely caused by his foot becoming entangled in the rope that was holding the girl down. Other than some abrasions around his ankle, there are no other signs of injury. But like the girl, the bluish discolouration around his nose and mouth is an obvious giveaway.'

As Tanner turned to gaze down at the girl again, still racking his brain to remember where he'd seen her before, the delicate touch of someone's mouth brushing against his ear had him jumping around with a start – only to find there was nobody there.

'Jesus Christ,' he gasped, raising a hand to his pounding heart.

'Are you alright?' he heard Vicky quietly ask.

'Yes, sorry. I thought...' he began, glancing furtively about. 'Never mind,' he eventually added, shaking his head before catching Johnstone's eye. 'How long before we can expect a post-mortem report?'

'Assuming you're more interested in the girl's body than the man's, and that you don't find anyone else for me in the meantime, I should be able to have something over to you by the end of play today.'

- CHAPTER NINE -

SEEING A POLICE constable endeavouring to garner his attention from the path leading through to the car park, Tanner left Johnstone to continue with his work to make his way over.

'Sorry to bother you, boss,' the young man began, 'but there's someone asking if it's alright for them to come through.'

'Not a reporter, I hope,' Tanner replied, looking over the constable's shoulder to see a grey-haired old man wearing a distinctly unfashionable brown corduroy suit, being held back behind a line of *police do not cross* tape.

'He says his name is Professor something, and he's demanding to know what's going on.'

'Then I suppose we'd better have a word with him, hadn't we,' Tanner sighed, glancing around to beckon Vicky over.

'DCI Tanner and DI Gilbert,' Tanner eventually announced, presenting his ID to the old man as Vicky stepped up beside him. 'I understand you'd like to know what's going on?'

'Well, I am in charge of the archaeological dig that was supposed to start today, so yes, I wouldn't mind.'

'And your name was again?'

'Professor Alfred Beaumont. I'm one of the senior

lecturers at Norfolk University.'

'OK, Professor Beaumont, I'm afraid it's unlikely that you'll be able to start today.'

'May I ask when we will?'

'At the moment, I'm not in a position to say.'

'I'm sorry, Detective Inspector, but that's not good enough. I've spent the best part of my life undertaking extensive research into where King Guthrum was buried, together with his ship, and having finally been granted permission from the local council to begin excavating the site to prove my theories correct, you're telling me I can't because – what – some half-drunk fisherman fell out of his boat and drowned?'

'Unfortunately, it's a little more complicated than that.'

'Why – because he wasn't drunk, or he wasn't a fisherman?'

'Because the body of a young woman was found with him.'

The professor opened his mouth as if to protest once again, only to close it a moment later.

'And it doesn't appear that she was either fishing or drunk,' Tanner continued, 'so I hope you can appreciate that we'll need a little more time to investigate.'

'I do, of course,' came his apologetic response. 'May I ask how much? It's just that we've hired a company who were supposed to start draining the broad this afternoon – at some considerable expense, I may add. We also have a team of construction workers booked in to start removing the surrounding vegetation tomorrow.'

'I'm sorry, Professor, but until our forensics team has finished their examination of the site, nobody will be allowed access.'

'Can you at least tell me how long you think that will take?'

'As I said, I don't know.'

'But you must be able to give me some sort of an idea?' the professor demanded, his eyes darting between Tanner's with agitated irritation.

'Well, it won't be today, I know that much.'

'Tomorrow, then?'

'I think that's a little unlikely.'

'I'm sorry, but that's not good enough!'

'It's the best I can do, I'm afraid.'

'Then you're going to have to give me the name of your superior officer.'

'It would be my pleasure,' came Tanner's enthusiastic response, digging out his wallet to prise it open. 'If you could make sure to mention my name,' he continued, handing the professor Forrester's card, as well as his own, 'and to let him know what I'm doing, I'm sure he'd appreciate the update.'

- CHAPTER TEN -

LEADING VICKY AWAY, Tanner stopped her in the middle of the car park to ask, 'How're you doing there, young Vicky?'

'Er... fine,' came her somewhat suspicious response. 'May I enquire as to why you're asking?'

'Because it looks like we have another murder on our hands.'

'Nothing new there,' she shrugged.

'You seem to have forgotten what we said last time.'

'Which was...?'

'That the next time something like this came up, you'd be taking the lead.'

'Oh right. I thought you were joking,' she laughed.

'So I was asking how you were doing in the context of becoming the Senior Investigating Officer?'

'To be honest, I was feeling better when I wasn't.'

'Well, look, we all have to start somewhere.'

'We do?'

'And being that there are no secret tunnels, five-pointed stars, or recently removed body parts left out on silver plates, I think this will be a good place for you to.'

'You mean – not *yet* there aren't.'

'I assume that's a yes?'

'That there aren't any tunnels, pentagrams, or wayward body parts, or if I'm happy to take the lead?'

'I was thinking of the latter.'

'Do I have a choice?'

'We all have a choice, young Vicky, as long as your answer is, "Yes, I'd be delighted to."'

'Then yes, I'd be delighted to.'

'Good choice!'

'On the condition that you help me, of course.'

'You mean – as if I'm your assistant?'

'I was thinking more along the lines of you doing the job of the SIO, whilst I go around pretending to.'

'Honestly, Vicky, it's not as hard as you're making it out to be. All you have to do is ask numerous people a variety of questions. If you're not comfortable doing that, you can get everyone back at the station to ask the questions for you.'

'OK, I'll do it, but I'd still like you to be by my side, at least for the time being.'

'Can I be by your side whilst in my office with my feet on my desk?'

'I was thinking more along the lines of you being by my side physically as well as mentally.'

'Being that I'm normally thinking about something else, that might be difficult, but I'll do the best I can. So, with you now officially the SIO, what do you think?'

'About what?'

'What do you mean – about what?'

'I've no idea,' Vicky shrugged. 'The last time we had this discussion, we ended up talking about mini-golf.'

'Fair enough, I suppose, but on this particular occasion I was thinking about the girl we found, and if it was just a coincidence that her death seemed to overlap with a university professor's lifelong search for a missing Viking ship – together with the Viking King who owned it.'

'To be honest,' Vicky began, 'that's exactly what I thought.'

'Can you be more precise?'

'That it was a coincidence.'

'I think you'll find that they don't exist – at least not in this job.'

'So, what do *you* think?' Vicky asked in return.

'That it may be an idea to start doing a little digging of our own.'

'Presumably not by having the broad drained to go in search of buried Viking treasure?'

'I was thinking more about his story: that it's been his lifelong obsession, and whether there's anyone who's shown themselves to be vehemently opposed to it.'

'Do you really think there's a connection between a girl beaten half to death before being drowned in the middle of Blackfleet Broad, and a planned archaeological dig?'

'At this stage, young Vicky, I have no idea. But with nothing else to go on, it would seem like a sensible place for us to start – sorry – I meant it would seem like a sensible place for *you* to start.'

- CHAPTER ELEVEN -

ARRIVING BACK AT Wroxham Police Station about half an hour later, Tanner climbed out to see first Vicky pulling into the car park behind him, then Sally, opening the station's glass entrance door to peer over at Tanner with a surprised look.

'Morning, boss,' she eventually said, before adding, 'Is that your car?'

Preparing to be on the receiving end of more comical, derogatory remarks, he locked the doors before turning back to say somewhat defensively, 'Actually, yes, it is.'

'Lucky you! I've always fancied buying myself a Triumph Stag.'

'You have?' Tanner replied, his head jerking back in surprise.

'My dad had one for years. His was in racing green, but personally, I always preferred it in yellow.'

'Well, thank you for saying so, Sally,' Tanner said with a relieved smile. 'No one else seems to like it.'

'That's because they don't have your impeccable taste.'

Beginning to wonder if she was about to ask for a pay rise – and thinking he'd probably give it to her – he called over to Vicky as she climbed out of her car. 'Did you hear that?'

'Did I hear what?' she replied.

'Sally likes my car!'

'Then she must be after a pay rise,' she grunted.

'My dad used to have one,' continued Sally, climbing down the steps to take a closer look.

'What, on purpose?' Vicky continued.

'He actually said it was the best car he'd ever owned.'

'But he eventually came to his senses and bought something else?'

'Well yes, but only because someone took it for a joyride and drove it into a tree.'

'Poor tree.'

'Do you think you'd be able to take me for a drive in it?' Sally asked, turning towards Tanner with an enquiring smile.

'I'd be delighted to!' Tanner exclaimed, returning the smile before smirking around at Vicky.

'Although, perhaps not now,' Sally continued.

'You can if you want.'

'Well, I'd love to, but there's a man in reception asking to speak to you.'

'Me, specifically?'

'Well, no, but he wanted to speak to whoever was in charge.'

- CHAPTER TWELVE -

'I UNDERSTAND YOU'RE looking for me?' Tanner enquired, having been guided towards a very normal-looking middle-aged man sitting on one of the blue plastic seats in the middle of the otherwise deserted reception area.

'Are you in charge?' the man asked, glancing up with an anxious frown.

'DCI Tanner,' Tanner nodded. 'I'm in charge about as much as anyone is around here. May I ask your name?'

'Richard Lowe.'

'And how may I help, Mr Lowe?'

'It's just that – well – it's my daughter, you see.'

Knowing what was coming next, Tanner sank slowly down into the seat beside him.

'She went to stay with her mother last week, but she never came home.'

'When was she supposed to?'

'Last night.'

'Perhaps she went to stay with a friend?'

Shaking his head, the man stared down at the floor. 'I spoke to her mother this morning. She was supposed to stay with her for the whole weekend, but apparently they had an argument on Friday, after which she packed her bags, telling her mother that she was coming back to see me.'

'It's still possible she went to stay with some

friends.'

'I suppose,' he sighed, 'but I keep calling her mobile only for it to click through to voicemail.'

'Where does her mother live?'

'Catfield.'

'And you?'

'Over in Tunstead.'

'And how did she travel between the two?'

'She has an old Mini Cooper I bought for her.'

'And there's been no sign of that anywhere?'

Again the man shook his head before sitting up to begin searching his pockets. 'I've got a photograph of her – somewhere,' he continued, eventually pulling it out.

Taking a moment to stare down at it, he handed it to Tanner with trembling hands. 'Her name's Tara. Tara Lowe.'

Hearing her name as Tanner stared down at the photograph featuring an attractive young woman, leaning back against an old yellow Mini with a carpet bag slung over her shoulder, a cold shiver ran the length of his spine. It was the same girl from his recurring nightmares – the same person they'd found submerged under the water less than two hours before. More than that, he now knew exactly who she was: the environmentalist he'd met when investigating the death of the young man found hanging in Bluebell Wood.

Handing the photograph back, the man glanced up to say, 'It's OK – you can keep it if you like.'

Pulling in a resilient breath, Tanner held the man's eyes. 'I'm sorry to say this, but I don't think that will be necessary.'

'What do you mean?'

'We found the body of a girl this morning. Having seen her photograph, I think there's a strong possibility that she's your daughter.'

The man blinked back at Tanner with a confused, incomprehensible frown. 'I'm sorry – but – what do you mean?'

'We found her submerged underwater at Blackfleet Broad. We're not sure yet, but after a preliminary examination, we believe she may have drowned.'

'But that can't be! What would she have been doing there? I doubt she even knows where it is. I'm not even sure myself.'

'That's something we're going to have to find out.'

'No, I'm sorry, Detective Inspector,' said Mr Lowe, vehemently shaking his head, 'but whoever you've found, it can't be my Tara. She's a happy young woman with a bright future ahead of her. There's just no way she'd have taken her own life.'

'At this early stage in our investigation, we're not sure that she did.'

'What are you trying to say?'

Tanner took another fortifying breath. 'It's our belief that someone may have had a hand.'

Mr Lowe's head jerked back in shock. 'You're trying to tell me that my daughter's been murdered?'

'As I said, we're at a very early stage in our investigation, but that is what we currently think.'

'Then you definitely have the wrong person! Why on earth would anyone want to do anything like that to Tara? She has nothing but love for the world. She spends half her life campaigning for the environment. Who would possibly wish anything bad to happen to her?'

'Perhaps someone who didn't share her environmental views?' mused Tanner.

'I'm sorry, Chief Inspector, but I came here to ask you to help me find my daughter, not to have to sit here listening to some ridiculous story that she's been murdered. Now are you going to give me some sort of missing person form to fill out, or am I going to have to speak to your superior officer?'

'Sorry, yes, of course,' Tanner replied, climbing to his feet. 'My mistake. I'll ask one of my colleagues to come out with a suitable form. And perhaps I'd be able to keep hold of that photograph as well?'

- CHAPTER THIRTEEN -

ASKING HENDERSON TO give Mr Lowe an appropriate form to fill out – if for no other reason than to get hold of his contact details – Tanner went in search of Vicky, eventually finding her in the kitchen.

'I think I know who our victim is,' he said, catching her eye as she made herself a coffee.

'Anyone I know?'

'You met her a year or so ago, outside her home.'

'Does she have a name?'

'Tara Lowe.'

'It does ring a bell,' came her contemplative reply.

'This will probably help,' he continued, handing her the photograph he'd been given. 'Her father just gave it to me, having told me that she's been missing for the last three days. That's the car she pulled up in. The carpet bag, as well.'

'Christ, yes, I remember!'

'She was also one of the environmentalists protesting outside the proposed Bluebell Wood development – which reminds me where I've seen those other people before as well. The ones we saw about to start a protest about the dig that's due to take place at Blackfleet Broad. If you remember, they said they were waiting for someone. I can almost guarantee that person was Tara Lowe. If it was, then it means we were right in thinking that there is a connection between what happened to her and the fact that the broad is about to be drained.'

'You mean *you* were right,' corrected Vicky. 'I seem to remember saying it was just a coincidence.'

'As I said – there's rarely such a thing.'

'OK, so what do you think we should do now?' asked Vicky, turning to look at Tanner with a steaming mug of coffee in her hand.

'That's your call, isn't it?'

'I thought I'd delegate the decision.'

'Fair enough,' he shrugged, glancing thoughtfully away. 'I think the first thing to do is to start finding out as much as we can about Tara's life over the last few months. We also need to let Johnstone know who we think the girl is. That should help him to formally identify the body.'

'Can't her father do that?'

'Unfortunately, he refused to believe that the body we found could be hers.'

'Despite coming in to tell us that she's missing?'

'Such is the power of denial,' shrugged Tanner. 'Once we've done that, then I suggest we head back to Blackfleet Broad, to see if those protestors are still there. We need to know if Tara was the person they were waiting for, and if they know of any reason why someone would have wanted to hurt her. Before that, I'd better give Forrester an update. Meanwhile, perhaps you could tell everyone what we've found, then delegate out the various tasks needed to find out what she's been up to. Once you've done that, perhaps you can do me a favour?'

'Which is...?'

'To look up the name of that housing developer we were dealing with during the Bluebell Wood investigation.'

'I can, of course,' came Vicky's hesitant response, 'the question is... why?'

'For now, let's just call it a hunch.'

'Did someone say lunch?'

'I didn't, but now that you mention it, I am rather hungry. Perhaps we can pick something up on the way back to Blackfleet?'

- CHAPTER FOURTEEN -

CLOSING THE DOOR to his private office, Tanner made himself a much-needed coffee before planting himself down behind his desk to reluctantly pick up his phone.

'Good morning, Forrester,' he began, slumping back in his chair, 'it's Tanner speaking.'

'I'm sorry – who did you say you were?'

'DCI Tanner?' Tanner replied, rolling his eyes. 'Average height, dark hair, ruggedly good-looking?'

With still no response, Tanner let out a petulant sigh. 'I work out of the Wroxham branch?'

'Do you mean John Tanner – the one with the sailing jacket, who drives around in that beaten-up old Jaguar XJS?'

'Actually, no. I'm the John Tanner who drives around in a beaten-up old Triumph Stag.'

'Why – what happened to your Jag?'

'The MOT,' Tanner replied, and not for the first time.

'And you thought you'd buy a Triumph Stag to replace it?'

'One came on the market, so I thought I'd give it a go.'

'That's very brave of you.'

'Your niece seems to like it.'

'That's probably because her father used to

have one. Anyway, I assume you're calling about that urgent email I sent you this morning – the one marked "urgent" – inside which I asked you to call me – urgently?'

'Yes, sir.'

'Then seeing that I sent it to you over three and a half hours ago, may I ask why it's taken you so long to pick up the phone?'

'Sorry, sir, what I meant to say was yes, I saw the email; I just haven't had a chance to open it yet.'

With the line falling silent, Tanner was forced to ask, 'Are you still there?'

'Yes, Tanner, I'm still here. I was just checking to see if any of the CVs we had in over the weekend are worth taking a look at.'

'Good one, sir,' Tanner replied, with a nervous laugh.

'So anyway,' Forrester continued, 'if you're not calling about my urgent email – because you haven't bothered to open it yet – then perhaps you could tell me why you are?'

'It's the same reason why I haven't had a chance to look at your email.'

'Which is...?'

'Because I was informed about the body of a man discovered at Blackfleet Broad, the very minute I was about to open it.'

'I assume you're about to tell me that he didn't die of natural causes?'

'It looks likely that he drowned, sir. Boating accident.'

'Then why – may I ask – are you calling?'

'Because it would appear that he got his foot caught around a rope.'

'Yes, and...?'

'At the end of which was a mud weight.'

'Is this leading anywhere, Tanner, or am I going to have to start arranging job interviews?'

'Unfortunately, at the other end was the body of a young woman.'

'Right, I see. Don't you think you could have started with that?'

'Well, yes, I suppose I could have, but then you wouldn't have understood the circumstances under which she was found.'

'Do we have a name?'

'We think she's a Miss Tara Lowe. Her father has just reported her as being missing, and the photograph he's provided would appear to confirm that. I'm also fairly sure that I've met her before.'

'Please don't tell me you had an affair with her – just before meeting your first wife?'

'Er, no, sir. I'm not sure she would have been born then.'

'Then how – may I ask – do you know her?'

'I spoke to her during the Bluebell Wood incident. She was one of the environmental activists protesting outside the proposed development, which is making me think there might be a connection.'

'To what?'

'Her environmental activist group, and the fact that Blackfleet Broad is about to be drained.'

'To build a housing development?'

'Well, no. According to the person in charge, it would be the first stage of an archaeological dig that's due to take place – in search of some sort of ancient Viking burial ground.'

'Then why do you think there's a connection?'

'It just seems too much of a coincidence that her body shows up in the middle of a broad that's about to be drained – especially when there was a group of environmental activists on site when we arrived, about to start protesting the dig. Even more so when I think they're the same group our victim was a part of.'

'Makes sense, I suppose. So – what's the plan?'

'First up, I wanted to ask if it was alright for me to make Vicky the SIO?'

'Oh, right. You don't think you can handle it?'

'Well, yes, of course – but I thought we agreed that she'd be given the chance to lead a murder investigation when the time came.'

'OK, but are we even sure it's a murder investigation?'

Having a flashback to his dream – and how he'd seen her being beaten and drowned, as if by his own hand – he glanced curiously down at one of them.

'Well, I suppose we're not one hundred per cent sure, but as she had been severely beaten beforehand, and given that her father just told me how happy she was, it would seem likely.'

'OK, but perhaps it would be worthwhile looking into her state of mind before jumping to any conclusions. Maybe see if she'd left a suicide note, as well.'

'Yes, of course,' Tanner replied – though with little intention of doing so.

'And how about Vicky – have you spoken to her about the SIO role?'

'I have.'

'And... what did she say?'

'She's agreed – albeit reluctantly.'

'She does know that it's a huge responsibility?'

'Yes, of course.'

'And you're confident she can do it?'

'If I work alongside her – at least for this first one

– then I'm sure she'll be fine.'

'OK, then let's see how she gets on. Oh, and Tanner?'

'Yes, sir.'

'Don't forget to take a look at that email I sent you – the one marked "urgent".'

'Of course.'

'And call me the moment you have.'

'Right.'

'And make sure to keep me updated as to how Vicky's getting on.'

'Is there anything else, sir?' came Tanner's resentful response, 'or may I get back to work?'

'Once you've responded to that email – I'd appreciate it if you did.'

- CHAPTER FIFTEEN -

OPENING THE EMAIL Forrester had been going on about, to find it was nothing more important than a stupid questionnaire, Tanner let out a petulant sigh before closing it again.

Climbing wearily to his feet, he made his way out into the main office to see Vicky talking quietly to Sally.

Beckoning her over, he asked, 'How's it going?'

'I've just been speaking to Sally about taking a look at Tara Lowe's social media accounts. Townsend and Haverstock are trying to access her finances, and Gina's doing the same with her email. I also thought it might be a good idea to get Henderson to see if he can dig up anything about that university professor we met, Alfred Beaumont.'

'OK, good,' said Tanner, gazing towards Henderson's desk only to see he wasn't there.

'But not before asking him to make everyone some coffee,' Vicky added, following his gaze.

'Did you have any luck finding out who that building developer was – the one we were looking into during the Bluebell Wood investigation?'

'Simon Balinger of SKB Holdings.'

'That's the one.'

'But I'm still struggling to see the relevance,' said Vicky. 'He builds houses. He doesn't fund archaeological digs. There's no money in them, for a start.'

'I know, but I'd still like him to be on our radar, just in case his name comes up in conversation.

'Speaking of names coming up in conversation,' Tanner continued, 'I've told Forrester that you're taking the lead on this one.'

'What did he say?'

'Oh, you know. The usual.'

'Which was…?'

'That I'm to update him on how you're getting on every five minutes, whilst filling out another one of his bloody questionnaires, which he seems to think will solve the question of God's existence, where the universe came from, if there's more than one of them, or if we're just a digital construct being played inside some sort of advanced multi-player computer game.'

'That's quite a questionnaire!'

'It's actually about our stationery supplies, but he seemed to think it was important.'

'I assume that means you haven't bothered to fill it out?'

'Strangely enough, no, I haven't.'

'Then why don't you give it to Sally? She manages our stationery supplies.'

'Because she's got more important things to do – as have we. Speaking of which, are you still up for a return trip to Blackfleet Broad, to see if those protestors are still there?'

'As long as we can grab something to eat on the way.'

'Of course!'

'And that I can take my own car.'

'You're not still going on about my Triumph Stag?'

'Not at all. I'd just prefer not to be seen dead in

it,' she smiled.

'Tell you what – being that you're the SIO and everything – and that my car could break down at any moment, I'd be willing to go in yours.'

'OK, but there is one condition.'

'Which is...?'

'That someone pays for the petrol. Someone apart from me, that is – which reminds me.'

'Let me guess. You want to know if your recent promotion to SIO comes with a pay rise?'

'I wouldn't mind.'

'I'm sure you wouldn't.'

'Well – does it?'

'To be honest, I don't know. I'll have to ask Forrester, which probably means having to fill out that bloody questionnaire of his.'

'What's that got to do with it?'

'I'm fairly sure it doesn't have anything to do with anything. However, I'm beginning to get the feeling that if I don't start doing what I'm told a little more often, he's going to stop talking to me – which will make it difficult to negotiate a pay rise for you, or anyone else for that matter. It will also mean he'll probably start looking for my replacement – that's if he hasn't started already.'

'Would that mean we could end up with another DCI?'

'I think that would be the idea.'

'One with a nice shiny new car for me to be driven around in?'

'Or perhaps one who wants nothing more than to sit behind his desk, barking out orders whilst recommending to HQ that everyone gets a pay cut – everyone except himself, of course.'

A moment of contemplative silence followed, before Vicky eventually looked at Tanner to say, 'Did

I ever tell you how much I like that new car of yours? The colour is also particularly attractive.'

'Does that mean you're happy enough for me to drive over to Blackfleet Broad?'

'If nobody's going to pay for my petrol, then I suppose I'll have to be.'

- CHAPTER SIXTEEN -

WITH VICKY PERCHED reluctantly inside Tanner's new-to-him car, ducking her head whenever she thought she saw someone she might know, they picked up some lunch before driving back into Blackfleet Broad's car park to find the small group of environmental activists still there.

Parking up alongside their Volkswagen van, which was nearly as old as Tanner's car, they climbed out to hear one of them call, 'Love the vintage look, Grandad.'

Glancing around to see an overweight teenage boy dressed like some sort of New Age hippy, smirking at him through stained yellow teeth, Tanner smiled back. 'Thanks, son – although it's not nearly as nice as your van.'

'That's where you're wrong,' the boy continued, grinning around at his hippy-styled friends. 'It isn't my van.'

'Then may I ask whose van it is?'

'Who's asking?'

'DCI Tanner, and my colleague, DI Gilbert,' Tanner replied, as they each held up their respective IDs.

'For fuck's sake,' he groaned, grimacing around at his friends. 'We haven't even started yet, and we're already being told to move on.'

'Don't worry, we're not asking you to move. We'd

just like to ask a few questions.'

'About what?'

'A certain Miss Tara Lowe.'

The mention of her name had everyone in the group staring around at him.

'Do you know where she is?' asked a stick-thin young woman with large, doleful brown eyes.

'So you do know her, then?'

'Yes, of course we do. She said she'd be here at eight o'clock this morning, but she hasn't turned up. She's not answering her phone, either!'

'May I ask when any of you last spoke to her?'

'It was Friday, I think,' she replied, glancing around at her friends. 'She was supposed to spend the weekend with her mother, but they ended up having a row, and she went back to her dad's house.'

'Did any of you speak to her after that?'

As they all shook their heads, the same girl glanced up to tentatively ask, 'Is she alright?'

Tanner drew in a fortifying breath. 'I'm afraid to say that the body of a young woman was found here in the early hours of the morning. We've yet to formally identify her, but it is our belief that it is your friend.'

As they all stared around at each other in muted horror, Tanner continued, 'Do any of you know of any reason why someone may have wished to harm her?'

'Do you think – do you think someone may have...?' the same girl tried to say, only for her words to falter as her voice broke with emotion.

'We believe it's possible, which is why we're trying to find out who saw her last.'

'It must have been me,' she said, gazing incomprehensibly up at Tanner. 'We went out for coffee, to discuss what we were going to do today.'

'Which was...?'

'To try and raise public awareness of the planned archaeological dig, and the long-term impact it will have on the local environment.'

'We thought they were only planning to drain the broad temporarily?'

'That's what they've been going around telling everyone, but Tara found out that it's all just an elaborate cover story. There's no buried Viking treasure. Their real plan is to get the council to pay for the broad to be drained, then have the entire site dug up under the guise of it being an archaeological dig, before announcing to the world that, unfortunately, there's nothing there. With the entire area having been drained and flattened, they're then intending to apply for planning permission to build a massive office block, to sell to the highest bidder.'

'That's quite a story,' said Tanner, crouching down to glance furtively behind him. 'Can you prove it?'

'We can't – but we're not freelance investigative journalists.'

'Are you saying Tara was?'

'She was hoping to be. She said that was the story that was going to launch her career.'

'It's also something that could end up getting her killed,' Tanner muttered.

As everyone in the group stared around at each other, the young woman took a breath to ask, 'Do you think that's what happened?'

'I don't know, but if I were you, I'd keep it to yourself.'

With them all nodding back, Tanner continued, 'Did she tell you any more – like the names of the people involved, for example?'

'She didn't, but she said the story was done, and

that she was going to send it off to *The Norwich Reporter*.'

'I don't suppose you know when she was planning on doing that?'

'On Friday. She was hoping that would mean it could be published today, to coincide with both our protest and the start of the dig.'

- CHAPTER SEVENTEEN -

TAKING DOWN THEIR various names and contact details, Tanner led the way back to his car, eventually stopping beside the door.

'I knew this had something to do with some dodgy building development,' he said, glancing back at the environmentalists. 'I can almost guarantee who's going to be behind it, as well.'

'You're thinking Simon Balinger, I assume.'

'Damn right I am! The challenge is now to prove it.'

'If what they were saying is true,' continued Vicky, 'we may not have to.'

'How d'you mean?' asked Tanner, unlocking the doors as Vicky made her way around to the other side.

'Because Tara Lowe may have already done it for us.'

'You seem to be confusing a newspaper story that only needs to entertain its readership with a police investigation that would need to stand up in a court of law,' commented Tanner, as they both climbed inside.

'It may not be enough for us to charge him with fraud, but it should at least get us on the right track.'

'And we'd need to find it, of course.'

'Can't we just go round to her house to access her computer?'

'Not until we have a formal identification. For all

we know, she could be alive and well, and living in Bournemouth.'

'Then who did we find in the middle of Blackfleet Broad?'

'My point is, we can't legally enter someone's property to start rifling through their personal belongings until we've been able to formally identify the body.'

'So, what are we going to do?'

'Chase Johnstone, for a start,' Tanner continued, digging out his phone to begin scrolling for his number. 'If he still hasn't been able to, then I think our next best bet would be to go round to *The Norwich Reporter*, to see if she was able to send it to them before someone got to her first.'

- CHAPTER EIGHTEEN -

WITH JOHNSTONE STILL waiting for Tara Lowe's identity to be confirmed by her dentist, Vicky found the address for *The Norwich Reporter* to direct Tanner towards it.

Arriving about half an hour later, they entered an empty reception area to see a high, curving white desk at the end.

Creeping their way inside, Tanner reached the desk to peer over the top, just in case there was somebody lurking behind it.

Turning back to Vicky, he leaned towards her to whisper, 'There's nobody there,' before continuing to glance curiously about.

'OK,' Vicky replied, in a similar low, clandestine voice, 'but why are we whispering?'

'I don't know,' Tanner continued, his voice barely audible. 'It just feels like we're not supposed to be here.'

'Maybe we're not,' she replied, 'and we were supposed to make an appointment.'

'The door was open,' he shrugged, glancing up at the ceiling to see a security camera pointing directly at them. 'Don't look now,' he continued, 'but I think we're being watched.'

Seeing Vicky turn to stare up at it, he let out an admonishing sigh. 'I told you not to look at it!'

'Sorry, but why shouldn't I look at it?'

'In case someone's seen us!'

'But – I thought we wanted someone to see us?'

'Yes, right. Good point,' Tanner replied, standing up straight for his voice to return to normal. 'Then perhaps you should wave at it, to try and attract someone's attention?'

'I'm not waving at it!' Vicky protested, folding her arms as if to make sure she didn't start. 'Someone might be looking!'

'I thought that was the idea.'

'Isn't there a bell to press, or anything?'

'Not that I can see.'

'Well, we can't stand around here all day.'

'We actually can,' Tanner shrugged. 'I'm just not sure I want to.'

With them both staring absently around, wondering what to do, Tanner eventually said, 'I suppose we could start a fire. That should get someone's attention.'

'And how would you propose we do that?'

'Simple! We could put some paper into a bin and use a cigarette lighter.'

'And you have a cigarette lighter, do you?'

'Well, no, but I thought you might have one in that handbag of yours.'

'Why do you think I'd have a cigarette lighter?'

'I thought you smoked?'

'What makes you think that?'

'I don't know,' he shrugged. 'You just look like the sort of person who might.'

'Well, I don't,' she huffed. 'Neither do I have a cigarette lighter.'

'You don't carry one around with you, just in case you have the inkling to start?'

'Surprisingly, no, I don't – but I can see now that I should. Tell you what, the next time we stop at a petrol station, I'll make sure to buy myself one.'

'OK, good, but that doesn't help with our current predicament. Perhaps we can find someone to ask?'

'You want to find someone to ask if they have a cigarette lighter, so enabling us to start a fire in order to attract someone's attention?'

'Uh-huh,' Tanner replied, making his way around to the other side of the reception desk to begin digging about.

'What are you doing now?' Vicky queried, peering over the top of the desk.

'I was just wondering if they have some sort of Tannoy system, or maybe there's someone we can call,' he continued, perching himself on a stool to pick up a phone.

Resting it against his ear, he was about to start pressing random numbers when a large woman came charging through a door to stare over at first Vicky, then Tanner.

'May I help you?' she enquired, in a distinctly unwelcoming tone.

'Sorry,' began Tanner, putting the phone gently down. 'There was nobody here.'

'So you thought it would be alright to sit behind my desk to start using my phone?'

'We were actually wondering if someone had a cigarette lighter?'

'You do know that you're not allowed to smoke here, just as you're not allowed to in any enclosed workplace or public area?'

'That wasn't the reason we were looking for one.'

'Then what was the reason?'

'We were thinking about starting a fire.'

'I beg your pardon?'

'Never mind,' Tanner replied, climbing down off the stool to slink his way around to the other side.

'Now perhaps you wouldn't mind leaving, unless, of course, you want me to call the police?'

'There's really no need.'

'So – you're leaving then?'

'No. We actually *are* the police.'

'Excuse me?'

'DCI Tanner and my colleague, DI Gilbert,' Tanner replied, as they each dug out their respective IDs.

With the woman glaring at them with incredulous contempt, Tanner put his away to continue. 'We were actually wondering if we could speak to your Editor-in-Chief?'

'Do you have an appointment?'

'I'm afraid not.'

'But I assume you are here on official police business?'

'We are,' Tanner confirmed.

With the receptionist remaining resolutely where she was, Tanner thought to add, 'If it helps, I have actually met him before – assuming it's the same man, of course.'

'And who do you think it is?' she asked, narrowing her eyes with suspicion.

'Simon Reynolds. He was kind enough to help with a previous investigation. If you mention my name, I'm sure he'll remember me.'

- CHAPTER NINETEEN -

BEING SHOWN INTO a spacious office with sleek, modern furniture, and large windows that flooded the room with natural light, Tanner glanced enviously around at the surrounding plants, just as the receptionist announced his name.

'A DCI Tanner and a DI Gilbert to see you, sir.'

'Mr Tanner!' said a familiar middle-aged man, standing up from a black ergonomic chair on the other side of a desk to smile over at him. 'What do I owe this honour – or more to the point, what have I done?' he laughed.

'Good afternoon, Mr Reynolds,' Tanner replied, leading Vicky inside. 'I was wondering if you'd remember me.'

'How could I possibly forget!'

'Quite easily, I'd have thought, especially given the fact that your office is at least twice as big as mine.'

'Do you think so?' Reynolds replied, gazing around. 'I thought it was at least three times the size.'

'Yes, you're probably right,' grumbled Tanner.

'Please – take a seat,' he offered, directing both Tanner and Vicky to the two chrome and black leather chairs neatly positioned in front of his desk. 'May I get you a coffee?'

'Is it any good?' Tanner enquired, failing to see anything that could be used to make one.

'It's actually my own special blend,' Reynolds

replied, reaching over to pick up a pristine white coffee mug from out of its saucer, only to find it was empty.

Replacing it with disgust, he snatched up his phone to press a button. 'Sorry to bother you, Susie, but would you mind making me some more coffee?'

Holding the phone away from his mouth, he looked again at Tanner and Vicky. 'Was that a yes?'

With them both nodding back, he returned to his phone conversation. 'Actually, Susie, could you make that three? If you could bring in separate milk and sugar, we'll take it from there. Oh, and if you could make sure to heat the milk, that would be appreciated. Thanks, Susie!'

Replacing the receiver, they each settled into their respective chairs.

'Now – how can I help?' Reynolds enquired.

Tempted to ask if he could have his job, his office, and whoever made his coffee, Tanner did his best not to let his resentment show by crossing one leg nonchalantly over the other. 'We were wondering if you've heard of someone by the name of Tara Lowe?'

'Is she that lunatic suing us for defamation?'

'Er – I don't think so.'

'Then she must be the one going out with that famous footballer.'

'She's actually an environmental campaigner who's apparently been trying her hand at freelance journalism.'

A knock at the door had Tanner turning around to see an attractive, dark-haired young woman wearing a tight-fitting blouse and an even tighter dark grey mini-skirt, glancing behind her as she reversed a tray inside.

Spinning elegantly around, she smiled first at Tanner, then Vicky, before turning to face Reynolds. 'Where would you like it?'

'On my desk would be fine.'

Standing up as he watched her place it carefully down, Reynolds eventually smiled at her to say, 'Perfect, thanks, Susie!'

'No problem. Let me know if you need anything else.'

As she spun around to make her way out, Reynolds poured some milk into the cup nearest to him. 'Please, help yourself,' he said, giving both Tanner and Vicky an encouraging nod.

Climbing eagerly out of his chair, Tanner poured milk into the remaining cups to hand one to Vicky before sitting back down with the other.

'What did you say her name was again?' Reynolds asked, placing his cup down to take hold of his mouse.

'Tara Lowe,' Tanner repeated, breathing in the intoxicating smell of the smooth, perfectly blended coffee before taking a sip.

'Yes, of course,' Reynolds announced. 'She's been sending us a few stories. Some of them were a little far-fetched – actually, some of them were *very* far-fetched – but she certainly has a talent for writing. The one she sent over recently actually looked quite good. It's just a shame it's not the sort of thing we cover. I was going to reply, advising her to send them to *The Norfolk Herald*; I just never got around to it.'

'The most recent one she sent you,' Tanner began, leaning back in his chair, 'it wasn't about some dodgy scheme to have Blackfleet Broad drained on the pretence of looking for Viking treasure, when instead it was to secure planning permission to build an office block?'

'Hold on – I'm just trying to find it now.'

They waited in silence as Reynolds moved his mouse erratically around while staring at his computer.

'OK, her most recent one was entitled *Mysterious Light Seen Over Broads Sparks UFO Debate*. It goes on to say that a local Norfolk resident reported seeing a strange, glowing orb moving silently over the Broads that has since led to a flurry of UFO sightings and speculation. As I said,' he continued, 'it's probably something *The Norfolk Herald* would be interested in.'

'Nothing about Blackfleet Broad being drained on the pretence of looking for buried Viking treasure?'

'Not that I can see,' he continued, 'but it sounds like the sort of thing she'd have come up with – again, more for *Norfolk Herald* readers than our own.'

'Are you suggesting that she just made the whole thing up?'

'Well, yes,' he replied, sitting back in his chair to present them with an amused smile. 'Obviously!'

- CHAPTER TWENTY -

EVENTUALLY THANKING REYNOLDS for his time, Tanner led Vicky out of the office and back to his car, all the while in contemplative silence.

'What did you make of that?' Vicky eventually asked, standing beside the Triumph's passenger door.

'That I'm definitely in the wrong line of work,' Tanner moaned, unlocking the car to climb inside.

'You want to move into journalism?' Vicky enquired, following him in.

'If it comes with a plush modern office that's at least three times the size of mine, with decent coffee on tap, and a secretary to make it for me, then yes, I'd love to move into journalism!'

'You could always ask Sally to make your coffee for you.'

'I suppose,' he replied, gazing soulfully out of the window.

'And if you want a bigger office, you could always move into ours.'

'And where would you all go?'

'Well, Sally and Townsend would probably be happy enough in the stationery cupboard. The rest of us could probably fit into yours.'

'You know, that's not a bad idea! Remind me to bring it up with Forrester the next time he calls.'

'And what about what Reynolds said?' Vicky

continued, clearly endeavouring to steer the subject back to the investigation. 'If Tara just made the whole thing up, then it doesn't bode well for our theory that she was killed for what she'd found out.'

'Just because he didn't think it was true doesn't mean it wasn't.'

'Well, no, but when you put it into context with some of the other stories she'd come up with, plus the fact that she was obviously just trying to think of something to help get herself published, I can see why he'd think that. And if he does think she made the whole thing up – given his profession and everything – then don't you think we should too? After all, we don't have a single shred of evidence to prove it was true. As yet, we haven't even seen the story. For all we know, her environmentalist friends made it up. Or, alternatively, Tara told them she had a great story involving Blackfleet Broad simply to incentivise her troops.'

'Maybe so, but that would mean Tara's body being found under the water there, and a dig to unearth buried Viking treasure at the exact same place, is just a coincidence – and you know how I feel about those.'

'Coincidences do happen,' Vicky replied.

Pulling his seatbelt on, Tanner glanced around at her to say, 'Maybe so, but until we have another theory, it may be sensible to stick with the one we've got.'

'Sounds good to me, but if you're about to ask me what we should do next, I'm not sure I'd be able to answer.'

Hearing his phone ring, Tanner began searching around for it. 'With any luck, that'll be someone to tell us.'

Digging it out to see it was Dr Johnstone, he added, 'Looks like it's our lucky day,' before answering, 'Tanner speaking!'

'Good afternoon, Tanner, it's your favourite medical examiner calling.'

Tanner glanced down at his watch before saying, 'You haven't completed the post-mortem already – have you?'

'Sadly not, but thanks to being given a name, I am at least able to confirm the victim's identity.'

'So, it was Tara Lowe, then?'

'Her dental records just came in to confirm it.'

Turning to nod at Vicky, Tanner continued, 'And the post-mortem report?'

'I should have that to you by end of play, but so far it's looking like we thought. Death was from drowning, and she was severely beaten around the head and face beforehand.'

'How long before?'

'About an hour.'

'Where do we stand on forensics?'

'Nothing yet, but with where she was found, I'm not sure there's going to be anything that'll be of much use. Bodies submerged under water rarely have much in the way of usable DNA or fingerprints. It may have been a different story if we'd found any skin underneath her fingernails.'

'I assume that means you didn't?'

'I'm afraid not, but we may have more luck with her clothes. Anyway, I just wanted to let you know her identity has been confirmed.'

Ending the call, Tanner turned to look at Vicky. 'Did you get any of that?'

'That her body's been identified, that she was beaten before being drowned, and there's nothing in the way of DNA or fingerprints?'

'That about sums it up.'

'Did he suggest what we should do next?'

'I forgot to ask.'

'Then may I suggest we go round to her house to let her father know?'

'Are you volunteering?'

'Er – I wasn't planning on.'

'Don't worry. I've already told him once. The second time should be easier.'

'Whilst we're there,' Vicky continued, 'hopefully he'll allow us to have a look around for that story of hers. He may even know something about it.'

'Sounds like a plan,' said Tanner, starting the engine, 'which means two things – at least two things that I can think of.'

'Which are?'

'Firstly, that it won't be long before you'll be able to do this on your own.'

'And secondly?'

'That you're going to have to give me his address. I know we've been there before, but for the life of me, I can't remember where it was.'

- CHAPTER TWENTY-ONE -

TURNING INTO THE driveway of a large, detached house with high, red-bricked walls and a sloping slate-grey roof, Tanner heard Vicky say, 'It doesn't feel all that long ago since we were here last.'

'I know what you mean,' Tanner replied, seeing Mr Lowe talking to a slim, middle-aged woman directly outside the front door. 'It's also difficult to believe that the young woman we were talking to when we were here is now dead.'

Seeing the man and woman's conversation becoming more animated, Tanner parked up alongside a silver-grey Saab 900 to climb quickly out.

The moment he did, the couple fell into what appeared to be a brooding silence as they each turned to glare over at him.

'May I help you?' the man called out, squinting as if struggling to see who it was.

'I'm sorry to bother you, Mr Lowe,' said Tanner, respectfully making his way over. 'It's DCI Tanner, Norfolk Police. We met earlier today – at Wroxham Station.'

'Have you found her?' the woman demanded, stepping towards him while wringing her hands.

'Are you a relative?' Tanner asked.

'I'm Tara's mother,' she stated, stopping immediately in front of him. 'Have you found her?'

Tanner took a moment to look first at Tara's father, then back at her mother, before pulling in a breath. 'I'm sorry,' he eventually began, 'I don't know if your husband mentioned this to you, but we found the body of a young woman this morning.'

The moment he said it, the woman's head sank towards the ground as her shoulders began to shake.

'I've already told you, Mr Tanner,' Mr Lowe began, marching forward to put an arm around his wife, the gesture as protective as it was comforting. 'Whoever you found – it isn't our daughter!'

'Regretfully, our medical examiner has since been able to confirm otherwise.'

'But – how?'

'By examining her dental records.'

As the man just stared unblinkingly back at Tanner while his wife continued to sob, Tanner glanced briefly towards Vicky before nervously clearing his throat. 'Again, I'm most dreadfully sorry. If there's anything we can do to help, please don't hesitate to ask.'

The sound of movement behind him made Tanner glance round – only to find himself staring into the striking green eyes of a pale young woman wearing a simple white cotton dress, whose resemblance to Tara Lowe was so strong that his heart lurched inside his chest.

'What's going on?' the young woman enquired, her eyes moving past Tanner's to rest on the couple standing behind him.

'It's nothing, Sasha,' Mr Lowe replied, in an offhand tone. 'Get back in the car.'

'But this man said they'd found someone. Is it Tara?'

'Your mother will talk to you about it later.'

'Is it her?' she demanded, her proud cheekbones flushing with colour. 'I have every right to know if it is.'

'Do as you're told and get back in the car!' Mr Lowe snapped.

Remaining resolutely where she was for a moment longer, the young woman's eyes eventually shifted back to Tanner's before spinning resentfully around to storm back to the nondescript car she must have come out of.

'You must forgive Sasha,' Mr Lowe eventually said, not even bothering to wait until she was out of earshot. 'She's never liked to do what she's told.'

'Who does?' said Tanner, hopefully loud enough for the young woman to have heard.

Hearing a car door slam, Tanner glanced around to see her staring resentfully down at her lap in the front passenger seat. 'Your daughter, I take it?' he asked, turning slowly back.

'She lives with her mother.'

'And Tara lives with you?'

'Mostly.'

'I'm sure it's not the best time, but would you mind if we asked you a couple of questions about her?'

'Who – Sasha?'

'I was actually thinking of Tara.'

'Yes, you're right, Detective Inspector,' Mr Lowe replied, gazing gently down at his wife's head as she buried her face into his chest, 'now is far from a good time.'

'Of course. We'll leave you in peace. But before we do, would it be alright if we took a very quick look inside her bedroom?'

'I beg your pardon?'

'We're looking for something that might help to

shed some light on who may have wanted to harm her.'

'And you think now's the right time to do that, do you?'

'To be honest, I can't think of a worse time,' Tanner admitted, 'but we have to start looking into what happened. The longer we leave it, the harder it will be to find who was responsible.'

'Then I suggest you come back another time.'

'How about this evening?' Tanner proposed.

'I'm sorry, Mr Tanner, but we're going to need longer than that.'

'Then tomorrow morning?'

'I was thinking more along the lines of next week.'

'I'm afraid we can't wait that long.'

'And why the hell not?'

'Because of the circumstances surrounding Tara's death, and the fact that we've already launched an investigation.'

'I'm not sure what that has to do with us.'

'Don't you want to find the person responsible?'

'Would it bring her back?' he suddenly demanded, tears appearing at the corners of his eyes.

Tanner opened his mouth to answer, only to close it again when he saw the demented look in the man's eye.

'No. I didn't think so,' Lowe continued. 'Now, if you'd be kind enough to leave us to grieve the death of our daughter, I'd be grateful.'

'Yes, of course. But we will have to return – you must understand that. You may not care who murdered your daughter, but we most definitely do. When we're able to, we'll need to ask where you were at the time of her death. There will also be the question of your fingerprints and DNA.'

'What?'

'We'll need to take samples – not only yours, but your wife's as well.'

'You're not seriously suggesting that either one of us could have been responsible?'

'I'm not suggesting anything, Mr Lowe, but in order to help eliminate you from our enquiries, we will need the aforementioned samples. If you refuse, then I'll have no choice but to arrest you for obstruction of justice. The same applies to allowing us access to your property. If you fail to give permission, then under Section 8 of the Police and Criminal Evidence Act, I'll be forced to apply for a search warrant.'

'Then I can tell you now – I'm not allowing you inside. Not after you've treated us with such callous insensitivity.'

'Then we'll just have to return with the necessary warrant,' said Tanner, with an indifferent shrug, 'but I have to warn you: any attempt by either of you to conceal, tamper with, or destroy what could be considered evidence could lead to a charge of Conspiracy to Pervert the Course of Justice. In the case of murder, that would mean your immediate imprisonment.'

- CHAPTER TWENTY-TWO -

TANNER LEFT HIS remarks to sink in for a moment before turning around to lead Vicky back to his car. Once they'd climbed inside and the doors were closed, as Tanner started the engine to begin reversing, Vicky caught his eye to ask, 'Did you get the feeling Mr Lowe was trying to hide something?'

'Because he didn't seem keen for us to take his fingerprints and DNA, or because he refused to let us inside his house?'

'I was thinking both.'

'I'm not sure,' came Tanner's eventual reply, glancing back at the house in the rear-view mirror as he steered the car out of the drive. 'He did seem genuinely upset, as did his wife, but that doesn't mean much. What we don't have is any reason to believe that either of them had a hand. We certainly don't have any evidence. All we know so far is that Tara was supposed to spend the weekend with her mother, but that they had an argument on Friday night, at which point she drove home – which does leave one rather obvious question.'

'Which is...?'

'If that was the case, then what happened to her car? If you remember, she had an old beige Mini. It wasn't there. It wasn't at Blackfleet Broad, either.'

'Maybe she'd sold it, and used her father's instead?'

'Maybe,' Tanner agreed. 'The problem is, with her parents proving to be on the uncooperative side, it might be difficult for us to find out.'

'Not necessarily,' said Vicky, diving into her handbag.

'What are you looking for?' asked Tanner, glancing curiously around.

'This!' she eventually replied, pulling out the photograph Mr Lowe had given Tanner when he'd reported her as missing. 'As you can see,' she continued, digging around for her phone, 'it has the car's number plate on it.'

'Good thinking, Batman,' said Tanner, refocusing his attention on the road.

'I'd prefer Batwoman.'

'So would I!' Tanner exclaimed, before catching the admonishing look in her eye. 'Anyway,' he said, clearing his throat, 'perhaps you could ask Townsend to find out whether she still owns it. If she does, tell him to check for any CCTV cameras along the route between her parents' houses. At least that'll help us to verify her father's story. And it might be wise for us to leave a squad car parked outside their house, just to keep an eye on him.'

Resting her phone in her lap, Vicky leaned her head back against the Triumph Stag's black vinyl seat to close her eyes, leaving Tanner glancing curiously around at her.

'I know you're the SIO, and everything,' he began, 'and that you're under no obligation to do what I suggest, but – are you going to?'

'I already have,' she replied, suppressing a smirk, 'although I asked Gina instead of Townsend.'

'Oh, right,' came Tanner's surprised response. 'Then perhaps you could ask someone to apply for a search warrant for Mr Lowe's premises?'

'I've done that as well.'

'But – when?' Tanner demanded, doing a double-take between her and the road.

'When you were busy telling me what to do. It doesn't take long – not when you're using WhatsApp.'

'Since when have we been using WhatsApp?'

'Since I set up a group chat for us.'

'When did you do that?'

'When we were talking to Mr Lowe.'

'Oh, right,' said Tanner, unsure what else to say. 'Have I been invited?' he tentatively asked.

'Of course!' Vicky exclaimed. 'I sent you an invitation at the same time as everyone else. I thought it was about time we brought ourselves kicking and screaming into the 21st century.'

'You don't think you could have asked me first?' he enquired, making himself sound even more insecure.

'Oh, sorry – I thought I was the SIO?'

'Well – yes – you are – but you could have at least run it by me.'

'You mean in the same way you run things past Forrester, before going ahead and doing them anyway?'

Forced to think about that for a moment, Tanner eventually shrugged. 'Fair enough, I suppose. Who did you ask to sort out the search warrant?'

'I didn't.'

'I thought you said you did?'

'I mentioned in the group chat that it needed to be done. Townsend came back to say that he'd be happy to.'

'Then it sounds like you're on top of things.'

'Thank you.'

'Have you told them about your new appointment?'

Vicky shook her head. 'I thought I'd leave that to you.'

'At least I still have one job to do,' he laughed.

'You can keep updating Forrester as well, if you like, but only because I'd rather not have to talk to him.'

'He's not that bad.'

'Really?'

'OK, he is. But either way, until you've mastered the art of being able to lie to him without flinching, it's probably better if I continue to.

'So, not-so-young Vicky,' Tanner continued, smiling around at her, 'what's next?'

'Unless we can think of another way to find Tara's alleged sensationalist news story – or at least find someone who'd be able to corroborate it – I'm not sure what else we can do.'

'Then perhaps I may make a suggestion.'

'Which is...?'

'That we go round to see that Balinger chap.'

'For what possible reason?'

'To ask if he knows anything about Tara's story – or perhaps, more to the point, when he saw her last.'

'But we don't have any evidence to suggest that he was involved. His name hasn't even been mentioned.'

'Yes it has.'

'When?'

'By me, just now. Also before, when we were first told about Tara's story.'

'You mean – Tara's *alleged* story.'

'That's the one.'

'Which – if I remember correctly – was you as well.'

'What was?'

'The person who mentioned Balinger's name.'

'There we are then! Not only have I mentioned his name on no fewer than two occasions, but you have as well.'

'When did *I* say his name?'

'Just now, when you said, "the person who mentioned Balinger's name".'

'Oh, right. Who needs evidence when you have logic like that?'

'Exactly! Besides, Tara was the one who was blocking Balinger's previous Bluebell Wood development plans – successfully, I may add. Who's to say she wasn't doing the same thing all over again, but this time he wasn't prepared to stand by and let her?'

'Well, yes, it's possible, but as I said before, Balinger's name hasn't even been mentioned.'

'And as I said before, I've said his name a number of times now – as have you – which is good enough for me. Besides, we're not exactly going to charge him with her murder. I just want to know if he knows anything about the story, and if Tara has ever spoken to him about it.'

'Would he tell us if he had?'

'I've no idea, but there's one thing I do know.'

'Which is?'

'That we're not going to find out unless we ask him.'

- CHAPTER TWENTY-THREE -

FOLLOWING VICKY'S DIRECTIONS to where Balinger's office was based, Tanner was soon leading her towards a large multistorey office block in the middle of Stalham.

'He can't own all of this,' Vicky whispered, as they stepped inside a large open-plan reception area defined by a gleaming dark grey marble floor, expansive smoked-glass windows, and a lofty high vaulted ceiling.

'I think you're right,' Tanner eventually replied, gazing about as they made their way towards a curving black reception desk, rising out of the floor ahead. 'At least I hope you are.'

Stepping up to one of two immaculately dressed female receptionists, each one as attractive as the other, Tanner cleared his throat in an effort to lure her eyes from the screen that her mascara-lined eyes were focused on.

Failing to do so, he glanced briefly around at Vicky before resting an arm on the desk. 'Sorry to bother you,' he began, 'but you wouldn't happen to know if a Mr Simon Balinger works here, by any chance?'

'Give me just one moment,' the woman replied, her perfectly manicured nails rattling over the keyboard before turning to face Tanner with a fixed, well-rehearsed smile. 'Sorry about that. Who were you looking for again?'

'Mr Simon Balinger.'
'From which company?'
'I believe it's called SKB Holdings.'
'And do you have an appointment?'
'I'm afraid not.'

'OK, hold on,' she replied, her head swivelling back to her monitor as if she were a humanoid robot.

As her fingernails tap-danced over the keyboard once again, she eventually looked back to say, 'Mr Simon Balinger of SKB Holdings does have an office here.'

'OK, good.'
'But unfortunately, he's not in.'
'Oh, right.'
'Would you like to leave him a message?'
'Do you know what time he'll be back?'
'I'm afraid I don't.'
'Do you know where he's gone?'

'Again, I don't have that information. Would you like me to make a note of your name and telephone number on our system, and ask him to give you a call?'

'I suppose that will have to do,' Tanner sighed, prising one of his business cards out from his wallet to present to her.

Taking the proffered card, she stared down her nose at it to read, 'Mr Detective Chief Inspector John Tanner?'

'That's correct,' Tanner replied, 'albeit without the "Mr".'

Placing the card down, she poised her fingers over the keyboard, staring first at the screen, then back at the card, before looking at him again. 'I'm afraid I don't have an option for Detective Chief Inspector in the title field. Would it be alright if I selected "Mr" instead?'

'By all means,' Tanner replied, beginning to wonder how long this was going to take.

'And your first name is John?'

'That's correct.'

'Surname Tanner?'

'Uh-huh,' Tanner replied, glancing incredulously around at Vicky.

'And which company do you work for?'

Discreetly shaking his head, Tanner replied, 'It's written on the business card.'

Glancing back at it, she returned to staring at the keyboard to mumble, 'Norfolk Police,' while her fingers rattled over the keys like the sound of a distant machine gun. 'And the best number for him to contact you on?'

'That would be my mobile – again, as written on the card.'

Another short machine-gun burst had her staring back at Tanner. 'If he can't get hold of you on the phone, would it be alright if he were to contact you by email?'

'He's free to contact me any way he likes. Carrier pigeon, if he has one.'

With her fingers dancing over the keyboard once more, curious to know if she was actually writing that down, Tanner leaned over the top of the reception desk to try and see her screen, only for her to turn her head to glare at him with admonishing disapproval.

'Sorry,' Tanner apologised, bringing his head back to where it was evidently supposed to be. 'I was just wondering how long this was going to take?'

'Nearly done,' she suddenly smiled. 'I just need to know if you'd be happy to sign up for our newsletter.'

'Your newsletter?' Tanner repeated.

'Just in case you're ever in the market for a new

office. We offer a wide range of modern, open-plan spaces – everything from what we call a shared "hot desk" to suites that can accommodate up to a hundred people. We also have a café, gym, sauna, and heated swimming pool, all on site. Our premier members also get free access to a local tennis court and golf club.'

'Do your offices come equipped with modern ergonomic furniture and plants?' Tanner enquired, remembering Simon Reynolds'.

'All our offices come fully furnished.'

'How about secretaries able to produce perfectly blended coffee at the push of a button?'

'I'm sorry, Mr Tanner, but we're unable to fulfil staffing requirements. However, our café does provide excellent coffee.'

'How about holding cells?'

'Holding cells?' she repeated.

'You know – secure rooms with locked doors, for the purpose of holding prisoners prior to either formal interview or transportation?'

'I'm – er – not sure we have any of those, but most of our doors do have locks. We also have security cameras that are monitored 24/7 by our in-house team.'

'OK – well – I'd have to run it past my boss, but it does sound rather appealing.'

'Is that a yes for our newsletter?'

'Why not!' Tanner exclaimed, turning to grin at Vicky, only to find her staring back at him with a disapproving glare.

'OK, Mr Tanner,' the receptionist continued, 'that's all set up for you. I'm sending Mr Balinger a text message now, and you'll be receiving our monthly newsletter at the beginning of each month. Is there anything else I can help you with?'

'That's it, I think,' Tanner replied, hearing something ping from somewhere behind him.

Glancing curiously around, he stared over towards the reception's tall, smoked-glass entrance doors to see none other than Mr Balinger pushing his way through one of them, only to come to an abrupt halt just inside to stare down at his phone.

'It would appear their messaging service is as impressive as their serviced offices,' Tanner remarked, glancing at Vicky. 'Not only does it deliver the message to the correct person, but it appears to teleport them to the required location as well.'

With Vicky shaking her head at him, Tanner turned back to gaze at the man still staring at his phone. 'Mr Balinger!' he called out, raising an enquiring hand as he stepped towards him.

As Balinger glanced up with a confused frown, Tanner pulled out his formal ID. 'DCI Tanner, Norfolk Police. You may remember me from that unfortunate incident at Bluebell Wood.'

'Mr Detective Chief Inspector Tanner,' Balinger began, returning to look at his phone. 'I've only just this second had a text message asking me to give you a call.'

'Yes, I know! I was telling my colleague, DI Gilbert here,' Tanner continued, glancing at Vicky as she reluctantly approached, 'that your serviced office's messaging system is even more impressive than the offices themselves – and that's saying something!'

'Dare I ask what you'd like to talk to me about? It's just that I have another meeting I need to attend – one I'm already late for,' he added, glancing peevishly down at his watch.

Waiting for him to look back up, Tanner held his gaze. 'We wanted to ask if you'd heard of a place called Blackfleet Broad?'

'Why – are you lost?' he replied, with just the hint of a smirk.

'Does that mean you have, or you haven't?'

'Alright, you've got me,' he sighed. 'I have heard of it. Should I call my lawyer now, or wait till we get to the station?'

'May I also ask if you remember someone by the name of Tara Lowe?'

'She's not about to give birth to my love child, is she? Because if she is, I've definitely never heard of her!'

'Unfortunately, her body was found this morning – held underwater by a mud weight – at the aforementioned Blackfleet Broad.'

'So she's not, then? Well, that's a relief. I'm not sure I could afford the child payments for yet another of my seemingly endless illegitimate offspring.'

'She was a member of an environmental action group called Nature First. If you remember, they were eventually able to stop you from bulldozing your way through Bluebell Wood to build a rather large housing development.'

'I'm sorry, Mr Tanner, but I've probably found myself up against more environmental action groups in my time than drunken tarts down my local pub,' he replied, presenting Vicky with a lurid, lopsided grin before returning to stare at Tanner.

'Oh, right,' Tanner continued. 'I must admit, I'm a little surprised. Judging by how much money her work with Nature First must have cost you on that one development alone – I'd have thought her name would've been seared into your brain, never to be forgotten again.'

'Sadly, my memory isn't what it used to be.

Now, if you'll excuse me, I really must be getting on.'

'Yes, of course,' said Tanner, stepping aside with an apologetic nod.

With Balinger remaining where he was for a moment, as if unsure whether he was really being allowed to leave, Tanner waited for him to step past before saying, 'Actually – sorry – but there was one more thing.'

'Well, there's a surprise,' Balinger replied, turning slowly around to meet Tanner's gaze once again.

'I also wanted to ask if you've heard of someone by the name of Alfred Beaumont.'

Seeing Balinger's eyes dart almost imperceptibly between Tanner's, he continued, 'He's a professor teaching History at Norfolk University, if it helps.'

'I'm sorry,' Balinger eventually said, 'but once again, I've never heard of him – though that's probably because I'm not a university History student. If I had been, then no doubt I'd be a little more use.'

'Then you don't know anything about an archaeological dig that's about to take place – again, at Blackfleet Broad?'

'No, I don't!' Balinger stated, staring belligerently at Tanner. 'May I go now?'

'By all means,' Tanner smiled. 'But if we find out that you've been lying to us, we will, of course, be back.'

- CHAPTER TWENTY-FOUR -

OPENING THE DOOR for Vicky to then follow her out, Tanner caught up to her to ask, 'So, what did you think?'

'That he's a weaselly little male chauvinist pig, one who should have been locked up a long time ago – but that's what I thought about him the last time we met.'

'Did you think he was lying?'

'About what?'

'Everything!' Tanner exclaimed, reaching his car.

'I wouldn't be surprised, but I couldn't tell from just talking to him.'

'You can often see it in the eyes,' Tanner commented, unlocking the doors to pull open his own.

'In the way people look away when they're talking to you?'

'Sometimes. Certainly with less confident people. But with individuals such as our Mr Balinger, more often than not they'll do the opposite.'

'Which is?'

'To stare directly at you without moving a muscle.'

'I assume he was?'

'Most of the time.'

'So you think he remembered who Tara Lowe was?'

'As I said, I'd have been surprised if he didn't, but it was his reaction when I mentioned the name Alfred Beaumont that was of greater interest.'

'Which was...?'

'His previously impenetrable gaze seemed to falter for just a fraction of a second, which I'm fairly sure means that he knew exactly who he was. And that leaves me thinking that my original hunch was right – that he is the building developer mentioned in Tara Lowe's story.'

'You mean, the story we still haven't even read yet, let alone had a chance to verify,' commented Vicky, in a less optimistic tone.

'You know what they say: where there's smoke, there's fire.'

'I'd normally agree with you, but we don't seem to have either.'

'We have a dead girl, that's what we have. Not just any girl, either. If we can prove what I strongly suspect – that Balinger does know Professor Beaumont, probably through some sort of dodgy financial dealing – then I think we'd be onto something.'

Hearing his phone ring from the depths of his sailing jacket, Tanner pulled it out to answer. 'Tanner speaking!'

'Good afternoon, Tanner, it's Dr Johnstone calling again. Is now a good time?'

'It's as good a time as any,' Tanner replied, as they both climbed into the car.

'Just to let you know that I've emailed Miss Tara Lowe's post-mortem report to you,' Johnstone continued.

'Anything of interest?' asked Tanner, glancing

around to see Vicky glued to her phone.

'Pretty much as we expected. Although she'd been beaten – quite severely, I may add – death was from asphyxiation by drowning.'

'Time of death?'

'I'd say sometime between nine o'clock in the evening and midnight on Friday.'

'Do you know how long it was between when she was beaten and when she drowned?'

'An hour – maybe two.'

'Was there any indication that she'd been attacked in any other way?'

'She hadn't been raped, if that's what you mean.'

'Had she been sexually active recently?'

'Not that I could see.'

'I assume you've included a toxicology report?'

'Yes, of course!'

'Was there anything there that could be of interest?'

'Nothing worth mentioning. Her blood sugar level was a little high, but nothing out of the ordinary.'

'She hadn't been drugged?'

'There was no sign of anything in her system, nor was there anything in her stomach – not so much as a paracetamol.'

'Alcohol? Marijuana?'

'Nothing at all,' Johnstone confirmed. 'And because she'd been in the water for what must have been at least six hours, there wasn't much in the way of DNA or fingerprint evidence either – but I think that was to be expected.'

'So, you can't really tell me anything at all?' said Tanner, with fractious irritation.

'Other than what she ate before she died, I'm

afraid not.'

'And what was that?'

'By the looks of it, I'd say it was a pizza – but it's all in my report, as you'll see.'

Ending the call with an indignant sigh, Tanner turned to find Vicky grinning at him like a cat who'd just eaten the proverbial canary.

'What are you looking so pleased about?'

'I had a hunch!'

'OK, well, try not to worry. They generally don't last very long, so you should be feeling more like your normal self soon enough.'

'You know what we were discussing before?' Vicky continued, ignoring Tanner's rather poor attempt at humour.

'You mean, before Dr Johnstone's post-mortem report came through telling us exactly nothing that we didn't already know?'

'I was thinking that if Balinger had been lying to us, and that he did know Professor Beaumont, then it was more likely to have been a business relationship than a personal one.'

'Go on,' Tanner prompted.

'So I thought I'd look up his name on the Companies House website, to see what came up.'

'Something involving the professor, presumably?'

'They're both listed as directors of a company called BBSE International Investments Ltd,' she replied, 'along with two other people, one of whom I think you know.'

'And who is that, may I ask?'

'Mr George Elliston,' Vicky replied, showing Tanner her phone's screen. 'Your favourite Member of Parliament.'

Studying the name with particular interest, a thin smile appeared on Tanner's face. 'Now that *is* interesting,' he eventually said, taking the phone from her to scroll down the screen. 'That last name rings a bell as well,' he added, drawing Vicky's attention to it. 'Jeremy Southcott?'

'I was thinking the same thing myself,' she replied, taking the phone back to navigate to another app, 'which is why I looked him up as well. He's the Chairman of Norfolk Council's Planning and Housing Committee. I'm pretty sure that his name came up during the Bluebell Wood investigation as well.'

'They're making it too easy for us,' Tanner grinned.

'Hardly! We still don't have any evidence to connect them to what happened to Tara. Neither do we have any idea if her story was true.'

'But at least we have something to go on – and sometimes that's enough.'

'OK, so – what do you want to do now?'

'What do you think we should do?'

'If Tara was killed because of what she found out about Blackfleet Broad, then we really need to get our hands on that story of hers.'

'And if whoever killed her managed to get to it first?'

'Then I suppose we'll need to research it for ourselves, which will mean getting everyone else involved.'

'Agreed,' replied Tanner, 'which means you'll need to brief the office as to what we've found.'

'What do you mean – me?'

'Because you're the SIO – or had you forgotten?'

'Can't I just send them all a WhatsApp message?'

'You're not scared of public speaking, I hope?'

'Of course I am!'

'Yes, me too,' Tanner grimaced. 'Anyway, sometimes, just occasionally, we do still need to talk to people face-to-face, even in today's increasingly prevalent age of social media. Briefing the office will also help to prepare you for when you have to speak to the press.'

'We're not holding a press conference as well, are we?'

'We may not have any choice, but I suggest we start with an office-wide briefing and see where we go from there.'

'Can't you at least do it with me?'

With Vicky staring at him like a lost puppy, Tanner let out a capitulating sigh. 'I suppose I need to formally introduce you as the SIO anyway, so I might as well.'

- CHAPTER TWENTY-FIVE -

'ALRIGHT, LISTEN UP everyone!' called Tanner, standing in front of the office about an hour later, with Vicky fidgeting nervously beside him.

As the various conversations drifted to an eventual close, he stared around at them all before continuing. 'As I'm sure you all know by now, the body of a young woman was found in the early hours of the morning by a couple of fishermen at Blackfleet Broad – one of whom sadly drowned in the process. We aren't treating his death as suspicious, but we are most definitely treating the woman's. Dental records have confirmed her as being Miss Tara Lowe,' Tanner continued, turning to point at the photograph they'd been given of her, now stuck to a whiteboard behind him. 'She was the leader of an environmental action group called Nature First. Having recently graduated from Law school, she was also endeavouring to launch a career as a freelance journalist.

'Dr Johnstone's post-mortem report concludes that death was from drowning, but she'd been severely beaten about two hours before. Time of death is thought to have been sometime on Friday night. She was supposed to be spending the weekend at her mother's house, but apparently they had an argument shortly after she arrived, at which point she was supposed to have driven back to her father's – only she never showed up. As you can probably tell, her parents are separated. Tara lived predominantly with her father.

'Before going into the details of what we've been able to find out so far, I'm pleased to announce that our very own DI Vicky Gilbert will be taking the lead on this one.'

As the office erupted into cheers, wolf-whistles, and generous applause, Tanner turned to watch her cringe with awkward embarrassment.

'As you can probably tell,' he eventually continued, turning back to face the office as the cheering gradually subsided, 'she didn't exactly volunteer, but the promise of a generous pay rise was enough to have her putting her hand up.

'So, with that said,' Tanner concluded, 'it's over to DI Gilbert!'

Amidst another spluttering of applause, Vicky stepped forward to say, 'Thanks, boss,' in a heavily sarcastic tone. 'Although, just for the record,' she continued, gazing around at everyone, 'I haven't been promised a pay rise. I certainly haven't been given one. The only reason I'm doing it is because our illustrious leader – DCI Tanner – didn't want to.'

A welcome ripple of laughter seemed to help her relax – enough, at least, for her to look more confidently around the room before continuing.

'Bringing the subject back to the investigation, we believe there may be a connection between her work with the previously mentioned environmental group and the broad where her body was found. When we arrived at the scene, a group of her activist friends were already there, preparing to protest what was supposed to be the start of an archaeological dig at Blackfleet Broad. They told us she'd apparently been writing a story about the dig for one of the local newspapers. According to them, she'd found out that the dig was simply an excuse to have the broad drained to make way for the construction of a large office development. Unfortunately, we've yet to unearth the story itself, but we have applied for a search warrant to have her house searched, so hopefully something will turn up there.

'What we have found is a connection to the person responsible for the dig, a certain Professor Alfred Beaumont. According to the Companies House website, he's one of four directors of a company called BBSE International Investments Ltd. The others are three men we've had dealings with before. One is Jeremy Southcott, Chairman of Norfolk Council's Planning and Housing Committee; another is Simon Balinger, who owns a local construction company; and fourth – but by no means least – is George Elliston, MP for Norfolk. So, as you can see, it's looking rather likely that Tara's story – if it does exist – was most probably true. If that is the case, the question then becomes who else knew about it, and whether what they discovered was enough to make them feel the need to silence her.'

'May I ask a question?' said Haverstock, raising his hand near the front.

'Please,' Vicky smiled.

'If the individuals mentioned did reach the conclusion that it was necessary to permanently silence her, then surely they wouldn't have wanted anyone to know what they were up to?'

'I think that would've been the idea,' Vicky replied, returning a confused frown.

'Then why would they have set up a company together, for all to see – including the taxman and just about everyone else? I mean, it's hardly the sort of thing criminal organisations go around doing, is it?'

'I've no idea,' came her honest reply, 'but it's certainly a remarkable coincidence that Tara Lowe's body was found with her feet tied to a mud weight, bang in the middle of Blackfleet Broad – a large body of water that was about to be drained in search of buried Viking treasure – and that the person leading the exploration just happens to be in business with three of the most influential people in the whole of Norfolk.'

With Haverstock left to first open, then close his mouth, Vicky continued by asking, 'May I continue?'

'By all means,' he eventually replied, returning an admiring smile.

'Unfortunately,' Vicky continued, casting her eyes around the room with a now steady confidence, 'as Tara's body is thought to have been left submerged underwater for several days, little in the way of physical evidence has been found. Something else that appears to be missing is her car. I don't suppose anyone's had any luck finding it?'

With her eyes returning to Haverstock, he cleared his throat to say, 'We're still checking CCTV footage.'

'How about ANPR?'

'Her number plate didn't come up.'

'Have any abandoned cars been reported?'

'Nothing we've heard about.'

'Then maybe try checking to see if it's been left in a public car park somewhere. Henderson, if I can leave that with you?'

Seeing the lanky young man obediently nod, Vicky continued.

'Apart from that, I think we need to focus our attention on those who had the most to lose if Tara's story had been published – that's if she even wrote it. As there are four individuals, perhaps they can be divided up between you. We'll need the normal background checks as well as access to their emails, finances, and social media, but what we're really looking for is anything that might lead back to Blackfleet Broad, or any communication they may have had with Tara Lowe.

'What about the victim's parents?' asked Haverstock, respectfully raising his hand again. 'Has anyone spoken to them yet?'

'DCI Tanner and I have – albeit briefly. Her father was reluctant to believe that it was his daughter. He's also been unwilling to let us inside his house, which is why I asked for someone to apply for a search warrant. Speaking of which, has someone been able to do that?'

'I emailed it over to them a couple of hours ago,' Townsend replied.

'OK, good. Let me know as soon as you hear back. We'll pick things up again with the father once we have. At some point, we'll also need to have a proper chat with the mother – if for no other reason than to find out what their argument was about – but again, that can wait until the search warrant has come through.

'Right, I think that's about it,' Vicky concluded, clasping her hands together. 'Any questions?'

Seeing Haverstock raise his hand again, Vicky continued to look around the room. 'I don't suppose anyone else would like to have a go?'

'It's actually a question for DCI Tanner,' Haverstock said.

'Oh, right!' Vicky replied, glancing around at him.

'I was just wondering,' Haverstock began,

catching Tanner's eye, 'if DI Gilbert – our brand-new Senior Investigating Officer – *will* be getting a pay rise? I don't know about everyone else, but from what I've seen so far, I really think she should!'

As everyone began cheering once again, and with Townsend beginning to chant, 'Pay rise! Pay rise! Pay rise!' while clapping his hands in time, Tanner raised his voice to step slowly forward.

'Alright, alright!' he called out, lifting his voice above the unruly noise. 'I certainly intend to mention it to the powers that be, but as I've already said to DI Gilbert, I wouldn't hold your breath.'

- CHAPTER TWENTY-SIX -

CREEPING INTO HIS home a few hours later, Tanner quietly closed the door to stand perfectly still, listening for the slightest sound of movement.

Wondering if it was possible that Baby Samantha was actually asleep, he was in the process of placing his keys down on the sideboard as quietly as was humanly possible when a sudden, ear-piercing shriek echoed around the house, followed by a loud, ominous thud.

With it sounding like someone had been murdered in the living room with a candlestick, he threw his keys down to hurry forward.

Bursting into the main living area to stare fitfully about, he let out a sigh of relief when he saw Samantha crawling across the carpet towards him with delirious excitement, whilst Christine was exactly where he thought she'd be – bumbling around the kitchen as if looking for a way out.

'For a minute there, I thought someone had been murdered,' he eventually said, crouching down to offer Samantha some encouragement.

'Oh, hello, darling,' called Christine, throwing something into the oven before spinning gracefully away. 'I didn't hear you come in.'

'I thought everyone was asleep. That was until I heard someone scream.'

'I think you'll find that was Samantha. Her hearing must be better than mine. I left her on the sofa while I started preparing your dinner. She must have climbed down to come and see you.'

'That would explain the loud, rather ominous thud,' he replied, as Samantha reached him to begin gurgling up at him through a wide, toothless grin.

'Which reminds me,' Christine continued, 'she has something to show you.'

'I sincerely hope you're not about to tell me that she's brought a boy around?' Tanner enquired, taking a cautious moment to glance fitfully about.

'Er... not that I'm aware of.'

'Then presumably she's just made her very first soufflé?'

Happy to ignore him, Christine said, 'If you prop her up against the side of her playpen, she might be willing to show you.'

'She's not finally ready to reveal that tunnel she's spent the last four months digging, is she?'

'You'll just have to see,' said Christine, continuing to gaze over at them with just the hint of a smile.

'Another mystery for me to solve,' commented Tanner, heaving Samantha up. 'What have you been up to, young lady?' he enquired, gazing lovingly into her impossibly large blue eyes.

As she began wriggling with indignant frustration, he did as he was told, manhandling her over to her playpen whilst trying not to drop her in the process.

Eventually setting her down, he stood back to watch her do nothing but to remain where she was sitting, examining her hands as though she'd only just realised she had them.

'She's not going to do some sort of magic trick, is she?'

'Something like that,' said Christine, joining

Tanner in watching Samantha as she turned her attention to the bars.

Having apparently made up her mind as to what she was going to do, she took hold of the bars to begin lifting herself up, until she was eventually standing a little precariously on her feet, both hands still holding tight to the bars in front of her.

'She's finally learnt how to stand up,' said Tanner, in an underwhelmed tone.

'Don't sound too impressed,' Christine responded, folding her arms to glare over at him.

'Sorry, but I thought she was about to cut someone in half.'

'Anyway, I don't think she's finished yet.'

Falling silent again, they watched her remain where she was for a moment before eventually letting go of first one hand, then the other.

Taking a moment to balance herself, she risked a mischievous glance at her father before pivoting around to begin walking towards him with an overconfident swagger.

Feeling himself welling up with emotion, Tanner crouched down to beam a broad, proud smile at her as she continued along, faster and faster, straight into his awaiting hands.

'Now that is a magic trick!' he exclaimed, hoisting her up to give her a well-earned, slightly damp kiss.

'I told you she had something to show you,' said Christine, smiling at them both before returning to whatever it was she'd been doing before.

'Well, you were certainly right about that. Now, where's that sexy young magician's assistant you were going to cut in half?'

Seeming to get his joke, Samantha shrieked with laughter before starting to wriggle all over again.

'Do you want to have another go?' Tanner asked, nodding into her now rather frustrated-looking face. 'How about taking a stroll down to the corner shop to get me a bottle of rum and some cigarettes?'

'You're not going to take up smoking, I hope?' came Christine's concerned voice.

'Aren't you more worried about me sending Samantha out to buy some?'

'If I thought she could make it past the living room door, then I probably would be.'

'Anyway,' Tanner continued, carrying Samantha back to her playpen to see if she wanted another go, 'I have run out of rum, unless you've just happened to buy some for me?' he asked, staring over at her with an optimistic frown.

'There's a brand-new bottle for you on the breakfast bar – which you would have seen if you'd looked.'

'So there is!' he replied, seeing it hiding in plain sight, in exactly the same place as the other one had been.

Making his way towards the breakfast bar, and the bottle resting on top of it, the sound of something made him glance around to see Baby Samantha come wobbling to an uncertain halt behind him.

'Looks like you're being followed,' commented Christine, glancing over.

'I think you're right,' he replied, picking her up to place her securely on his hip, only for her to start squirming again in a desperate effort to get down.

'If I were you, I'd let her walk around for a bit. It might help to wear her out before bedtime.'

'If you say so,' Tanner replied, placing her back down on her feet for her to immediately begin walking off, this time heading towards the half-open patio doors that led out to the veranda, and the river beyond, 'but that will mean having to put up some safety gates. She may be able to walk now, but I'm fairly sure she can't swim.'

'I think she'll be all right out there,' said Christine. 'I've already had a good look around. There's no way she'd be able to fit through the balustrade fencing, and it's too high for her to climb over the railing.'

'May I suggest we don't risk it?' he said, heading past the perambulating toddler to reach for the patio door.

As he slid it closed, Samantha stopped where she was to give him a long, hard stare before seeming to shrug her shoulders to begin heading towards the fireplace.

'We may need to put something around the fire as well,' added Tanner, grateful at least that it wasn't on, but deciding to chase after her nonetheless to gently guide her away.

Watching her amble straight towards the television and the tangle of plug sockets beside it, Tanner steered her away again – only to see her make for the kitchen, just as Christine drew an enormous, razor-sharp knife from its wooden block to begin attacking some poor, innocent vegetables.

'How about I carry you around for a bit,' he said to her, scooping her up in his arms.

Placing her down on his hip, half-expecting her to start squirming again, he was pleasantly surprised when she looked up to smile at him before resting her head against his chest.

Happy enough to start pacing up and down with her whilst thinking about all the things he was going to need to do to make the house toddler-safe,

Tanner caught Christine's eye to ask, 'How was your day?'

'Apart from Samantha walking, very much like every other one. Yourself?'

'Eventful,' came his brusque response.

Christine stopped what she was doing to gaze over at him. 'I'm sorry – I completely forgot.'

'About what?'

'About the call you had this morning – and the man who drowned over at Blackfleet Broad?'

'Yes, of course. That feels like weeks ago!'

'How did it happen?'

'Apparently, it was a fishing accident.'

'Oh, right. I'm sorry to hear that. Perhaps you could pretend he was murdered?'

'Fortunately, I didn't need to.'

'You mean – it wasn't an accident?'

'No, we're fairly sure it was. He fell out of the boat, only to get his foot caught around a rope tied to a mud weight at the bottom.'

'Then why are you back so late?'

'Because, at the other end of the rope was the body of a young woman. She'd been badly beaten before being drowned with the help of the afore mentioned mud weight.'

'That's a relief. For a minute there I thought you had to go an entire day without having a murder to investigate.'

'The problem is, this time around I actually knew the victim.'

'I thought you knew the last victim as well, being that he was my ex-boyfriend?'

'I never did tell you about that, did I,' mused Tanner.

'You never told me about what?'

'Never mind. No doubt it can wait until another

day. Is it all right if Samantha falls asleep?' he asked, deciding to steer the conversation away from the letter he'd found inside the book a former murder suspect had given him for Christmas – the contents of which he'd decided to keep firmly to himself.

'Yes, that's fine,' Christine replied, returning to her dinner preparations. 'If you could put her down in her cot for me, she'll probably sleep through the night.'

Having done what he was told, Tanner returned a few minutes later to find a plate of steaming hot food waiting for him on the breakfast bar.

'Did she go down OK?' asked Christine, now busy loading the dishwasher.

'She was out like a light,' he replied, propping himself up on one of the breakfast bar stools to stare down at the food. 'This looks nice,' he said, picking up the knife and fork whilst trying to work out what it was. 'At least, I think it does.'

'It's Pithiviers de Canard aux Foie Gras et Morilles,' she replied, in a near-perfect French accent.

'I see,' said Tanner, still staring suspiciously down at it. 'May I ask what that is in English?'

'It's a pie made with puff pastry filled with duck, foie gras, and mushrooms.'

'How delightful. And what are these?' he added, pointing at something on the side.

Lifting her head to glance over, Christine replied, 'They're vegetables. You've seen those before, haven't you?'

'Well, yes, but I must admit, it's been a while.'

'Anyway, I hope you like it. With Samantha

becoming increasingly independent, it's certainly nice to be able to start cooking again.'

'Isn't it,' Tanner remarked in response, albeit with less enthusiasm.

'So, are you going to tell me about that girl?'

'Which girl was that?' Tanner replied, prodding at the food before taking his first tentative bite.

'The one whose body you found, who you said you knew.'

Finding Christine's cooking surprisingly delicious, Tanner ploughed merrily away whilst answering between mouthfuls.

'Tara Lowe.'

'Do I know her?'

'I don't think so. I barely did myself. I only met her a couple of times. It was in connection with our Bluebell Wood investigation, just before we had Samantha.'

'You mean, before *I* had Samantha?'

'Yes, of course. Sorry. I must admit I sometimes forget that I wasn't the one who gave birth to her.'

'What do you mean, you *sometimes* forget?' Christine queried, stopping what she was doing to stare over at him.

'You know – when I'm not thinking about it,' came his rather vague response.

Glancing up at the look on her face, he returned to his meal to say, 'You know, this food really is remarkably good. You must give me the recipe.'

'Going back to what you were saying,' Christine continued.

'You mean about the girl?'

'About struggling to remember that it wasn't you who gave birth to Samantha.'

'Oh, right. I thought we'd moved past that.'

'It's just that your comment would seem to imply

that there are times when you think you did.'

OK, well, that's not what I meant.'

'I should hope not!'

'So anyway,' Tanner continued, making a mental note to avoid the use of the word "we" when discussing the birth of Samantha, or anyone else for that matter, 'at the time she was a final-year Law student, one who was actively involved in an environmental campaign group.'

'Who, Samantha?' Christine asked, returning to the dishwasher.

Er... no,' Tanner replied, glancing up. 'The girl we found.'

'Oh, right. That's a relief. For a minute there I thought I'd blacked out at the thought of you giving birth to Samantha, waking up to find I'd missed the first twenty-one years of her life.'

'It was because of Tara's work with the environment group,' Tanner continued, happy to ignore Christine's glib remark, 'that Bluebell Wood wasn't bulldozed over to build what would have been the largest housing development Norfolk had seen since World War Two.'

'Is it safe for me to assume that you think that had something to do with what happened to her?'

'We're not sure yet, but it's looking increasingly likely, especially when we found out that she'd been trying to make a name for herself as a freelance journalist, and had apparently come up with a story about Blackfleet Broad being drained as part of some sort of Viking treasure hunt, when in fact it was to cover up a commercial development project.'

With Christine stopping what she was doing to gaze sagaciously off into space, Tanner looked up to ask, 'Has something I said triggered a bell?'

'Sorry, I thought I heard something.'

'I think that was me – talking.'

'No – it was something else.'

'Something else – like...?'

'More like the sound of someone inside the house.'

Feeling the hairs on the back of his neck stand up, Tanner stopped chomping on his food to listen.

When the sound of a gentle thud came from somewhere near the hall, he slowly turned to face Christine to eventually whisper, 'I think you might be right.'

Glancing around for some sort of weapon, he added, 'How the hell did they get inside? I definitely closed the front door.'

'To be honest, I think they've always been here,' Christine replied in a similar whispered tone.

'Now you're really freaking me out! The estate agent didn't say anything about the place being haunted. Nor did he mention anything about it being built on an ancient Indian burial ground.'

A sudden bang on the door that led out to the hall had him jumping in his seat.

With both of them now staring at it with their eyes wide open, Tanner eased himself off the chair to creep over towards the dining-room table, and the tall floor lamp they kept beside it.

'What on earth are you doing?' whispered Christine, as Tanner lifted it up to begin feeling its weight.

'What do you think I'm doing?'

'You're not using that as a weapon!'

'Why not?'

'Well, for a start, it's still plugged in.'

'Good point,' he replied, following the cable to the wall.

'Besides, why would you want to use a lamp?'

'Because we don't have any candlesticks, obviously!'

'Don't you have a golf club you can use?'

'I don't know if you've noticed, but I don't actually play.'

'I thought every self-respecting man had a golf club inside their house, whether they play or not.'

'You're thinking of guitars.'

'Oh, right. Have you got one of those?'

'Well, yes, of course!'

'Then why can't you use that?'

'You mean – as a weapon?'

'No, to play. Perhaps something from Coldplay's new album?'

'Well, I would, of course, but I'm not very good. Even if I was, it's in the bedroom.'

'Where Samantha is,' said Christine, before staring at Tanner with a look of panicking dread.

'Quick, give me one of those knives,' Tanner demanded, holding a hand whilst staring dementedly at the thankfully still closed door.

'Which one?' asked Christine, turning to the long magnetic rack fixed to the wall, where knives of every shape and size could be seen lined up in a neat, orderly row. 'I've got a Santoku knife, a paring knife, a boning knife, a fillet knife, a Nakiri knife, and a Usuba knife. I used to have a Kiritsuke knife as well, but I've lost it somewhere.'

'For Christ's sake, Christine. Don't you just have a normal knife?'

'Of course I do,' she replied, sounding a little put-out. 'Which one do you fancy? I've got a bread knife, a cake knife, a carving knife, or a cheese knife.'

Shaking his head, Tanner glanced earnestly around the kitchen. 'What was that one you were using before – to cut the vegetables?'

'Oh, that's my chef's knife.'

'Can't I use that?'

'No, you can't!'

'Why not?'

'Because it's a Wüsthof Classic Ikon that's worth over a hundred pounds, and I'm not having you ruin it by using it to stab some poor intruder to death.'

'Then which knife can I use?'

'Actually, none of them,' she replied, turning around to begin opening various cupboards. 'How about having a go with a frying pan instead?'

'Just give me something, will you?'

'Actually, they're both in the dishwasher. I can give you a sauté pan, but it's not very big. How about a paella pan? I hardly get the chance to use it, so now might be a good time.'

'Never mind,' Tanner muttered, stepping lightly back to the breakfast bar to grab hold of the bottle of rum.

Inverting it to hold by its neck, he lifted it above his head like an axe to begin creeping towards the door that led out to the hallway.

Reaching for the handle, he was about to turn it when he heard Christine say, 'Please be careful, John.'

'Don't worry. I'll be fine.'

'I meant about the bottle. I've only just bought it!'

Shaking his head, he turned the handle ever so slowly, eventually opening the door an inch at a time to peer cautiously through the widening gap.

Seeing Baby Samantha, sitting on the doormat by the front door, Tanner let out a relieved breath.

'I think I've found our intruder,' he looked back towards Christine to say.

'Not an axe-wielding maniac?'

'She probably would be if you gave her one,' he replied, disappearing into the hall to return a moment later carrying a wriggling baby.

'How on earth did she get out of her cot?'

'I've got no idea, but I definitely put her in it.'

'OK, time for bed, young lady,' said Christine, rinsing her hands to begin marching over.

'Do you want me to fetch some straps from the garage?'

Taking Samantha from him, Christine asked, 'What for?'

'To tie her down. I've got a sturdy pair of ratchet straps which should do the job.'

'I'm not sure that will be necessary.'

'Fair enough. I'll see if I can find some bungee cords instead.'

- CHAPTER TWENTY-SEVEN -

Tuesday, 16th June

ARRIVING AT WORK the next day, Tanner managed to avoid having to say hello to anyone before reaching the peaceful sanctuary of his office.

With a freshly made cup of coffee in his hand, he slumped behind his desk to fire up his computer.

Sitting back in his chair, he waited for it to do its thing before eventually reaching forward to open his email.

'For fuck's sake,' he moaned, seeing what must have been at least two dozen messages had arrived since he'd last bothered to look.

Scrolling down to see if any were worth opening, he was about to close it to look for something more interesting on YouTube when a new email appeared at the top, its subject line shouting VERY URGENT! in all caps.

Seeing it was from Forrester, he rolled his eyes. 'It bloody better be,' he muttered, opening it – only to find it was the same questionnaire Forrester had sent the day before. 'Has he never heard the story about the boy who cried wolf?' he asked himself, before having the genius idea to forward it on to Henderson.

With that done, he opened YouTube to begin a search for *best home security for wayward toddlers*, when he heard a knock at the door.

'Come in!' he called out, immediately doing what he normally did when caught doing nothing in particular – at least nothing work-related – to begin bashing at random keys while staring at the screen with apparent demented intensity.

'Sorry, boss,' came Vicky's hesitant voice. 'Have you got a minute?'

'Hold on,' he replied, continuing to hammer at the keys before finally pressing *enter*. 'Sorry about that,' he said at last, glancing briefly at her before returning to the screen to see what he'd managed to search for.

Seeing a video called *What side of a cat has the most fur*, he raised an intrigued eyebrow. 'I was just responding to one of Forrester's urgent emails.'

'Oh, right,' Vicky said. 'I thought you might have been replying to Townsend's.'

'Which one was that?' he asked, bookmarking the video before reopening his inbox. 'I get so many these days, half the time I end up missing the ones that are actually important.'

'He sent it about ten minutes ago.'

'Yes, I see it – at least I think I do. Perhaps next time you could tell him to change the subject line to something other than *urgent*.'

'You mean – like *very urgent*?'

'Unfortunately, Forrester's already tried that. If someone really wants me to open an email, I think the subject needs to be a little more alluring.'

'You mean like "Get sexy pics here"?'

Tanner shook his head. 'I get loads of those already.'

'Then how about, "You've just won ten million pounds – now we just need access to your bank account"?'

'Again, I get quite a few of those – or at least ones that sound remarkably similar.'

'Don't you have a spam folder, where all that sort of stuff gets automatically sent?'

'Well, yes, but that's where I keep my sandwiches.'

With Vicky staring at him as if he had three heads, Tanner grimaced at his own admittedly rather peculiar joke. 'Do you mean an email junk file?' he eventually asked.

'Of course I meant an email junk file!' Vicky responded. 'What did you think I meant?'

'Sorry, I thought you were talking about my secret stash of spam sandwiches – the ones Christine doesn't know about. But rest assured, young Vicky, I do have an email junk file. It's just that my computer seems to get confused between what's junk and what isn't, which means I have to keep checking both.'

'That's not right,' she muttered, making her way around to his side of the desk.

Quickly closing the chess game he'd lost the night before – then the game of Battleships he'd managed to win – Tanner leaned back to let her look at his screen.

Taking a firm hold of his mouse, she began navigating her way around his email account.

'Why are all these emails from Forrester in your junk file?' she eventually asked.

'Because that's where I keep them, obviously!'

'You transfer them there from your inbox?'

'Only the ones marked *urgent*.'

'Then I'm not surprised your email can't tell the difference between what's junk and what isn't. If you want to file them separately, may I suggest you create a new folder, and keep them in there?'

'And how do I do that?'

'Simple!' she replied, quickly creating one for him. 'What do you want to call it?'

'How about *Junk File?*'

'You've got one of those already.'

'Yes, I know – which is why I keep them in there.'

'Why don't we call it *Forrester's Emails*,' she said, typing that in.

Taking back control of his computer, Tanner added the word *Junk* in the middle, before sitting back to admire his handiwork.

'And what if Forrester happens to see your screen?'

'Good point,' Tanner replied, leaning forward again to replace the word *Junk* with *Pointless*.

'And now perhaps we can get back to the one Townsend sent you.'

'No problem, but I can't see it now.'

'That's because it's in your junk file,' she said, shoving Tanner out of the way to grab the mouse, 'along with just about everything else,' she added, navigating to Townsend's yet-to-be opened email.

'So you're saying that if I stop putting Forrester's emails into the junk file, then the computer will stop putting everything else there too?'

'Something like that.'

'Which means I'm going to get even more!' he moaned.

'If you managed your emails a little more efficiently, you probably wouldn't find them to be quite so daunting.'

'I thought that's what I *had* been doing!'

'By creating different folders – not by simply shoving everything you don't want to read into your junk file.'

'That's what I used to do back in the day. Everything I wanted to read stayed on my desk. Everything else went straight in the bin.'

'As you may have noticed, things have moved on a bit since then.'

'Then perhaps I need to go on an email management course.'

'I'm not sure such a thing exists.'

'Oh, I'm fairly sure they do.'

'Actually,' said Vicky, gazing sagaciously away, 'you're probably right. I think my grandfather went on one during the Boar War.'

'Are you trying to imply that I'm old?'

'Not exactly, but you do seem to enjoy living in the past.'

'What makes you say that?'

'Apart from your antiquated approach to email management – you *have* seen that car of yours, haven't you? The one that's bright yellow and named after a horny antelope?'

'It's called a Stag, not an antelope.'

'It could be named after a reindeer for all I care. Now, can we get back to Townsend's email?'

'Which email was that again?'

'This one!' she said, pointing at it on the screen.

'Oh yes, I nearly forgot. Thanks for reminding me. Do you have any idea what it's about?'

'It's what came back from his search warrant application for Tara's father's house.'

'Don't tell me it was turned down.'

'It's been approved, but they've limited the scope.'

'In what way?'

'We're only allowed to search through Tara's possessions.'

'Didn't Townsend tell them that she lived with her father?'

'Uh-huh.'

'Then how do they expect us to search through her stuff without looking through his as well?'

'I've no idea.'

'Did they at least give a reason?'

'They said it was because her father isn't being viewed as a suspect – but feel free to read it for yourself,' Vicky added, moving aside for Tanner to see.

'I'll take your word for it,' he replied, lurching up to fetch his keys, wallet, and phone from the top of his desk.

'Where are you going?' asked Vicky, stepping back in surprise.

'Not me. *We.* And where we're going should be obvious.'

- CHAPTER TWENTY-EIGHT -

WITH VICKY PERCHED self-consciously in the seat beside him, Tanner was soon driving them down the road towards Tara Lowe's father's house.

Rounding a bend to see a squad car parked on the road opposite the entrance, Tanner pulled up alongside it to wind his window down.

'Has anything been going on?' he asked, only for the young man slumped behind the steering wheel to blink nonchalantly over at him.

'Er... *hello!*' Tanner prompted, causing the young man to jump in his seat.

'Shit!' he exclaimed, straightening himself up as his colleague did the same. 'Sorry, boss. I didn't recognise your car.'

'It's new,' Tanner replied. 'At least for me. Has there been any movement?'

'Not since we took over this morning.'

'And before that?'

'Only Mrs Lowe and her daughter leaving in their car, shortly after you did yesterday.'

'OK, thank you. We've managed to get hold of a search warrant, so perhaps you can give us a hand.'

'Yes, of course!' the driver replied, with surprising enthusiasm. 'Shall we follow you in?'

Heading off with a nod, Tanner turned into the drive to see the same Saab 900 that had been parked there before, seemingly in exactly the same place.

Checking in the rear-view mirror to see the squad car following them in, Tanner turned to Vicky. 'Did you bring a printout of that search warrant?'

'How could I forget?' she replied, holding it out for him.

Turning off the engine, he glanced around at her. 'Keep hold of it for now,' he said, before thinking to add, 'Actually, you may as well give it to him. He might be more receptive to you asking if we can go inside than if I do.'

Seeing her place it back into her handbag to climb quickly out, he followed her up to the front door. When she reached for the bell, he held out a hand to stop her. 'Do you know what you're going to say?'

'Actually, I'm not sure,' she replied, lowering her hand. 'I was going to ask him out on a hot date, but with you being here and everything, it's probably not appropriate.'

With Tanner staring back at her with an unamused expression, she glared directly back. 'Of course I know what to say! I'm not twelve!'

'Sorry. I just wanted to be sure, that was all.'

'May I ring the doorbell now?'

'Be my guest, but you might want to get your ID out first, just in case he asks to see it.'

Vicky gave him a peevish look before digging around inside her handbag.

'Perhaps the search warrant as well,' Tanner added, taking the opportunity to peer inside to see what else she kept in there.

With seemingly everything apart from a kitchen sink – and the necessary tools to install it – he leaned forward for a closer look, only to find her staring at him.

'Nice bag,' he said, offering her a guilty smile. 'What do you keep in there, anyway?'

'Just the essentials,' she replied, closing it firmly.

To rob a bank, or to invade a third world country? Tanner muttered to himself, before asking, 'Are you ready?'

'I was ready before!' she replied, reaching up to press the doorbell.

'And you know what you're going to say?'

Hearing hurried footsteps approach from inside, she shook her head at him before finding herself staring into the glaring eyes of the home's owner.

'Good morning, Mr Lowe,' she began, presenting her ID. 'DI Gilbert and my colleague, DCI Tanner, Norfolk Police.'

'It took you long enough,' he muttered, staring past them with an agitated expression.

'I'm – er – sorry about that,' Vicky replied, glancing uncertainly at Tanner. 'We had to wait for the search warrant to come through.'

'The search warrant?' he demanded, glaring down at her as she held it up.

'We have a warrant to search your premises in connection with what happened to your daughter.'

'You're not here about the break-in?'

Hearing the sound of an approaching siren, Vicky glanced again at Tanner, before turning back. 'What break-in?'

'The one I just called you about! Someone broke into my house last night. My wallet's gone. So is my laptop!'

Stepping forward, Tanner caught the man's eye. 'I sincerely hope, Mr Lowe, that this isn't some sort of misguided effort to destroy evidence relating to the murder of your daughter?'

'Of course it bloody isn't!'

'It's just that it does seem rather convenient that your house was broken into just a few hours before we arrived at your front door with a warrant to search it.'

'I can assure you, Mr Chief Inspector Spanner – or whatever your name was – the whole thing is the exact opposite of convenient. But apart from that, if I didn't want you inside my house to conduct a search, why would I have called you to say someone had broken in?'

'So when we came calling, you had an excuse as to why your laptop just happened to be missing.'

'You're seriously suggesting that I murdered my own daughter, and that the plan I had for doing so was kept on my laptop?'

'I don't know. Was it?'

'This is ridiculous,' he muttered, shaking his head. 'If you don't believe me, then I suggest you come in to take a look for yourself.'

'If we may, that would be appreciated.'

'Well, come on then!' he said, turning on his heel to lead them inside.

Following him through to a large but dated kitchen, Mr Lowe stopped beside the central island. 'As you can see,' he said, directing their attention towards the back door, and the window that had been smashed, 'they must have come in through there.'

'And where was your laptop?'

'I'd left it on the kitchen table.'

'And your wallet?'

'Inside this,' he replied, resting a hand on a suit jacket, hanging on the back of a high kitchen chair. 'I always leave it there.'

'Is anything else missing?'

'I don't think so, but I haven't had a good look around yet.'

'Where were you at the time?'

'Asleep upstairs! Where do you think?'

'And you didn't hear anything?'

'Well, no, but I am quite a heavy sleeper.'

'So you don't know what time this was?'

'Sometime between when I went to bed and when I woke up.'

Tanner took a quiet moment to glance curiously about. 'Do you mind if we have a look around?'

'What for?'

'To see if they took anything else.'

'I can do that, thank you very much.'

'Yes, of course, but we still need to search the house. With the possibility that the break-in is connected to what happened to your daughter, we're going to have to get forensics in anyway.'

'Is that really necessary?'

'If you want us to catch who did this, then yes, I'm afraid it is.'

'Then I suppose you'd better let me have a look at this supposed search warrant of yours.'

With Vicky stepping forward to present it to him, he fished out a pair of reading glasses to begin leafing studiously through.

'You do know that this only gives you the right to search through Tara's things?'

'We are aware of that,' Tanner replied, a little annoyed that he'd managed to work that one out.

'You didn't mention it before,' he said, staring suspiciously up at Tanner over the rims of his glasses before continuing to read.

'The subject of where we were able to search never arose.'

'Uh-huh,' Lowe mumbled in response.

Reaching the end, he removed his glasses to hand the document back to Vicky. 'Very well,' he eventually said. 'Tara's bedroom is at the top of the stairs, first door on your right.'

'Thank you,' Tanner replied, 'but the warrant gives us the right to search through all Tara's possessions.'

'Which you'll find in her bedroom.'

'You're trying to tell me that nothing of hers is in any other part of the house?'

'That's exactly what I'm saying. And unless you have a search warrant that says otherwise, the second I see you trying to look anywhere else, I'll be calling my lawyer. And just in case you happen to find yourselves stumbling into the wrong room to begin searching it by accident, I'll be happy to take you up there myself.'

- CHAPTER TWENTY-NINE -

FOLLOWING MR LOWE up a nondescript staircase to the floor above, he opened a door for them before standing to one side, allowing them into a small single bedroom with sunlight streaming in through a pair of half-drawn orange curtains.

As they waited for him to disappear, they stared around at the walls plastered with environmental awareness posters, picturing everything from burning forests to dried-up riverbeds.

'What a delightful chap,' Vicky eventually said, checking the coast was clear before closing the door.

'I don't think we can blame him if he's a little upset,' Tanner replied, gazing over at a small dressing table in the corner, where tangled clumps of jewellery could be seen lying amidst tealight candles, half-burned incense sticks, crumpled leaflets, old concert tickets, and a couple of passport photographs featuring Tara posing with various of her hippy-styled friends.

Trying to shake the unsettling feeling that he'd somehow been there before, he turned slowly around to look at a single, unmade bed. 'Any sign of that newspaper story she'd been working on?'

'Nothing obvious,' came Vicky's response, as she stepped towards a desk on the other side of the room that was even more cluttered than the dressing table.

Stooping down to look under the bed to find nothing more than what appeared to be an old Christmas tree covered in dust, Tanner stood up to take a look at the bedside table.

'You know what,' he heard Vicky say, as he opened the table's drawer to peer inside, 'there's something missing.'

'Yes, I know,' Tanner muttered. 'It's called the story we're looking for.'

'I was thinking more about a laptop. I mean, she must have had one. How else would she have been able to write it?'

'That's a good point,' Tanner replied, straightening himself up to continue staring about.

'Do you think whoever broke in could have taken it as well?'

'Assuming someone actually did break in, and the father didn't just say that to cover up the fact that he's the one who's dumped everything into the nearest river, that's most likely what they were looking for.'

'Well, anyway,' Vicky continued, having given up with the desk to begin examining a shelf above it, 'other than some really boring-looking legal textbooks and a collection of crime fiction novels, there's nothing here.'

'Then I think we need to ask the father if she had one. Assuming she did, then it's probably been taken, along with his own – which unfortunately means that we're still missing her increasingly elusive story.'

'Unless she kept it on an SD card?' suggested Vicky.

'Have you seen one of those?'

'Well, no, but if she had, and had an inkling that

someone might have been looking for it, then it could be anywhere.'

'Then I suggest we get forensics up here to have a proper look around. I think it might be an idea for us to apply for another search warrant as well – this time for the whole house. If she was keeping it on an SD card and thought it necessary to hide it, then I doubt she'd have left it in her bedroom.

'Anyway,' he sighed, 'I don't think there's all that much more we can do here. Perhaps we should head downstairs to have another chat with her father. For all we know, she never had a computer, and did all her work the old-fashioned way.'

'I think that's him now,' commented Vicky, as the sound of raised voices came drifting up towards them from somewhere outside.

Stepping over to the window, Tanner peeled back the curtains to see Mr Lowe having some sort of argument with two of his police officers.

'Can you see what's going on?' questioned Vicky, trying to see for herself.

'I've no idea,' Tanner moaned, shaking his head. 'But one thing I do know is that our Mr Lowe is turning out to be one giant pain in the arse.'

- CHAPTER THIRTY -

FOLLOWING THE SOUNDS of raised voices, Tanner led Vicky back down the stairs and out through the front door, where they found Mr Lowe, being prevented from getting into his car by the officers who'd been watching the house when they'd arrived.

'If you shove me once more,' the taller of the two officers warned, 'I'll be arresting you for assault.'

'I didn't shove you,' Lowe replied, his voice simmering with indignation. 'I accidentally touched your uniform with the tip of one of my fingers while endeavouring to make a point – that point being that you can't keep me here against my will!'

'Alright, alright!' said Tanner, stepping between them. 'What's going on?'

'The suspect is attempting to leave the premises,' replied the officer, his eyes still fixed on the man who'd apparently assaulted him.

'I've run out of milk!' Lowe snapped, glaring at Tanner. 'In order to get some more, I need to go down to the corner shop. I normally walk, but with you lot here, I thought it would be quicker if I took the car. Now, unless there's some sort of special milk-buying licence I need to apply for before doing so, may I suggest that you let me leave?

Unless, of course, one of your officers would be kind enough to buy some for me? If that's the case, then I could do with some bread as well.'

'Under the circumstances,' Tanner began, 'it may be better if we were to buy some for you.'

'You're not being serious?'

'Just until we've been able to complete a full search of your property.'

'I thought we'd already established that you don't have the authority to do so?'

'That was before we were unable to find certain items that we believe your daughter should have been in possession of – like a laptop, for example.'

'You're saying it isn't there?'

'Not that we could find.'

'Then whoever broke in must have stolen that as well.'

'We're also looking for any SD cards, or memory sticks she may have had. You wouldn't happen to know where she might have kept them?'

'I'm sorry, I don't.'

'She didn't mention anything about having to hide them?'

'Why would she have wanted to do that?'

'One of her friends mentioned something about a story she'd been working on – something concerning Blackfleet Broad. I don't suppose you know anything about that?'

'I know she was trying to become a journalist, but she never discussed the stories she was working on.'

'OK, well, we believe it's possible that whoever was responsible for what happened to her may have found out, and had been trying to stop her.'

'You think someone killed her over some stupid story?'

'As I said, it's possible, which is why we're trying

to find her laptop, or perhaps something she used to keep the story on.'

As Mr Lowe opened his mouth to respond, a loud thud came from one of the windows behind them.

Glancing around with a start, Tanner looked up to see something roll down the tiles before landing on the driveway, just to the side of the front door.

'What the hell was that?' muttered Lowe, as Vicky stepped quickly forward.

Crouching down in front of it, she looked back at Tanner. 'It's a sparrow!' she exclaimed. 'It must have flown into the window.'

'Is it OK?' Tanner asked, joining her to stare down at it with concern.

'I – I don't know,' she replied, 'but with the way its head's hanging like that, I'd say it was dead.'

'Did you say it was a bird?' Lowe asked behind them.

'A sparrow,' Tanner replied, stepping back to look up at the window it must have hit to recognise the curtains they'd seen hanging in Tara's bedroom.

'Well, I hope it didn't break the glass,' Lowe muttered. 'I've got enough on my plate without having to worry about getting someone round to fix it.'

'The window looks fine,' Tanner said, shaking his head at the man's callous remark.

Thinking he saw something move in the trees behind him, he turned sharply around, just in time to glimpse what he could have sworn was Tara's deathly pale face staring back. But when he looked again, there was nobody there, just the flaking trunk of an old silver birch tree.

'Is someone going to buy me some bloody

milk?' came Lowe's irritated voice, 'or are we going to hold a funeral service for a bird that must've been as blind as it was stupid?'

Tanner took another moment to cast his eyes over at the treeline before turning back. 'Not a fan of our feathered friends, Mr Lowe?'

'Not if it means being unable to have a decent cup of coffee.'

'Fair enough, I suppose,' Tanner said, in a more sympathetic tone.

Turning to the constable he'd spoken to earlier, he caught his eye to say, 'Could one of you pop down to the local shop to buy Mr Lowe some milk?'

Seeing the constable nod, Lowe interjected, 'I need some bread as well – preferably seeded wholemeal, if they have it.'

'Anything else?' Tanner asked.

'I suppose that depends on how long you're planning to keep me here. If it's going to be more than a day, then someone's going to have to go to Sainsbury's for me.'

'Get the man some bread as well,' Tanner said, glancing at the constable, who nodded back before heading for his car.

'Am I allowed to go back inside my house now?' Lowe demanded.

'Be my guest,' Tanner replied, exhaling in relief as the man turned to stomp back inside.

Hearing the door slam closed, Tanner caught Vicky's eye to mutter, 'Miserable git,' before scanning the treeline once again.

'Looking for anything in particular?' asked Vicky, following his gaze.

'Not really,' he said quietly, glancing up at the window the bird had flown into. 'I just thought I saw something. Can you call the office to have someone request another search warrant?'

'Yes, of course,' she said, digging out her phone.

'But this time, for the whole house. Once you've done that, I think it might be useful to have another chat with the professor.'

'I was actually thinking that maybe we should go and talk to Tara's mother.'

'For any particular reason?' Tanner asked, turning to look at her.

'Only because we haven't had the chance yet. Hopefully she can tell us what they were arguing about before Tara left. I'd also like to ask about Tara's relationship with her father.'

'You're thinking he might've had something to do with what happened to her?'

'I'm only saying we shouldn't rule it out. It's possible something happened between them – another argument, perhaps. Maybe he *did* know about the story she was working on and is trying to make it look like she was killed because of it, which would explain why her body was left in the middle of Blackfleet Broad. And don't forget, he's been oddly reluctant to let us inside his house, and that break-in he reported came at the perfect time, especially for someone wanting to hide any evidence he might have had about her story.'

Remembering his dream – of Tara being beaten inside what he now believed to have been her own bedroom, Tanner nodded. 'Sounds like a plan, young Vicky. All the more reason we need that warrant for the whole property. If you can get that sorted on the way, I'll drive us over there now.'

- CHAPTER THIRTY-ONE -

ARRIVING AT A small semi-detached house on the outskirts of Catfield, Tanner parked his Triumph Stag outside to climb slowly out.

'Do you want to do all the talking?' he asked Vicky, turning to watch her step out from the other side.

'Not particularly,' she shrugged. 'How about I do some of the talking, and you do the rest?'

'Tell you what – let's see if she's in first,' he replied. 'If she is, then I suggest you start, and I'll jump in if you need me to. Just remember, she's probably still very upset.'

Nodding at him, she led the way up to the front door to ring the bell.

Hearing the sound of approaching footsteps, they glanced around at each other before pulling out their respective IDs.

'Mrs Lowe?' Vicky enquired, holding hers up to the shrivelled, almost unrecognisable face of the woman peering out at them. 'DI Gilbert, and my colleague, DCI Tanner. We met briefly the other day at your husband's house.'

'Do you have any news?' she suddenly demanded.

'If you're asking if we've found who hurt your daughter, I'm afraid we haven't – at least not yet.'

'You're not here to tell me that you made a mistake?'

'I'm sorry,' Vicky replied with a sorrowful frown.

'As I think my colleague mentioned before, our medical examiner has been able to positively identify her.'

'Yes, of course,' came the woman's quiet reply, her bloodshot eyes drifting to the ground. 'I just thought there might have been a mix-up – and that she'd been found staying at a friend's house.'

'I'm sorry again,' Vicky repeated, unsure what else to say.

Wiping away an escaping tear, Mrs Lowe lifted her head to offer them both a faltering smile. 'Would you like to come in?' she asked, glancing a little awkwardly behind her. 'I've only just put the kettle on.'

Vicky looked briefly at Tanner before saying, 'If you don't mind?'

'Not at all,' Mrs Lowe replied. 'To be honest, I could do with the company.'

Following her through to a small, cluttered kitchen, with a tortoiseshell cat staring curiously at them from on top of a wooden table, Mrs Lowe shooed it gently off before moving to the kettle. Switching it on, she began fishing items out of the cupboards.

'Tea or coffee?'

Viewing the own-brand jar of instant coffee she'd just pulled out with wary suspicion, Tanner closed the kitchen door before replying, 'I'd rather not, thank you,' only for Vicky to jab him sharply in the arm before shooting him an admonishing glare.

'But then again,' he quickly added, 'if it's not too much trouble, I'd love a coffee.'

'I'll have one as well, thank you,' said Vicky, as the cat began curling itself around her leg. 'May I ask what your cat's called?'

'Her official name is Amber, but Sasha tends to use slightly more derogatory terms.'

'Sasha being your daughter,' Vicky continued, ambling towards a shelf crammed with decorative items and family photographs, 'the young woman we met the other day?'

'That's right,' Mrs Lowe replied, glancing round to see Vicky studying the photos. 'That's her on the left – although she's changed quite a bit since then.'

'Do you mind me asking why Sasha decided to live with you, while Tara chose to stay with her father?'

Having finished making the drinks, Mrs Lowe lifted two steaming mugs to place them on the table where the cat had been.

'My husband and I separated a few years ago. We left it to Sasha and Tara to decide who they wanted to live with. We felt they were old enough to make up their own minds. Sasha chose to stay with me, while Tara wanted to remain with her father.'

As both Vicky and Tanner reached for their mugs, Vicky waited for their host to pull out a chair for herself, 'Was there any particular reason why?'

'No reason in particular,' she replied, lowering herself into the chair. 'Tara was always close to her father. To be honest, they both were, but as Sasha grew older, she just seemed happier to stay here with me.'

Just then, a faint creaking sound could be heard from the hallway, just outside the kitchen door.

Tanner's brow creased as he turned slightly towards it.

'Is Sasha in?' he asked.

'She is.'

'I don't suppose it would be possible for us to have a chat with her as well?'

Mrs Lowe hesitated, her expression tightening. 'I'm afraid she's very upset,' she eventually said. 'The doctor prescribed her some sedatives to help her cope. She's been sleeping on and off all day.'

Tanner nodded, glancing at Vicky before turning back. 'Then perhaps another time?'

'Yes, of course.'

Making a mental note for them to return the following day, he heard Vicky ask beside him, 'May we ask what your husband is like?'

'Normal enough,' she shrugged.

'Do you know if they ever argued?'

'Who, Richard and Tara?'

As Vicky nodded behind her mug, Mrs Lowe held her gaze for a moment before sitting up. 'You're not suggesting it was my husband, I hope?'

'At the moment, we're simply looking to establish what the relationship was like between them.'

'Well, it wasn't him! I mean, yes, he has a bit of a temper, and he could certainly be a pain to live with, but he could never have done something like that – certainly not to Tara. He worshipped the ground she walked on.'

'I was just thinking that as both Tara and Sasha used to be close to him, with Sasha becoming more distant as she grew older, I wondered if the same thing might have been happening with Tara.'

'A little, perhaps,' she admitted, 'but only because she was becoming more independent, and my husband's always been a little controlling. But that doesn't mean he'd have hurt her.'

'But did they argue?'

'Well, yes, of course – doesn't everyone?'

'Then perhaps an argument could have got a little out of hand?'

'I'm sorry,' she said, vehemently shaking her head, 'but what you're suggesting is unthinkable. Even if they weren't as close as they used to be, he'd never have done anything to hurt her – intentionally or otherwise.'

With Vicky glancing at Tanner as if asking for help, Tanner rested his elbows on the table to gently ask, 'Perhaps you could tell us a little about Tara?'

Taking a moment to compose herself, Mrs Lowe looked first at Vicky, then at Tanner. 'What do you want to know?'

'We heard she was a freelance journalist?'

'She was trying to be,' she replied, as fresh tears welled up in her eyes.

'Did she ever talk to you about the stories she was working on?'

'Only when she was particularly excited about something. Although, to be honest, she spent more time moaning that no one wanted to publish them than actually writing,' she added, glancing down at the table with a wistful smile.

'Did she mention what she'd been working on most recently?'

'I'm not sure. She seemed to have quite a few stories floating around in that head of hers.'

'Something about Blackfleet Broad, and an archaeological dig that was supposed to take place there?'

'Was that the one about it being drained under the pretence of searching for a long-lost Viking burial ground – when the dig was actually just an excuse to prepare the site for a commercial building development?'

'That's the one,' Tanner replied, leaning forward. 'I don't suppose she showed it to you?'

'I think so,' she nodded. 'At least, she normally

would – if only to ask what I thought.'

'Can you remember any of the names she mentioned in connection with it?'

'I'm not sure I can.'

'What if I read some out – do you think that might help to jog your memory?'

'I'm sorry, Detective Inspector, but I doubt it. I'm ashamed to say that I never took the time to read them properly. I'd simply glance through before offering her a few words of encouragement.'

'Did she leave you with a copy?'

Mrs Lowe shook her head. 'She'd show them to me on her laptop.'

'So you don't remember any details?'

'I'm afraid not. The only thing I remember about the one she'd written about the Viking burial ground was the name of the professor she mentioned – Alfred Beaumont.'

Tanner turned to Vicky before looking back. 'Do you remember what she said about him?'

'Only that he was involved somehow. But as I said, I didn't read the whole thing.'

'But you're sure about the name – Professor Alfred Beaumont?'

'Quite sure,' she replied. 'I studied History at Norfolk University – what must have been about three lifetimes ago. He was one of my lecturers. I must admit, I thought he must have died by now, so I was very surprised to find out that he hadn't.'

- CHAPTER THIRTY-TWO -

'AT LEAST WE know the professor's involved,' said Vicky, the moment they stepped outside for the front door to close behind them.

Tanner turned back to glance at the house, just in time to see what he thought was a curtain twitch in one of the upstairs windows.

Pausing for a moment, wondering if it had moved or if it was just the sun catching the glass, he shook it off to lead the way back to his car.

'Maybe so,' he eventually replied, 'but we still haven't seen the actual story.'

'What did you make of what she said about her husband?'

'To be honest, not much.'

'You didn't think it was strange that one daughter chose to stay with the father while the other went to live with the mother?'

'Not really,' came Tanner's dismissive response. 'I'm fairly sure that sort of thing happens all the time.'

'Even though they were both daddy's girls – until Sasha reached a "certain age".'

Unlocking the car, Tanner stopped to look around at her. 'Are you about to propose that Sasha chose to live with her mother because her father had been showing an unnatural interest in her?'

'I was thinking about it,' came Vicky's sheepish reply.

'If that were the case, then surely they'd both have decided to live with their mother.'

'Not if Sasha didn't feel able to tell anyone.'

'But surely she'd at least have told her sister?'

'What – that if she stayed with her father, he might try to have his way with her when she grew up?'

'OK, I suppose that is a little unlikely.'

'Anyway, if forensics finds anything in his house that might give us reason to suspect him further – anything at all – then I'd like to bring him in for questioning.'

'Fair enough, I suppose, but it'll have to be something fairly substantial. Otherwise, you'll have Forrester to deal with.'

'Yes, of course,' she replied, tacking on a nervous laugh. 'I must admit, I'd kind of forgotten about him. I don't suppose you'd be willing to talk to him on my behalf?'

'You mean as an intermediary?'

'Exactly as an intermediary!'

'Fat chance!' he laughed – only to hear his phone ringing from the depths of his threadbare sailing jacket. 'That's probably him now.'

'Surely not,' Vicky replied, watching as Tanner fumbled through his various pockets.

Eventually finding it, he pulled it out to stare at the screen. 'Told you,' he said, turning it round for Vicky to see that it was indeed Forrester calling.

'Do you think he has some sort of rare psychic ability to know whenever someone's talking about him?' questioned Vicky.

'I think it's more likely that he calls so often, he was bound to catch us eventually. Anyway, I'd better take it – unless you want to, of course?' Tanner asked, holding it out for her.

'I'd rather have my brain removed with a spoon, thank you very much,' came her decisive response, recoiling from the phone as if it were a poisoned chalice.

'Me too,' sighed Tanner, finally lifting it to his ear. 'Tanner speaking!'

'Ah, Tanner, there you are! I was about to ask Sally to fill out a missing person's report.'

'Sorry, sir. I was just talking to Vicky.'

'Presumably about the investigation?'

'We were actually discussing last night's Celebrity Traitor.'

'Then perhaps you could talk to *me* about the investigation?'

'What would you like to know?'

'Whatever's been happening since we last spoke.'

'Sorry, sir, but when was that again?'

'My point exactly, Tanner!'

'Yes, of course, sir – but that doesn't answer my question.'

'It was yesterday. Does that help?'

'Not really.'

Tanner heard Forrester sigh down the line before drawing in a rasping breath.

'Is Vicky there?'

'Vicky?' Tanner repeated, lifting his eyes to meet hers.

'You remember,' Forrester continued, 'the detective inspector you said you were talking to when I called?'

'Oh, *that* Vicky!'

'Is she there?'

'I'm – er – not sure,' said Tanner, pretending to look around for her.

'If she is, then I'd like a word.'

'OK, hold on. Let me see if I can find her.'

Placing a finger over the phone's microphone, Tanner caught Vicky's eye. 'Would you like to speak to Forrester?'

'About what?'

'The investigation, presumably.'

'That'll be a no, then.'

Nodding, Tanner returned to the call. 'I'm sorry, sir, but I don't seem to be able to find her.'

'But I thought you said you were just talking to her?'

'Yes, sir, I was.'

'Then where the hell has she gone?'

'Presumably off chasing a lead.'

'You don't know where?'

'Er – not exactly. Would you like me to ask her to give you a call when I next see her?' he asked, smiling at Vicky before looking away.

'For Christ's sake, Tanner, all I want is an update!'

'Then why didn't you say!'

'I thought I did.'

'And from when would you like to be updated?'

'From when we last spoke.'

'Which was when again?'

'Are you going to tell me how you've been getting on, or am I going to have to come over there to take control of the investigation myself?'

'There's not really that much to report.'

'There must be *something*.'

'Well, sir, we have confirmed the victim's identity.'

'Was it who you thought it was?'

'The environmental activist, Tara Lowe.'

'And she was definitely murdered?'

Recalling his dream, Tanner nodded. 'Dr Johnstone believes she was beaten before being drowned.'

'How about witnesses?'

'Only the person who found the body.'

'You haven't heard from anyone who may have seen something around the time she was killed?'

'Not yet.'

'Have you at least asked?'

'We haven't had the chance to hold a press conference, if that's what you mean.'

'But you are intending to?'

'Of course!' Tanner replied, even though he hadn't been.

'How about suspects?' Forrester continued.

'It's a little too early to name anyone in particular.'

'But you must have someone in mind?'

'We have a number of people in mind, sir – just nobody we have any evidence against.'

'Then how about a motive? Didn't you mention before that it might have something to do with where she was found?'

'That still remains a possibility.'

'More so, or less so?'

Tanner hesitated. As much as he didn't want to, he knew he had to give Forrester something – even if it wasn't much.

'We spoke to some of her environmental friends, one of whom told us that Tara was trying to become a freelance journalist. Apparently, she'd been writing a newspaper article about the archaeological dig being nothing more than an excuse to have Blackfleet Broad drained to make way for a commercial development project.'

'So you were right, then?'

'We still don't know – only because we've been unable to find her story. We met with the newspaper editor she was supposed to have sent it to, but he hadn't seen it. Then we tried searching her home, only for her father to refuse us entry, so we applied for a warrant. When it was finally granted, it only gave us permission to search Tara's possessions – which didn't make much difference, since by the time we arrived, her father claimed the house had been broken into overnight, and both his laptop and Tara's had been stolen.'

'That sounds like quite a coincidence.'

'That's what we thought.'

'Do you believe him?'

'The jury's still out on that. We've applied for another warrant, this time for the whole house. If he was lying and staged the break-in to hide evidence, we've yet to find a motive. According to Tara's mother, he worshipped the ground she walked on.'

'But it's still a possibility?'

'Which is why we need that warrant.'

'What about her story on Blackfleet Broad? Have you found anything to suggest it's true?'

'Well, yes – but not enough to start going around arresting people.'

'Can you tell me what you *have* found?'

'Just the details of an investment business registered with Companies House, together with a list of directors.'

'And they are?'

'Jeremy Southcott – Chairman of Norfolk Council's Planning and Housing Committee, Professor Alfred Beaumont – head of the archaeological dig, Simon Balinger – the developer who was trying to bulldoze Bluebell Wood for a housing development project, and last but by no means least, someone else whose name I'm fairly sure you won't want to hear.'

'And why's that?'

'Because it's none other than our local MP – George Elliston.'

'You're not seriously telling me he's a director of some dodgy investment company?'

'Unless there are two of him, or he's resigned since being elected, I'm afraid I am.'

The line went quiet for a moment before Tanner continued, 'But as I said, we've no direct evidence linking any of them to Tara's murder.'

'Have you spoken to any of them?'

'You mean – have we spoken to George Elliston?'

'Well, have you?'

'Not yet.'

'Any of the others?'

'Briefly with the professor, when we first found Tara's body. Later with Balinger – but that was before we knew about the company.'

'May I ask what your next move is?'

'I was about to discuss that with Vicky when you called. Having just spoken with Tara's mother, I thought it might be worth another chat with the professor.'

'For any particular reason?'

'According to her, Tara showed her the story about Blackfleet Broad. She hadn't read it all, but confirmed the professor's name was in it.'

'But you *are* going to hold a press conference first, aren't you? For all we know, someone might have seen her being attacked or drowned, and is just waiting for us to ask.'

'Press conference first,' Tanner agreed – albeit reluctantly.

'And given that you make a complete hash of it every time you hold one,' Forrester continued, 'perhaps you could ask Vicky to do it instead of you?'

Ending the call, Tanner caught Vicky's eye.

'Was that Forrester, telling us to hold a press conference?' she asked.

'No, that was Forrester telling *you* to hold a press conference.'

'Oh, right,' came her less-than-enthusiastic response.

'Are you up for it?'

'Is it really necessary?'

'If it helps persuade someone to come forward, then for once, I think Forrester's right. As much as neither of us may want to, it's probably worth doing.'

'Then how about we do it together?'

'Are you sure? Every time I hold one, in Forrester's words, I do seem to make a complete hash of it.'

'But you always manage to win them over – eventually.'

'I do?'

'Well, most of the time.'

'Tell you what,' said Tanner, 'how about you take the lead, and I'll stand beside you – for moral support.'

'But you will step in if I make a hash of it myself?'

'If you really want me to.'

'Yes, please.'

'OK, deal. Perhaps you could give Sally a call to arrange it?'

- CHAPTER THIRTY-THREE -

A LITTLE OVER two hours later, Tanner stopped in front of Wroxham Police Station's reception doors to stare warily out at the group of journalists Sally had assembled in the car park outside.

Taking a shallow breath, he turned to look at Vicky standing beside him.

'Are you ready for this?'

'About as ready as I'll ever be,' came her nervous reply.

'Just remember what I told you earlier, and you'll be fine.'

'What was that again?'

'To not make any sudden movements, and whatever you do, don't look them in the eye.'

'I thought you told me to focus on what I wanted to say, and not to let their constant irrelevant questions distract me?'

'I did?'

Turning to offer him an unamused glare, she returned to staring hesitantly out through the double glass doors. 'I suppose we'd better get started, before I change my mind to let you do it instead.'

'Yes, of course,' replied Tanner, surging suddenly forward, just in case she did. 'Let me get the door for you.'

Pulling it open, he stood back to allow her to head

out first – only to realise she hadn't moved.

'Are you alright?' he whispered back, as a few cameras began to flash beyond the now wide-open door.

'I was just wondering if I had time to change my shoes,' she replied, glancing down. 'I've got a pair of Nike trainers in the car.'

'Why do you have a pair of Nike trainers in the car?' came Tanner's curious response.

'For when I go for my lunchtime jog, of course!'

'You go for a run at lunchtime?'

'Well, no, but I think now might be the perfect time to start,' she replied, glancing down at her watch.

'Don't worry, Vicky. You'll be fine.'

'I will?'

'Of course. But if you're not, Wroxham Medical Centre's only just down the road.'

'That's reassuring.'

'I know!'

'I assume you're still going to introduce me?'

'Naturally.'

'So, we're doing this, then?'

'Well, you are, yes!'

'But we're still doing it together?'

'Don't worry, I'll be right behind you.'

'How are you going to introduce me if you're right behind me?'

'Good point,' he replied. 'I'll go first then, shall I?'

'If you could.'

'And you'll be right behind me?'

'I'll be as far behind you as you were planning on being behind me.'

'So about two and a half miles?'

'Something like that.'

'Right then,' Tanner replied, facing forward to take a fortifying breath. 'Once more unto the breach,' he muttered to himself, before stepping cautiously forward.

Coming to a halt behind a table on which sat two small piles of leaflets, Tanner waited for Vicky to take up a position beside him before clearing his throat.

'Thank you all for coming at such short notice,' he began, glancing around to see if he could recognise any of the bustling journalists.

'That's alright,' replied one of them, much to the amusement of the others.

'We're here to tell you about a body that was discovered yesterday morning, over at Blackfleet Broad.'

'Which one?' the same man asked.

Realising it was the loud-mouthed reporter from *The Norfolk Herald*, Tanner discreetly rolled his eyes.

'It's just that one of my sources told me that two bodies were found,' the reporter continued, 'one was a fisherman who drowned, the other a young woman who was apparently murdered.'

'Mr Fletcher, isn't it?' Tanner enquired.

'From *The Norfolk Herald*,' the man replied, offering Tanner a thin smile in return.

'And may I ask who told you?'

'I'm sorry, but unfortunately, I can't –'

'– reveal your sources,' Tanner finished for him. 'Yes, I know.'

'Then you can understand why I can't say.'

'The next time you speak to him, perhaps you could ask him to give me a call? I may be able to offer him a job working for Norfolk Police – that's if he doesn't already.'

'Who said it's not a policewoman?' Fletcher replied, lifting his pen to point at Vicky. 'Speaking of which, may I ask who your friend is?'

'Yes, of course. This here is Detective Inspector Gilbert.'

Glancing around to see Vicky go a little red around the edges, Tanner heard Fletcher call out, 'Is she your chaperone – to try to stop you from putting your foot in it, like you did last time – and the time before that?'

Hearing a ripple of laughter, Tanner chose to ignore the remark. 'From this point forward, she'll be leading the investigation.'

'You haven't told us what the investigation is yet.'

'DI Gilbert,' Tanner continued, turning to face her. 'Perhaps you'd like to continue from here?'

'Thank you, DCI Tanner,' came her formal response.

Turning to address her audience, she lifted her chin to continue. 'As my colleague has already mentioned, yesterday morning a body was found at Blackfleet Broad.'

'Are we talking about the one who drowned, or the one who was allegedly murdered?'

'Her name was Tara Lowe...'

'So the one who was murdered, then,' Fletcher muttered loudly to himself while returning to his notes.

'She was twenty-two, had recently graduated with a degree in Law from Norfolk University, and was a member of an environmental action group called Nature First.'

'I don't suppose you know who killed her, by any chance?' came Fletcher's irritating voice again.

Vicky made the mistake of glancing over to find him staring at her with his pen poised.

Forcing herself to look away, she cast her eyes around at the other, more respectful reporters. 'She was also working towards becoming a freelance journalist.'

'At least that's one less hack we have to worry about,' she heard Fletcher mumble, much to the amusement of those surrounding him.

'Excuse me,' Vicky suddenly announced, turning to glare at him with a darkening face, 'but would you mind being quiet?'

Glancing curiously over his shoulder, Fletcher turned back to say, 'Sorry, but – are you talking to me?'

'I'd also appreciate it if you could show a little more respect for the victim.'

'The fisherman, or the girl?'

As Vicky was left seething with indignation, Tanner felt it necessary to take a step forward. 'Mr Fletcher, if you could refrain from making any comments until the end, I'm sure we'd all appreciate it.'

'I was only trying to establish which victim I was supposed to be showing a little more respect for,' came his insolent response.

Seeing him return to his notes, Tanner turned to look back at Vicky. 'Would you like to continue?'

'Not really,' she muttered, but only loud enough for Tanner to hear.

Lifting her head again, she shifted her weight from one foot to the other. 'Now, where was I?'

'You were telling me to show a little more respect for some dead girl.'

'Mr Fletcher!' Tanner exclaimed, meeting the reporter's gaze with an indignant glare. 'If you're unable to remain silent, then I'll be forced to have you escorted off the premises.'

'I suppose that's better than being locked up inside it,' he mumbled, leaving a handful of his fellow reporters doing their best not to laugh.

Feeling like a headmaster addressing a class of unruly teenagers, Tanner took a moment to glare around at the group as a whole. When they finally fell silent, he cleared his throat. 'I think what my colleague was about to tell you was that Miss Tara Lowe was last seen leaving her mother's house on Friday evening, at around seven o'clock. She would have been driving a beige Mini and should have been heading in the direction of Tunstead. If anyone thinks they may have seen her at around that time, or shortly afterwards, possibly in or around the entrance to Blackfleet Broad, we'd very much appreciate hearing from you.

'Now, we have some leaflets we'd like to hand out,' he continued, as both Vicky and himself picked up a pile each. 'The photograph is of Miss Lowe. It was taken fairly recently, so it should provide an accurate likeness. It also features the beige Mini she would have been driving.

'Once again, if anyone thinks they may have seen either Miss Lowe or her car on Friday night between the hours of seven o'clock and midnight, then we urge you to call the number provided at the bottom of the leaflet. All calls will naturally be treated in the strictest confidence.

'Does anyone have any questions?' Tanner asked, glancing around.

'I've got one,' said Fletcher, raising his hand.

'Anyone else?'

'It's actually something I asked before, one that neither of you answered.'

'That was probably because we didn't know.'

'Or maybe you didn't hear?'

'Would you like to ask it again?' sighed Tanner.

'Yes please!'

'Well, go on then.'

'I was just wondering if you knew who killed her?'

'If we knew that, then we wouldn't have the joyful task of standing out here talking to you lot, now would we?'

Amid another round of laughter, Fletcher continued. 'Then how about suspects?'

Lining them all up in his head, Tanner glanced around at Vicky. 'Nobody we're able to mention – at least not publicly.'

'How about Professor Alfred Beaumont?' asked Fletcher.

Hearing the name, Tanner whipped his head around to meet the reporter's penetrating gaze. 'May I ask how you came across that name?'

'He's in charge of the archaeological dig, isn't he? The one that was about to start at Blackfleet Broad – before the bodies of the fisherman and the girl were found.'

'He is,' Tanner confirmed, 'but that doesn't automatically make him a suspect.'

'Then how about the people he's in business with?'

'I'm sorry?' asked Tanner, struggling to believe that this moronic-looking reporter from *The Norfolk Herald* had somehow managed to stumble over the same line of enquiry they were now following.

'The property developer, Simon Balinger,' Fletcher continued, reading from his notes, 'the person responsible for Norfolk Council's new-build development proposals, Jeremy Southcott, and our local MP, Mr George–'

Knowing half of Norfolk would be listening –

including Forrester, before Fletcher had the chance to read Elliston's surname out, Tanner lept around the table. 'Right, that's quite enough of all that!'

'That's quite enough of all what?' Fletcher asked, glancing up from his notebook to present Tanner with an innocent smirk.

'Of you reading out a list of random people's names in an effort to connect them with an ongoing murder investigation.'

'But they're not exactly random, though, are they?'

'OK,' Tanner said, casting his eyes around at the other journalists, 'thank you all for coming, but this press conference is officially over!'

'But – you'd only just started,' chirped Fletcher, as his colleagues let out a collective groan.

'Don't worry,' Tanner said, leaning towards him while the other journalists began packing up their equipment. 'I thought I'd give you an exclusive.'

'Not seriously?'

'Very seriously. So much so that I'd like to chat about it with you inside the station.'

'You can't arrest me!' Fletcher protested, as the surrounding reporters began to take more of an interest. 'Not for doing nothing more nefarious than asking you a couple of questions – which, by the way, is my job!'

'Of course I'm not arresting you,' Tanner said, lowering his voice to an insistent whisper. 'Do you want the scoop, or not?'

Fletcher glanced nervously around before looking at Tanner with narrowing eyes. 'OK,' he eventually said, 'but you'd better be telling the truth.'

'Surprisingly,' Tanner replied, 'unlike the

newspaper you work for, I'm not in the habit of telling a never-ending series of blatant lies.'

- CHAPTER THIRTY-FOUR -

ASKING VICKY TO join them, Tanner virtually frogmarched Fletcher inside the station and didn't stop until reaching the door leading through to the imaginatively named Interview Room One.

'Where the hell are you taking me?' the reporter eventually protested, as Tanner brought him to an ungainly halt in front of the already open door.

'Do you want an exclusive, or not?' he asked, inviting him to step inside.

'Well, yes, of course, but why does it feel more like I'm being arrested than about to be briefed on a career-defining news story?'

'Would it help if I offered you some tea and biscuits?'

'It wouldn't go amiss,' he shrugged.

'Tell you what. Why don't you take a seat, and I'll sort some refreshments out for us when we take a break.'

'Why do I feel I'm not being given much of a choice?' Fletcher asked, leaning cautiously forward to cast his eyes around the small, windowless room ahead.

'You're not,' came Tanner's terse response, shoving him suddenly forward.

'Oi! Watch it, mate!'

'Now, sit down and stop moaning.'

'What if I don't?'

'Then I will arrest you.'

'What for?'

'For being a pain in the arse, that's what for. Now, are you going to sit down, or am I going to have the duty sergeant formally process you?'

'How about telling me what you want to talk to me about first?'

'I'd like to know where you got that list of names from,' Tanner replied, leading Vicky inside before closing the door.

'What list of names?'

'The one you were so keen to read out in front of half the nation's press.'

'Oh, I don't think half the nation's press were there. It was probably more like a quarter.'

'Are you going to tell me, or are you going to have an unfortunate accident with the edge of the table?'

'You're not seriously threatening me, are you? I mean, you do know what I do for a living?'

'I'm fully aware of what you do for a living, which is why I wouldn't be stupid enough to threaten you. However, if you did just happen to trip over to end up cracking your head on the edge of the table – before standing up to do it all over again – I doubt anyone would believe you if you were to contradict such an event, given your job, who you work for, and everything.'

'Then it only leaves me to thank you for such reassuring words. It's always comforting to know that all the stories floating around about police brutality are actually true.'

'Does that mean you're going to tell me?'

'Sorry – what was the question again?'

'Where you got that list of names from?'

'The same place I get pretty much all of my

information.'

'You mean... one of your sources?'

'How did you guess?'

'Then, unfortunately, in this particular instance, I'm going to insist that you tell me their name.'

'You know I can't do that. Nor am I under any legal obligation to.'

'I'm afraid the Police and Criminal Evidence Act of 1984 says otherwise.'

Fletcher's eyes flickered with nervous hesitation before his face broke out into an uncertain grin. 'You just made that up.'

'Feel free to search it up on the interweb, but you'll save us both a lot of time if you just told me.'

Fletcher took a moment to look at Vicky, glaring at him from the corner of the room with her arms folded, before turning back to Tanner. 'OK, I'll tell you, but this isn't some sort of confession.'

'Let me guess – it was the murdered girl, Tara Lowe?'

Fletcher first opened, then closed his mouth.

'I take it that means I'm right?'

'Well – yes – but... how did you know?'

'Because we've been told that she'd written a story that sounds remarkably similar to the one you're evidently working on yourself.'

'I didn't steal it from her, if that's what you're inferring!' Fletcher exclaimed, a ripple of sweat breaking out over his greasy forehead. 'And I didn't murder her in an effort to cover it up, either!'

'There's no need to look so worried. I believe you.'

'You do?'

'Well, at least the part about not having been responsible for her murder. What I'm not so sure about is what you said before – that you didn't steal it from her.'

'I didn't!'

'Listen, Mr Fletcher, I really don't care who came up with the story. What I want to know is if it's true – and, more to the point, if you know whether the people involved knew she'd been writing it.'

'How should I know?'

'Did she tell you that she'd spoken to them about it?'

'No.'

'Then what *did* she tell you?'

Fletcher held Tanner's gaze for a moment with a defiant glare before breaking eye contact to lower his eyes.

'Mr Fletcher?' Tanner prompted.

'Alright, alright! She phoned the office, saying she had a story – something about a scheme to build a commercial development on Blackfleet Broad. I just happened to be the one who picked up the phone.'

'What happened then?'

Fletcher shrugged. 'It actually sounded quite good, so I invited her out for a coffee, to talk about it – at which time she was stupid enough to tell me the whole thing.'

'So you *did* steal it from her, then?'

'I got the idea from her, but I wouldn't say I stole it.'

'Then what would you say?'

'That I was inspired by her idea and decided to develop it,' he smirked.

'Without her consent.'

'She didn't say I couldn't, but she didn't say I could, either.'

'Just because someone doesn't give you permission to take something, doesn't mean it isn't theft.'

'You can't steal an unpublished story – certainly not when she decided to tell me the whole thing.'

'Anyway, as I said before, I really don't care who came up with the idea.'

'If you want to know if the people who were named knew about her writing it, then as I said before, I don't know!'

'You didn't ask if she'd spoken to any of them about it?'

'Nope!'

'Did you at least ask who her sources were?'

'Actually, yes, I did.'

'And...?'

'She said what I was expecting her to say.'

'That journalists never reveal their sources,' Tanner replied, shaking his head with despondent frustration.

A knock at the door had Tanner glancing around to see Sally's head appear from the corridor beyond.

'Yes, Sally, what is it?' came Tanner's terse response.

'Sorry to bother you, boss,' she replied, glancing around at Vicky before presenting Tanner with a guilty frown, 'but something's come up that I thought you should know about.'

'If it's to tell me that the printer's run out of ink, then do you think it can wait?'

'It's just that – er –,' she continued, lowering her voice as her eyes rested briefly on Fletcher's, 'something's been found at Norfolk University.'

'Don't tell me that a student's been discovered

attending a lecture?' came Tanner's amused response.

Shaking her head, Sally leaned through the gap in the door to whisper, 'The body of a man's been found – and it looks like foul play.'

'Whoever it is,' came Fletcher's insistent voice, 'I didn't kill him!'

Tanner turned to face him with a belligerent glare. 'I suggest you remain where you are for a moment, whilst DI Gilbert and I have a quick word with our colleague.'

'I wasn't aware I had much of a choice,' muttered Fletcher, slumping in his chair to begin staring despondently down at the table.

Leaving him to it, Tanner gestured for Vicky to join him as he led the way out into the corridor.

Closing the door quietly behind him, he turned to give Sally his full attention. 'Sorry about that. You were saying...?'

'I've just taken a call from a Mrs Denise Fairburn at Norfolk University,' Sally continued, her voice remaining a clandestine whisper as her eyes stayed fixed on the interview room door. 'She works there as one of the department coordinators.'

'I don't suppose we can move on to the part about a body being found?' urged Tanner, tilting his head in an effort to re-engage eye contact.

'Sorry, yes, of course,' she replied, her lashes flickering under the weight of a thick line of mascara as her eyes lifted to meet with his. 'The body of a man's been found.'

'So you said,' came Tanner's curt response. 'What you haven't is who the person is.'

'Professor Alfred Beaumont,' Sally eventually said. 'At least, the woman on the end of the phone seemed to think it was.'

After holding her eyes for a moment, Tanner's gaze drifted away, only to find Vicky staring expectantly at him.

'I suppose we'd better head over there,' he heard her say.

'Yes, I suppose we had,' came Tanner's measured reply.

'What about the reporter?'

'Who?'

'Mr Fletcher? The man we were just talking to?'

'Oh, him!' Tanner exclaimed, glancing back at the door behind them. 'I suggest we leave him there for a while. One less reporter roaming the streets can't exactly be a bad thing.'

- CHAPTER THIRTY-FIVE -

ARRIVING AT NORFOLK University's burgeoning car park some thirty minutes later, Tanner stepped out of his rather conspicuous Triumph Stag to take in the building's vast, angular façades, its many glass windows gleaming in the late morning sun.

Seeing Vicky step surreptitiously out from the other side to begin glancing furtively about, Tanner called over to her, 'Are you alright?'

'Yes, fine,' she replied, ducking herself down while continuing to scan the surrounding cars, and the various people that could be seen milling about between them – most of whom appeared to be trendy-looking students, somewhere between eighteen and twenty-one. 'I'm just regretting having forgotten to bring my widest-brimmed hat and a pair of sunglasses.'

'You're not still going on about my car, are you?'

'Of course I'm still going on about your car! You've no idea how embarrassing it is to be seen within a mile of it – let alone climbing willingly out!'

'You're being ridiculous,' came Tanner's reproachful response, just as an impossibly attractive young man dressed in dark, loosely fitting jeans, a tight black T-shirt, and a chunky silver chain swaggered past to say, 'Nice car, Grandpa!' as if rapping out a lyric.

When the young man winked at Vicky before strolling casually away, Tanner glanced around to find her staring dementedly towards the ground.

As her eyes lifted to follow the young man away, she shifted them back to Tanner. 'You see!' she eventually exclaimed, in a heavily chastising tone. 'He probably thought I was your girlfriend!'

'Not my daughter?'

'That would have been even worse!'

'I don't see how,' Tanner replied, staring wistfully away.

'Anyway, can we go in now, before anyone else sees me?'

'After you,' came Tanner's magnanimous response. 'But I'm not selling my car just because you find it a little embarrassing.'

'Then I suppose I'll just have to live in hope that it will have been towed away by the time we get back – especially given the fact you've left it in a disabled parking bay.'

'Shit,' muttered Tanner, gazing up at the small blue sign Vicky was referring to.

Looking back at the car before staring around at the myriad of others jammed tightly around it, he drew in a breath. 'I suppose I'd better find somewhere else to park, although I've no idea where.'

'Yes, I suppose you should,' Vicky agreed. 'It's just a shame there aren't any dangerous cliff edges nearby.'

With Tanner shaking his head as he reopened the door, Vicky glanced over her shoulder. 'Do you mind if I wait for you inside? That rather attractive young man has stopped in front of the entrance and is looking this way. If I can catch him up, with any luck I'll be able to explain to him that you're my boss, not my boyfriend – which is why I'm being forced to be driven around in a car I wouldn't normally be seen dead in. If I can do that, then there's every chance he might just ask for my phone number.'

- CHAPTER THIRTY-SIX -

HAVING FINALLY FOUND somewhere to park, without risking his car being towed away, Tanner found Vicky standing in the middle of the university building's foyer, enjoying what must have been a hilarious joke with a young female police constable.

'Anything you'd like to share?' he asked, stepping up to offer them each a disapproving scowl.

As the constable's grin vanished instantly to stand to attention, Vicky's amused expression lingered a little longer as she turned slowly to face him.

'We were actually talking about your car,' she eventually replied, stealing a glance back at the policewoman. 'PC Dunning here was just saying how much she liked it.'

'Really?' Tanner enquired, in a cautious, albeit optimistic tone.

'Obviously not. We both think it's hideous.'

'Yes, of course you do,' he replied, rolling his eyes.

'Shall we head up?' Vicky continued, evidently keen to move the conversation along. 'The victim is on the first floor.'

'Then you'd better lead the way.'

Following her over to a wide concrete staircase,

built more for function than style, he caught her up to ask, 'Did your friend back there know anything more about the body?'

'She was only able to direct me,' came Vicky's brusque response.

As they made their way up, Tanner heard himself saying, 'May I ask how the conversation about my car came up?'

'It didn't – at least, not directly.'

'Then what were you laughing about?' he persisted, knowing the question must have made him sound a little paranoid.

Reaching the top, Vicky glanced over her shoulder at him. 'Don't worry, boss, it wasn't about you.'

'Then what was it about?' he continued, nodding at a couple of male PCs busy comforting a plump, middle-aged woman who was dabbing her eyes with a tissue.

'Just men in general,' he heard her say, as he followed her down an empty corridor. 'In particular, how useless they are – present company excepted, of course,' she added, glancing back at him with just the hint of a smile.

Reading between the lines, Tanner caught her up to say, 'I take it that young man you were eyeing up didn't have the courage to ask for your phone number?'

Drifting to a halt, Vicky turned to present Tanner with a quizzical expression. 'How did you know?'

'It's obvious,' he shrugged. 'Nobody wants to be rejected. The easiest way not to be is to avoid the possibility – which is why very few men go around asking attractive young women for their phone numbers, or anything else for that matter.'

Tanner's observation appeared to make Vicky blush.

'Sorry,' he apologised, looking away. 'I didn't mean to say anything that might make you feel awkward.'

'It's my fault,' she replied, glancing down. 'I'm not used to men telling me I'm attractive – certainly not when they just happen to be my superior officer.'

Coming to the conclusion that it might be wise to steer the conversation away from whether he did, or did not find her attractive, Tanner cleared his throat. 'You know, you still haven't told me what was so funny – when you were chatting to PC whatever-her-name-was.'

'Oh, that! It was just some silly meme on Insta.'

'Insta...?' Tanner enquired, feeling older by the second.

'Er... Instagram?'

'Oh, right. Yes, of course.'

'It's alright, you don't need to pretend that you knew what "Insta" meant,' she laughed.

'I must admit that I didn't, but at least I know what Instagram is!'

'Don't tell me you have an account!'

'Er, no, but Christine does. Samantha, as well.'

'Really?' asked Vicky, in an incredulous tone.

'Well, no, but it wouldn't surprise me. I caught her playing with my phone the other day, which probably means she's already set herself up on Facebook, Instagram, TikTok, and Twitter – and has already gained over a million followers by gurgling the tune *Stayin' Alive* by the Bee Gees with a whimsical smile.'

'You forgot Snapchat,' Vicky remarked.

'I forgot what?'

'It's another...' she began, before shaking her head. 'Never mind. Perhaps we should see if we can find this reported body before rigor mortis sets in?'

'Yes, of course,' Tanner replied, glancing vacantly about. 'I don't suppose you know where it is?'

'It should be down here,' she replied, leading the way once again. 'When we've found it,' she continued, waiting for him to catch up, 'maybe you can give me the name of Samantha's Insta account? I'm not sure I've ever seen a baby gurgling a tune to anything – let alone a classic like *Stayin' Alive* by the Bee Gees.'

- CHAPTER THIRTY-SEVEN -

SPYING A LINE of blue-and-white *Police Do Not Cross* tape ahead, they followed the corridor to its end, where a uniformed constable could be seen standing to attention, gesturing them towards a half-opened door.

Finding Johnstone lurking just outside it, rummaging through his black leather medical bag, Tanner called out, 'Morning, Johnstone!' whilst leading Vicky towards him. 'Have you forgotten something?'

'Examination gloves,' he mumbled, burying his head inside the bag. 'I had half a box full a few days ago. I can't believe they've gone already!'

'Don't worry,' chirped Vicky, delving into her own, much larger bag. 'I have enough in here to last a lifetime.'

Fishing out a tangled clump of pale white latex gloves, she set about handing a pair to first Johnstone, then Tanner, before donning a pair for herself.

'Bloody things,' muttered Tanner, struggling to find the right holes for his fingers, only to see Johnstone had already pulled his second on with practised ease.

'How the hell did you do that so quickly?' he demanded, pulling his hand free to shake the glove out before trying again.

'They are a little on the small side,' Johnstone commented, 'but I think you'll find that, like most things in life, there's a knack to it.'

Seeing Vicky was also struggling, Tanner held one of his gloves out to him. 'I don't suppose you'd like to share what that knack is?'

'Try placing your thumb in first,' Johnstone suggested, snapping one of his gloves off to give a practical demonstration. 'The rest of the fingers should then follow.'

Doing just that, Tanner found himself able to slip the glove on within a few short seconds.

'For Christ's sake,' he groaned, doing the same with the other. 'Is there a reason why nobody's told me that before? I must have spent half my life trying to put these bloody things on.'

'Perhaps you should have asked someone,' mused Johnstone.

'Perhaps someone should have told me,' Tanner continued, 'preferably twenty years ago during basic training.'

Offering him a stoic smile, Johnstone placed his re-gloved hand on the door handle. 'Shall we go in?'

'I simply can't wait,' came Tanner's sardonic response.

Drawing in a fortifying breath, Tanner waited in subdued silence as Johnstone gently pushed open the door to reveal a small, cluttered office, its walls covered from floor to ceiling with an abundance of dust-covered textbooks.

Following him through, they saw the figure of a stick-thin elderly man, leaning back in a worn leather chair behind an untidy varnished desk.

As Tanner stepped a little closer, he was able to see

the man's deathly pale face – staring unblinkingly up at the ceiling through a single blue eye, the other obscured by the handle of what appeared to be a silver letter opener.

'Not suicide, then,' Tanner remarked, prompting Johnstone to turn around to present him with an admonishing glare.

'Time of death?' Tanner continued. 'Approximately?'

Pushing his glasses up the ridge of his nose, Johnstone returned his attention back to the body.

'At a very rough guess, I'd say about twelve hours ago.'

'Anything to indicate that the cause of death might have been something other than the obvious?'

Leaning towards the body's stone-like face before casting his eyes over the rest of him, Johnstone eventually straightened himself up. 'Nothing immediate, but I'll be able to give you a better idea after the post-mortem.'

'And how long will that be?' Tanner enquired, glancing behind him to see a couple of overall-clad forensic officers stacking a series of transparent plastic containers outside the still-open door.

'I'm still working on the man you fished out of Blackfleet Broad yesterday,' said Johnstone, 'so it won't be until tomorrow, I'm afraid.'

'Alright – but if you could make this a priority, I'd be grateful.'

With Johnstone giving him an affirming nod, Tanner turned on his heel to lead Vicky out.

Elbowing their way through a growing number of forensic officers, Tanner eventually reached the end of the corridor to stop and wait for Vicky.

'Any thoughts?' he asked, the moment she'd caught up.

'Only that it was Professor Beaumont, and that someone had stabbed him through the eye with what looked like a letter opener.'

'Also that there didn't appear to be any sign of a struggle,' added Tanner, glancing absently around, 'which suggests he was attacked with deliberate intent, as opposed to an argument that got out of hand.'

'Not necessarily,' Vicky countered. 'The injury could easily have been the result of a disagreement. The fact that there were no obvious signs of resistance could simply mean he wasn't given a chance to defend himself.'

'Fair enough,' said Tanner. 'What would you say our next step should be?'

'To speak to the person who found him,' Vicky replied, guiding Tanner's attention towards the woman they'd passed at the top of the stairs, still deep in conversation with two uniformed constables. 'With any luck, that's her over there.'

- CHAPTER THIRTY-EIGHT -

WITH VICKY LEADING the way, they stepped up to the woman the two uniformed constables were still speaking to – just in time to hear her blow her nose on the tissue she'd been using to dab at her eyes.

'Mrs Denise Fairburn?' Vicky enquired, leaning forward to offer her a gentle smile.

Seeing her respond with a cautious nod, Vicky presented her ID. 'DI Vicky Gilbert and my colleague, DCI Tanner. Is it alright if we ask you a few questions?'

'I've already told these two nice young men everything I know,' came her hesitant reply.

'I'm sure you have,' Vicky said, smiling at the officers in question. 'Would you mind if we had a word, anyway?'

With the question directed as much at the constables as at the witness, the two officers stood briefly to attention before turning to amble slowly away.

'Sorry to have to put you through this again,' began Vicky, 'but could you start by confirming that the man you found is definitely Professor Beaumont?'

As tears welled at the corners of her eyes, Mrs Fairburn nodded jerkily at Vicky a couple of times before her gaze sank slowly to the floor.

'Were you the one who found him?' Vicky asked.

She nodded again. 'He was supposed to be giving a lecture at nine o'clock this morning. At half past, a student came into my office to ask if I knew if he was in. I told her that his car was in the car park – I can see it from my office window – so I assumed he was. I then asked if she'd tried his office. She said she had, that she'd knocked, but there'd been no response, and the door was locked, which was why she came to find me.'

'What happened then?' prompted Vicky.

'I went to take a look for myself, only to find she was right – the door was locked and there was no reply, so I had to come all the way back to my office to get the spare set of keys.'

As another bout of tears spilled down her face, Vicky dug a fresh tissue from her handbag to press it into the woman's trembling hand. 'I assume that was when you found him?'

Seeing her nod again, Vicky waited for her to compose herself before continuing. 'Did you see him at all yesterday?'

'When I left to go home. I have to pass his office on the way out, and his door just happened to be open.'

'Did you speak to him?'

'Only to say goodnight.'

'And how did he seem?'

'Cheerful enough to wave at me, but not enough to smile.'

Joining the conversation, Tanner caught her eye. 'Was his door normally open?'

'I'm sorry?'

'You said his door just happened to be open. Was that normal?'

'Well, no, but someone was in there with him – someone who'd either just arrived, or was on his way out.'

Tanner exchanged a glance with Vicky before continuing. 'I don't suppose you knew who his visitor was, by any chance?'

'I'm sorry, I don't.'

'A student, perhaps?'

'He was wearing a suit, so I sincerely doubt it!'

'Not another member of staff?'

'If he was, then it wasn't anyone I know. Although... now that I think about it,' she continued, gazing away, 'I remember thinking at the time that I'd seen him somewhere before.'

'You can't remember from where?'

As she shook her head, Tanner asked, 'Then perhaps you could describe him for us?'

'As I said, he was wearing a suit. A tie as well,' came her unhelpful reply.

Remaining patient, Tanner tried again. 'Was he short or tall?'

'About average?'

'How about his build?'

'He wasn't fat, if that's what you mean. But he wasn't thin, either.'

'So – about average again?' Tanner sighed.

'I suppose. He *was* rather good-looking,' she continued. 'I remember that much. He also had neatly cut brown hair, and his suit was navy blue with a crisp white shirt and a polka-dot dark red tie.'

'I don't suppose you heard what they were talking about, by any chance?' asked Tanner, as the image of someone all too familiar began forming in his mind.

'I don't eavesdrop, mister whatever-your-name-was!' came her defensive response.

'I was thinking more along the lines of you just

happening to overhear something as you passed,' Tanner added, in an apologetic tone.

With Mrs Fairburn continuing to glare at him, Tanner was about to give up when she turned to Vicky. 'I don't make a habit of deliberately listening to other people's conversations,' she said, in precisely the way someone who did exactly that would have said.

'I'm sure you don't,' Vicky replied, in an understanding tone.

The woman pursed her lips to emphasise the point before eventually turning back to Tanner. 'That said,' she continued, 'I did just happen to hear something.'

'Which was?' Tanner asked, leaning forward.

'Something about a commercial development project being delayed, and how much it was going to cost.'

'Anything else?'

'That was it,' she replied, shaking her head.

As Tanner cast a quick glance at Vicky, the woman added, 'I did also hear one of them mention Blackfleet Broad, and the bodies that had been found there – but I didn't think much of it, as pretty much everyone here's been talking about the same thing.'

Becoming increasingly certain that he knew exactly who the professor's visitor was, Tanner pulled out his phone to do a quick Google search.

'Could this be the man you saw?' he asked, turning his phone around to show her a photograph of none other than George Elliston – Norfolk's most recent Member of Parliament – grinning at the camera like a cat that had devoured an aviary full of canaries.

The woman took a moment to study the photograph before offering Tanner a look of uncertain doubt. 'It could be, but the man who was here had a red tie. That person's is blue.'

Suppressing the urge to unleash a tirade of verbal abuse at her for lacking even the merest fragment of imagination, Tanner took a fortifying breath. 'What if he changed his tie?'

The woman studied the photograph again. 'I'm not sure,' she eventually said. 'The man I saw wasn't smiling like that, either.'

Shaking his head, Tanner deliberately turned his back on the witness to begin stomping away, leaving Vicky to offer her an apologetic grimace.

'Thank you for your time, Mrs Fairburn. You've been most helpful.'

- CHAPTER THIRTY-NINE -

LEAVING THE WOMAN where she was, Vicky spun around to chase after Tanner, only to find that he'd stopped by the top of the staircase to glare dementedly down at his phone.

'Was it really necessary to be quite so discourteous?' she demanded, coming to an ungainly halt beside him to see what he continued to stare at – the same thing he'd shown the witness: the grinning photograph of the Right Honourable George Elliston.

'How was I being discourteous?' he enquired, tucking his phone away to direct his gaze down the stairs towards the university's glass-doored entrance.

'By not even bothering to thank the witness for her time.'

'Oh, sorry,' came Tanner's distracted response. 'I thought I'd leave that to you. Besides, she wasn't being particularly helpful.'

'Why's that? Because she was unable to provide a positive identification that the man she saw talking to Professor Beaumont in his office was your favourite MP in the whole wide world, only shortly after having found the body of one of her colleagues?'

'More because she lacked the cognitive ability to accept that it was possible for a person to have more than one tie in their wardrobe.'

'You can't blame her for that.'

'Actually, I think I can.'

'I meant for her not having the confidence to identify someone from a single photograph.'

'Do you think I should have shown her more?'

'I think you're missing the point.'

'I am?'

'The point being that she was clearly traumatised, and that you could have been a little more understanding.'

'That would have been difficult, I'm afraid.'

'And why's that?'

'Because, young Vicky, I was unable to understand how it could be possible for a human being to lack so much of their God-given imagination that they'd be unable to look beyond the colour of someone's tie!'

'I'm only saying that you could have been a little more empathetic, given what she'd been through.'

'So you agree with me, then, about the tie?'

'Well, yes, of course.'

'OK, good,' Tanner replied, returning his attention to the building's entrance, and the car park that could be seen through the glass doors beyond. 'Then you wouldn't object to us heading off to have a chat with him?'

'To have a chat to who?'

'Mr Elliston, of course!' Tanner replied, turning to face her with a look of bemused incredulity.

'I'm – er – sorry, boss, but I think that's a bad idea.'

'Why's that? Because he's just been implicated in the murder of a university professor, or because he's the most likely suspect in the death of a young woman found beaten and drowned in the middle of Blackfleet Broad?'

'More because the witness wasn't able to confirm that it was him she saw, and that we don't have any evidence to suggest that he was involved in what happened to Tara Lowe.'

'Not yet, we don't.'

'And I suggest that we avoid talking to him until we do.'

Tanner let out a disagreeable huff.

'Meanwhile,' Vicky patiently continued, 'perhaps we can work towards establishing with a little more certainty if Mr Elliston *was* here yesterday afternoon.'

'And how do you propose we do that?'

'By checking the footage from the university's various CCTV cameras,' she replied, bringing Tanner's attention up to one directly above their heads. 'I saw two more in the foyer below,' she added, 'and at least one in the car park.'

Tanner gazed thoughtfully around, as if looking to see if there were any more. 'Fair enough,' he eventually said. 'Perhaps you could make a start – or at least delegate the job to one of the officers I can see milling aimlessly around. Maybe you could also ask them to speak to some of the other members of staff, to see if they saw the same person.'

As Tanner's attention drifted towards the car park once again, Vicky gazed at him with a suspicious eye. 'And what, may I ask, are you going to do?'

'Find us something to eat!' he announced, before staring enthusiastically down at his watch. 'It is lunchtime, after all. Close enough – at least – for me to be in desperate need of a decent coffee.'

- CHAPTER FORTY -

OPENING HIS CAR door, Tanner stopped for a moment to stare back at the university building to picture Vicky in his mind, gazing suspiciously after him from one of its many gleaming windows.

Given the fact that he'd been forced to leave his car at the far end of the car park – meaning she'd have needed a telescope to see him – he shrugged off the feeling of being an errant schoolboy to climb inside and dig out first his phone, then his little used satnav.

After several minutes spent faffing about, trying to get the contraption to do what it was supposed to, he finally stuck it onto the windscreen, started the engine, and reversed out of the bay.

Just over twenty minutes later, he was taking the steps two at a time up towards the entrance of Norfolk District Council's headquarters – a vast, monolithic structure that made the university he'd just left look like a child's sandcastle by comparison.

Refusing to allow himself to be intimidated by the building's imposing presence, he pushed on towards the entrance, heaving open one of the heavy glass doors before staring vacantly about.

Without the faintest idea where to go, he turned slowly around whilst taking in the foyer's sleek, modern interior, before finally spotting what he'd been looking for: a sculpted wooden desk in front a lavish marble wall, etched with a gold-lined map of Norfolk.

Very much aware of the time – and that he was only supposed to be out buying something to eat – he hurried over to what he presumed was the reception desk, where a smartly dressed man and woman could be seen stationed behind it.

Being presented with identical smiles from both, unsure which one to address, he returned their smiles before pulling out his formal ID.

'Detective Chief Inspector Tanner,' he began, curious to see their reaction.

With neither even so much as flinching, he took a breath to continue. 'Would it be possible for me to have a very quick word with Mr George Elliston?'

'Do you have an appointment?' the male receptionist asked, briefly glancing at Tanner's ID before tapping at his keyboard.

'It's a police matter,' came Tanner's curt response. 'An urgent one, as well.'

Returning what appeared to be the exact same smile he'd used before, the receptionist gestured towards a nest of plush cream leather sofas. 'If you'd like to take a seat, I'll see if he's available.'

With the man remaining as he was – clearly waiting for Tanner to obey before proceeding – Tanner glanced anxiously down at his watch. 'How long do you think this will take?'

'I really can't say, but if you could take a seat, I'd be happy to look into his availability.'

Realising that probably meant anywhere between several hours to sometime next week, Tanner spent a full moment glaring at him with a look of threatening consternation, hoping that might hurry things along. But with the man remaining motionless, his hand extended like a human statue, Tanner sighed in resignation.

About to ask if there was anywhere nearby to buy coffee and sandwiches, he turned his head to see a large meeting room off to the side.

Leaning back to peer through the smoked-glass partition, he saw an insipidly dull-looking meeting was in full swing. When he saw a clock on the wall above, reminding him that he'd already wasted half an hour chasing what was undoubtedly going to be a lost cause, he made the executive decision to beat a hasty retreat back to his car.

Thanking the receptionist for his time, in the most disingenuous tone possible, he turned on his heel to leave.

Glancing over at the meeting room as he did, it was only when he recognised one of the people inside – sitting with his legs crossed at the head of the polished oval table – that he came to an ungainly halt.

Waiving triumphantly at the receptionist, he called over, 'It's alright, I've found him!'

With the receptionist staring after him in alarm, Tanner marched straight over to the meeting room, heaving open the door without even bothering to knock.

'Sorry to interrupt,' he began, glancing around at the dozen or so startled faces he could see before fixing his eyes on the man at the end. 'DCI Tanner, Norfolk Police,' he continued, holding up his ID. 'If it's not too much trouble, I'd like a quick word with your illustrious leader, Mr George Elliston.'

As every head turned towards Elliston, Tanner

gleefully watched him squirm in his leather bound chair before forcing himself up to his feet.

'If you'll excuse me,' he muttered, offering his colleagues a placatory smile. 'It's probably about my dog. He ran off after a squirrel this morning. Hopefully, there's been some news.'

As those most likely to be fellow dog-owners offered him sympathetic smiles, Elliston scooped up his phone to stride quickly out.

'This better be good,' he muttered to Tanner in a low, menacing voice as he brushed quickly past.

'It's concerning an area of outstanding natural beauty,' Tanner began, allowing the meeting room door to swing slowly closed.

'What?' Elliston demanded, scowling impatiently at him.

'Blackfleet Broad?' Tanner replied. 'I assume you've heard of it?'

'Why – are you trying to find it? If you are, there are easier ways – like using a map, for example.'

'You may have heard in the news that a couple of bodies were found there yesterday.'

'Yes, of course – although I'm not sure what that has to do with me.'

'One of the deceased was a local fisherman.'

'Uh-huh.'

'The other was a young woman by the name of Tara Lowe.'

'Yes, and...?'

'I was wondering if you knew her?'

'I'm sorry, but what makes you think I should have?'

'Because she was the leader of an environmental group called Nature First, who were trying to stop the area being turned into an archaeological dig in search of Viking treasure.'

'And what, exactly, has that got to do with me?' came Elliston's seething response.

'She was also a freelance journalist.'

'You don't say,' Elliston muttered, folding his arms to look deliberately away.

'She'd been working on a story shortly before she was killed.'

'I thought that's what freelance journalists did.'

'It was about how the dig was just an excuse to prepare the area for a far more lucrative building development project.'

'Sounds like you need to be talking to someone in our planning department. Perhaps I can make you an appointment.'

'If you don't know Tara Lowe, perhaps you know someone by the name of Alfred Beaumont?'

'Who?'

'He was a History professor at Norfolk University.'

'Are you nearly finished, Mr Tanner?' Elliston snapped, peering over his shoulder towards the meeting behind him. 'It's just that I appear to have a room full of people waiting for me.'

'He was also in charge of the archaeological dig.'

'I take it that's a no.'

'Or at least he *was*,' added Tanner, studying Elliston's face.

As Tanner fell silent, Elliston turned back. 'Does that mean you're finished?'

'Are you honestly trying to tell me that you don't know Professor Beaumont?' Tanner demanded.

'Yes, I am. Now, if you'll excuse me,' he said, shoving past, 'I really must be getting back.'

'Even though you were seen talking to him in

his office yesterday evening – only a few hours before he was found stabbed to death behind his desk?'

Tanner watched Elliston stop mid-stride to turn slowly around.

'I sincerely hope you didn't come all the way over here to accuse me of murdering some random university professor?'

'Are you going to deny that you were there?'

'You didn't answer my question.'

'Even though we have a witness who saw you with him – along with CCTV footage to back it up?'

'I take it that's a yes?'

With Tanner staring silently back, Elliston clapped his hands together. 'Right then! Thank you for taking time out of your busy day to come and see me. Always a pleasure to meet someone from our local police force, even at such short notice. You will, of course, be hearing from my lawyer.'

Offering Tanner his trademark smile, Elliston turned to head back towards his meeting – only to stop once again.

'Actually, while you're there, if you could give my regards to Superintendent Forrester – his wife as well,' he continued, 'I'd be eternally grateful.'

- CHAPTER FORTY-ONE -

WITH IT BEGINNING to dawn on him that he'd made what could easily turn out to be a rather serious error of judgement, Tanner slunk out of the building and back to his car.

Keen to avoid Vicky – to no doubt end up having to explain to her where he'd been – and where her lunch was – he bypassed the university to head back to the station instead.

Once inside, he crept into the peaceful isolation of his office to await the inevitable call from Forrester.

After making himself a much-needed coffee, and having spent an exceptionally dull hour weeding through his emails to try and separate the wheat from the chaff, he was both relieved and mildly surprised that his boss still hadn't called.

Picking up the phone, he decided to check in to see how his new SIO had been getting on.

'Vicky, hi – it's Tanner.'

'Hello, boss. Where are you?'

'Back at the office.'

'Oh, right. I thought you'd gone out in search of our lunch.'

'Yes, sorry about that. Something came up.'

'OK, well, not to worry. I managed to pick something up from the university canteen.'

'How have you been getting on?' Tanner continued – as keen to move the subject away from where he'd been as he was to find out whether she'd had any luck finding another witness who could confirm, with a little more certainty, that Elliston had met Professor Beaumont in his office the previous evening, or at least that he'd been caught on one of the university's CCTV cameras doing so.

'Nothing so far, I'm afraid.'

'Nothing so far, as in...?' Tanner asked, holding his breath.

'We've been speaking to various members of staff – none of whom could remember seeing the man our witness said she saw.'

Tanner cursed quietly to himself. 'What about the security cameras?' he demanded, with growing desperation.

'Well, yes, we did have a little more luck there, in that they managed to pick up a man dressed in a suit and tie entering the building at just after five o'clock.'

'But...?'

'But they were all facing down at him from the ceiling, and he never looked up – at least, not at the right time for them to capture his face.'

Tanner shook his head in frustrated consternation. 'What about the cameras outside the building?'

'I've asked Townsend and Henderson to try to gain access to the footage from where they are.'

'Can't you from there?'

'They're managed by a security company that looks after the car park.'

'Then I suppose I'd better have a word with them,' Tanner muttered, glancing through his office partition window to see if they were there.

'Don't – worry,' came Vicky's fragmented voice, as

the signal began to drop, 'I'm hitching a ride back now. I'll chase them up when I get there.'

- CHAPTER FORTY-TWO -

RESISTING THE URGE to chase after them himself, Tanner returned his attention to the mess that was his email's inbox to impatiently wait for Vicky's return. When he saw her step out of a squad car he'd seen reversing into a parking bay outside his window, he jumped up to make his way out to reception to meet her. But instead of finding her hurrying through the doors, he found himself being formally greeted by a tall, middle-aged man with a long grey face, and an equally grey pin-striped suit.

'Mr John Tanner?' the man enquired, stepping up to him with an unsettling air of confidence.

'Er... yes?' Tanner replied, eyeing him up with cautious uncertainty.

As Vicky pulled open the door behind him, the man produced a formal-looking document from his inside jacket pocket.

'My name's Edward Hargreaves. I work as a solicitor for Hollis, Langley, Fenwick and Merriweather, LLP.'

Tanner raised an eyebrow. 'And all that fits on the business card, does it?'

'I've been requested to present this to you,' the solicitor continued, holding the document out.

Taking it from him, Tanner prised it open to briefly scan its contents. 'What does LLP stand for?'

he eventually asked.

The solicitor met Tanner's eyes with a questioning gaze, as if trying to determine whether or not he should answer.

'I was just wondering if it was a typo,' Tanner continued, returning his attention to the letter, 'and if it should be LOL instead.'

'As you'll see from its contents,' the solicitor replied, 'it's a restraining order against you.'

'I think the clue was in the title,' Tanner mused, glancing around to see Vicky appear behind him to begin reading the letter over his shoulder. 'Have you met my colleague?' he asked the man. 'DI Gilbert. I believe she's currently single, and her interests include reading other people's letters whilst being unable to mind her own business.'

'Should you need further clarification,' the solicitor continued, 'you'll find my name and contact details at the top of the letter.'

'I will?' Tanner replied, bringing the letter a little closer.

'Now, if you'll excuse me, I have some more errands to run.'

Lowering the letter to watch the solicitor pivot around to head for the door, Tanner turned his head to find Vicky was still there.

'What on earth have you been up to?' she eventually demanded, snatching the letter out of his hands to continue reading.

'Would you like to take a look?' he asked. 'Sorry, you already are.'

'This is a restraining order!'

'Yes, I know. As I mentioned to the nice solicitor, the clue was in the title.'

'From George Elliston!'

'Oh, right. I was wondering who'd sent it.'

'But – what have you done for him to have had this sent to you?'

'Honestly, I've no idea,' he replied, tacking onto the end a nervous laugh.

'You must have done something,' Vicky continued. 'People don't have restraining orders issued against them for no reason.'

'I suppose it might have something to do with what we were talking about earlier.'

'You mean – me and you?'

'No – me and Elliston.'

'But – when did you see Elliston?'

'When I popped out earlier.'

'You said you were going out in search of lunch.'

'Yes, I know, but I found myself driving past the council offices, so I thought I'd stop by to see if I could have a quick chat with him.'

'By the contents of this letter, I assume you were able to.'

'Well, yes – although I did have to drag him out of a meeting first.'

'What then?'

'I proceeded to ask him some questions,' Tanner shrugged.

'Please don't tell me that you accused him of murdering Professor Beaumont?'

'Not in so many words.'

'For Christ's sake, John. What the hell were you thinking?'

'I was trying to make him admit to being inside the professor's office at the time of his death.'

'I assume he didn't.'

'Well, no, but in my defence, I thought we'd have a little more in the form of evidence by now that he had been.'

'Whereas instead, you've been handed a

restraining order – meaning that you're not allowed to have any contact with him for the next twelve months, nor can you go within a hundred metres of his home or place of work.'

'Yes, I know. However, the good news is that I don't have to.'

'And why's that?'

'Because you can, in my place – being that you're the Senior Investigating Officer, and everything.'

'That's all well and good, John, but it's hardly ideal. How's it going to look when the press finds out that you've been harassing our local MP to the point where he's had to take out a restraining order against you?'

'With any luck, they won't.'

'What about Forrester?'

'I don't think he's taken out a restraining order against me. He'd more likely try to do the opposite – although I'm not sure there is such a thing.'

'I meant, when Forrester finds out?'

'Oh – I can't see any reason why he should.'

'You don't think Elliston would let him know?'

'Er...' Tanner began, thinking back to the last thing Elliston had said to him – only to hear someone calling for him from the doors through to the main office.

Glancing up to see Henderson's gormless face, Tanner fixed his eyes on him to say, 'Yes, what is it?'

'Sorry to bother you, boss, but Superintendent Forrester is waiting on the line for you. I wouldn't normally have disturbed you, but he says it's rather urgent.'

- CHAPTER FORTY-THREE -

ARRIVING HOME LATER that evening, Tanner was greeted by a sudden crescendo of pots and pans, clattering down onto the kitchen floor.

Smiling to himself as he listened to Christine mutter some sort of inaudible curse, he called out, 'Honey, I'm home!' before throwing his keys onto the sideboard.

Not hearing a response, he made his way inside to pop his head into the main living area, only to find neither Christine nor Samantha were there.

With a prickle of concern, he gripped the door handle to creep further inside. 'Hello?' he said, listening to a strange swirling sort of a noise. 'Is anyone here?'

'I'm on the floor,' came Christine's disembodied voice.

'Oh, right. Sorry,' he said, stepping into the kitchen to see her on her hands and knees behind the breakfast bar, mopping something up with a cloth. 'I wasn't sure if you'd heard me come in.'

'What made you think I hadn't?'

'Because whenever I come home I always call out, "Honey, I'm home," to which you normally respond by saying, "I'm in the kitchen."'

'That's probably because I'm *always* in the kitchen – cooking your bloody dinner!'

Sensing it may not be the best time for his usual

irreverent banter, he glanced around the room. 'Where's Samantha?'

'Isn't she in her playpen?'

Crouching down to lift a blanket from the baby's mobile holding cell, he found nothing but a stuffed bunny rabbit with a pink nose and large floppy ears.

Standing back up, Tanner stared around the room with growing unease.

'Wasn't she there?' he heard Christine ask.

'Not unless she's turned into a stuffed rabbit with unfeasibly large ears.'

'That's Floppy,' came Christine's response, picking herself off the kitchen floor to arch her back.

'What's floppy?' Tanner asked, glancing down at himself.

'The name of her special bunny rabbit,' Christine replied, making her way to the sink. 'Not whatever it is that you've got down there.'

'What do you mean, whatever it is that I've got down there? You must know what it is that I've got down there. I'm not sure how Samantha could have arrived without you knowing *exactly* what it is that I've got down there.'

'Artificial insemination?' Christine posed, wringing the cloth out with a determined frown to leave Tanner looking a little dejected.

'Speaking of Samantha,' Christine continued, 'perhaps you could find her for me while I get your dinner.'

'Yes, of course,' Tanner replied, spinning around in a circle, unsure where to start.

Stepping quickly over to the patio doors to make sure they were locked, he glanced out at the veranda, on the off-chance she'd somehow managed to slip out. 'Any idea where she might have gone?'

'Try the bedroom,' Christine suggested. 'She might have crawled under the bed.'

Becoming more concerned about Christine's flippant attitude towards their baby's whereabouts as he was about finding their missing child, Tanner headed into the bedroom – only to return about thirty seconds later.

'She wasn't there,' he announced, still staring around.

'Did you look under the covers?'

Without replying, Tanner returned to the bedroom to conduct a more thorough search.

'She's not there either,' he eventually replied, a few minutes later. 'Neither is she in the laundry basket, behind the curtains, under the dressing table, or inside the wardrobe. I even checked the bin beside the bed!'

'Why on earth did you look in the bin?'

'Because I didn't know where else to look!' Tanner exclaimed, staring fitfully about.

'Don't worry,' said Christine, glancing over to offer him a pacifying smile, 'she'll turn up somewhere.'

'She's not a wayward hamster, one that's managed to chew its way through its cage.'

'Really? I'd no idea.'

With Tanner looking as if he was about to have a cardiac arrest, Christine glanced casually over at him as she pulled a plate down from a cupboard. 'Have you tried the bathroom?'

'What would she be doing in there?'

'Well, she is a girl, so it could be any number of things. Her hair, for a start.'

With Tanner staring at her with unamused reproach, Christine continued. 'OK, I don't know, but if she's not in here, and she's not in the bedroom, then I can't think where else she could be.'

Shaking his head, Tanner turned on his heel to go back out into the hall – only to return a moment later. 'She's not there, either!'

'Have you checked behind the door?'

'Which door?'

'The one you're standing in front of.'

'Why would she be –?' Tanner began, turning around to see Samantha, sitting there quite happily with what appeared to be the head of a stuffed dinosaur hanging out of her dribbling mouth.

'Found her!' he announced, lowering himself down to catch her eye. 'Hello, Baby Samantha,' he cooed, unable to stop himself from grinning. 'What on earth are you doing behind the door?'

Chewing the head off a Tyrannosaurus Rex, obviously, he imagined her saying.

'Your dinner's ready,' came Christine's voice. 'Where do you want it?'

'On the counter's fine, thank you,' he replied, scooping Samantha up – dinosaur and all – to spend a few happy moments perambulating her around the room before gently lowering her back down into her mobile holding cell. 'Do me a favour and stay there, will you?' he said, stroking her impossibly soft hair as if she were a Persian cat. 'At least until I've finished my dinner.'

As if completely oblivious to her relocation, Samantha discarded the dinosaur over her shoulder to grab hold of the floppy-eared bunny rabbit.

Watching her begin to chew on that, Tanner left her to it to make his way to the breakfast bar, where a steaming plate of food was waiting for him, smelling even better than it looked.

'Looks good!' he said, feeling suddenly ravenous. 'May I ask what it is?'

'Tagliata di Manzo,' Christine replied, replacing various things back into the fridge.

Glancing up to see Tanner staring blankly over at her, she added, 'Sliced sirloin steak with rocket, shaved Parmesan, and balsamic glaze.'

'Oh right. Sounds intriguing. Thank you!'

'Did you solve any cases today?' Christine asked, as Tanner tucked in with ravenous delight. 'Apart from the one about the missing toddler, of course?'

'I must admit, being a detective chief inspector, and everything, you'd have thought I'd be able to find a small child in a house with only a handful of rooms with a little more ease.'

'Don't be too hard on yourself. I seem to spend half my life trying to find her. Life was a lot easier when she did nothing but lie on her back screaming.'

'It was?'

'Well, maybe not,' she grimaced, as if recalling that happy time. 'Anyway, how was your day?'

'Oh, you know. Same old, same old.'

'I take it that means you found another body?'

'Uh-huh,' he replied, between mouthfuls.

'Anyone I know?'

'Professor Alfred Beaumont?' Tanner replied, glancing up to hold his breath.

'Never heard of him.'

Exhaling sharply, Tanner muttered, 'That's a relief,' before returning to his meal.

'And how's Forrester?'

'Cheerful, as always. Even more so when he found out that one of our prime suspects has filed a restraining order against me.'

'Not seriously?'

'The restraining order, or Forrester's reaction to it?'

'How about both?'

'The restraining order *was* filed,' Tanner clarified. 'Sadly, Forrester's reaction wasn't quite so agreeable.'

'I'm not surprised. May I ask what you did?'

'Nothing out of the ordinary.'

'You must have done something.'

Tanner gazed contemplatively up at the ceiling. 'Thinking back, I really don't think I did. I simply asked the suspect about his whereabouts at the time of the professor's death – being that a witness saw them talking together.'

'Then why did he file a restraining order against you?'

'Probably because of who he is,' Tanner replied, returning to his meal with a nonchalant air.

'And who's that?'

'The MP for Norfolk.'

'You mean the MP for Norfolk as in George Elliston, the MP for Norfolk?'

'Is there another?'

'And he's the suspect in a murder investigation?'

Tanner finished his meal to push the plate away. 'That was delicious, thank you!'

'You didn't answer my question.'

'Sorry, which question was that?' he asked, reaching for the bottle of rum kept in the corner to examine the label.

'That the MP for Norfolk is a suspect in a murder investigation.'

'Yes and no.'

'What does that mean?'

'*I* think he is. I just need to convince Forrester.'

'Do you have any evidence against him?' Christine asked, sounding more like Forrester with every passing moment.

'As I said, a witness saw him talking to the victim at around the time he was thought to have been killed – or at least she thinks she did.'

'And on that basis you decided to accuse him of murder?'

'Something like that.'

'Then I'm not surprised he filed a restraining order against you.'

'The fact that he did makes me even more certain it's him.'

'Well, you're going to have a job interviewing him about it if you're not allowed within striking distance.'

'That's not a problem. I'll just get the Senior Investigating Officer to do it.'

'But – aren't you the Senior Investigating Officer?'

'Not this time.'

'Then who is?'

'Vicky kindly volunteered.'

'Before or after George Elliston filed a restraining order against you?'

'Before. She was supposed to take on the role during our last murder investigation, but she chickened out.'

'I don't blame her.'

'So far it's working out rather well,' Tanner said, smiling happily to himself while pouring out a drink. 'I'm free to go around accusing whoever I like of murder, while she's able to continue the investigation irrespective of who I end up being unable to talk to.'

'Sounds like the perfect partnership.'

'Anyway, she's a far better SIO than I ever was – she just needs a little more confidence. But that will come with experience.'

'If it's experience of solving mysteries she's in need of, then perhaps you can give her a call to come over here.'

'Why, what's happened now?'

'Samantha's done a runner again,' Christine said, drawing his gaze to the empty playpen. 'And I, for one, can't be arsed to find her.'

- CHAPTER FORTY-FOUR -

Wednesday, 17th June

DANIEL CARTER NUDGED his van up onto the kerb, a few feet away from the unlit entrance to the vast, crumbling block of flats that could be seen lurking in the shadows beyond.

'So that's what's left of the Longmeadow Estate,' the man perched beside him muttered, undoing his seatbelt to lean against the dashboard.

'Soon to be the Riverside Gate Business Park,' said Daniel, joining his colleague in staring through the windscreen.

'You're sure the copper piping's there?'

'I stacked it up myself – all one 'undred and fifty kilos of it.'

'And we'll definitely be able to flog it?'

'Liam, relax, for Christ's sake. I've already told you – I've got a buyer willin' to pay six quid a kilo. So if we get the lot loaded before the foreman shows up, that's a hundred and fifty, times six, divided by two.'

'Which is 'ow much?'

'Didn't they teach you nuff'n at school?'

'They taught me how to stick batteries into a calculator – the one I forgot to bring. But in my defence, I fought we came to nab some copper pipin', not for a lesson in long division.'

'It's not long division – it's simple maths.'

'Go on then, Mr Algebra. How much is it?'

'How the fuck should I know? I forgot my calculator.'

After glaring over at each other with similar looks of malevolent indignation, they suddenly collapsed into fits of laughter.

As the giggling ebbed away, Liam caught his breath. 'Seriously, Dan – how much d'you reckon we'll get?'

'About nine hundred quid. Somethin' like that.'

'Each?'

'Divided by two. So more like four-hundred and fifty.'

'Is that it?'

'What d'ya mean, is that it?' snapped Daniel. 'You'd 'ave to work three days in a row to make that, and you'd still end up 'aving to pay tax on top!'

'Sorry, I know. I just fought we'd make more, with the risk, and everythin'.'

'What risk? All we've got to do is load it into the van.'

'And not get caught doing so.'

'Do you see anyone who's gonna catch us?'

'Well, no,' Liam admitted, glancing around at the seemingly deserted building site, and the equally empty road behind them. 'What time d'you think everyone will turn up?'

Daniel checked his watch. 'We've got two hours, so we'd better get a move on.'

Shoving open the door, Daniel stepped out into the eerie stillness of the breaking dawn to immediately head around to the back of the van. There he opened first one door, then the other, before returning to the front – only to find Liam hadn't moved.

'Are you comin'?' he hissed.

'Are you sure about this? I mean – if we do get caught...'

'We won't – I told ya – unless you just sit there, of course. Now – are you comin' or not? I can't shift a 'undred and fifty kilos on my own – not in two hours.'

With a grudging sigh, Liam clambered down to hurry after his best mate, towards the seven-foot high security gates, each one lined at the top with coils of lethal-looking razor wire.

Heaving up one of the gates, just enough to create a man-sized gap between them, Daniel nodded for Liam to squeeze through before sucking his own pot-bellied stomach in to follow after.

As soon as they were both inside, Daniel passed Liam to lead him across the cracked tarmac towards what remained of the Longmeadow Estate – a crumbling edifice of concrete flats, thrown up in the 1960s during yet another attempt to solve Britain's seemingly never-ending housing crises.

As the tower block loomed above them, Daniel reached the steps leading up to its empty rectangular entrance. There he stopped to turn back to Liam.

'Right,' he whispered, 'I left the piping in a pile opposite the lifts. I suggest one of us brings it out here, then the other can carry it to the van. That way, even if we run out of time, we'll still 'ave most of it.'

'Makes sense,' nodded Liam. 'Which one of us goes in?'

'I suggest you go. It'll be easier to bring it from the lifts to here, rather than from here all the way to the van.'

'Apart from avin' to go up and down all these steps.'

'Swap if you want. I just thought it'd be easier for

you.'

Liam took a moment to assess the distances, before eventually nodding his approval. 'All right – but don't forget – I know where you live, just in case you decide to drive off without me.'

'Why the fuck would I do that? We're not exactly stealing the Crown Jewels. Besides – I'm gonna need your help unloading it when we get back to the lock-up.'

Liam gave him a wary look before casting his eyes up to the entrance. 'OK – deal!' he eventually said.

'Did you bring any gloves?' Daniel asked, glancing down at Liam's pale, chubby hands.

'Nobody said nuff'n about gloves!'

'Don't worry – you can use mine,' said Daniel, handing his over. 'I've got some more in the van. Now we'd better get a move on,' he added, glancing over his shoulder to see a pale blue strip of light stretching across Norfolk's wide, open horizon. 'The sun'll be up soon.'

As Liam donned the gloves to start up the steps, Daniel called after him, 'Watch where you tread. Some of the tiles are loose.'

'Now you tell me,' he muttered, continuing on.

'And whatever you do, don't try to use the lifts. There's nuff'n in them but a twenty-foot drop to the basement.'

'Don't tread on anythin' – and don't use the lifts,' Liam repeated. 'Got it!'

Turning back towards the stairs, Liam shook his head to mutter, 'What the fuck have I got myself into?'

Stepping through the entrance, as his boots crunched over broken glass and shattered tiles, he paused to stare into the inky blackness beyond.

Unable to see anything at all, he was about to call back for a torch when he heard Daniel's voice drift towards him from somewhere outside.

'Are you all right in there?'

'All good,' he called back, his voice echoing around the damp, cold, empty space. 'Don't suppose you've got a torch, 'ave you?' he decided to ask. 'I can't see a fuck'n thing!'

'Don't worry. Your eyes just need time to adjust.'

Liam was about to argue that they weren't, when the lobby surrounding him began to take shape, enough at least for him to see a narrow communal staircase leading up to the right, and two rectangular voids just beyond, where a couple of lift doors must have once been.

Spying the pile of copper piping – glimmering in the shadows like a stash of gold – his first reaction was of pure, unadulterated greed, until remembering that he still had to carry it out.

'This is going to take forever,' he muttered, stepping over with a weary sigh.

Grateful for the gloves he'd been given, he crouched down to begin bundling the first dozen or so lengths up into his arms. He then straightened himself up to turn around before staggering back towards where he'd come in.

Thinking he could probably take more next time, his eyes danced between the floor and the entrance ahead, until finally emerging to find Daniel was nowhere in sight.

'Where the fuck has 'e gone?' he asked himself, gawping absently around.

About to shout his name into the darkness, he took a relieved breath when he saw Daniel hanging out of the van's window, reversing it back towards the security gates.

Bringing his mind back to the task at hand, he negotiated his way down the steps, eventually allowing the piping to clatter to the ground.

'How's it going?' came Daniel's breathless voice, tugging on a pair of gloves while jogging over.

'Alright, I suppose,' Liam replied, eyeing his meagre pile with a guilty frown. 'I can probably carry more next time.'

'Then I suggest you crack on,' Daniel replied, bundling the piping up into his arms before marching off, as if they weighed no more than a loaf of bread.

Determined to do better, Liam turned on his heel to take the stairs two at a time. Once back in the lobby, he picked his way back to the copper piping, and was about to crouch down to grab hold of a larger bundle, when he suddenly froze.

Something had moved behind him.

Holding his breath, he tilted his head to listen – but the noise – whatever it had been – had gone.

'Probably a mouse,' he muttered, trying to steady his nerves.

Knowing it was more likely to have been a rat, he scanned the shadows around his feet. Rats weren't exactly his favourite animals in the world, and the idea of one brushing up against his boots made him shudder.

Dragging his mind back to the job at hand, he bent forward – only to hear the sound again, but this time it was far louder.

'What the fuck *is* that?' he whispered to himself, remaining glued to the spot.

Hearing nothing again, he spun around, hoping to catch sight of whatever it was – but there was nothing there. Just dust and debris, and the two empty lift shafts.

'How're you doing in there?' came Daniel's impatient voice.

Jumping out of his skin, Liam called back, 'Just coming!' before shaking his head to reface the copper piping.

Then the sound came again, but it wasn't a mouse – nor was it a rat. He couldn't be sure, but it sounded like the voice of a man, coming from one of the abandoned elevator shafts.

'I've just seen one of the side gates 'as been left open,' came Daniel's voice again, the sound moving gradually away. 'I'm gonna try to bring the van around. It'll save us a shed-load of time if I can.'

'Hold on, Dan,' Liam called quickly out. 'I–I think someone's in here.'

'Dan?' he called again, only to be left listening to his own voice, echoing off the walls around him.

'Shit,' he muttered, his eyes now fixed on the shaft where he could have sworn the sound had come from.

Staying perfectly still, he listened again before taking a short, shallow breath.

'Hello?' he called. 'Is anyone there?'

Hearing what sounded like rubble being moved, followed by what he could have sworn was a groan, his heart began to pound as he crept slowly forward.

Reaching the edge of one of the shafts, he braced his hands on the walls on either side to lean slowly forward.

'Hello? Is anyone down there?'

Another faint groaning sound had him leaning further out, his eyes wide as they tried to penetrate the darkness.

'I can call for help, if you want?' he offered, before immediately regretting it. Drawing attention to what he was doing there wasn't exactly his best idea. 'Or I can try to find a way down?' he suggested instead.

The shaft fell into a cold, sterile silence.

Beginning to wonder if he'd simply imagined it, he leaned his head even further out. 'If you're down there, you'd better say something, or I'm gonna 'ave to leave you to it.'

Hearing nothing but his own voice, he said, 'Last chance!' before listening again.

Managing to convince himself that there was no one down there after all, he started to haul himself back when he heard another, altogether different sound, this time coming from the shaft above.

With his curiosity piqued, he squinted his eyes to glance up, only for the blackness above to explode into a screaming mass of wings and teeth.

As the flickering mass descended onto his head, he tore his hands from the walls to protect his face, only to feel himself falling steadily back, further and further down, until the shadows surrounding him burst into a blaze of brilliant white.

- CHAPTER FORTY-FIVE -

TANNER WOKE NATURALLY to spend an idyllic moment staring up at the ceiling. Allowing his eyes to rest for a moment, he listened to the peaceful sounds: Christine breathing softly beside him, Baby Samantha turning over in her sleep, and the gentle murmur of the river running sedately past their riverside bungalow.

Curious to know the time, he blinked open his eyes to glance at the bedside table – only to find his radio alarm clock wasn't there. In its place sat the Airfix model of a jet-black Jaguar XJS he'd painstakingly glued together the previous weekend. Behind it stood a box containing another new model, waiting to be built – a bright yellow Triumph Stag. He remembered getting it for Christmas the year before, but had yet to get around to building it. He must have left the box there as a reminder, although, now that he thought about it, he didn't recall Airfix ever making a kit for the Triumph Stag. He wasn't even sure they'd made one for the XJS either – but they must have done, as both were sitting there on his bedside table, waiting for him to play with.

Reaching over to pick up a miniature Luke Skywalker and Darth Vader standing next to the XJS, he lay back on the pillow to hold them above his head. As they commenced a deadly lightsaber battle, he heard a knock on the door.

Wondering who on earth that could be, he lifted his head. 'Come in?' he said, peering towards the door.

Watching it inch open, he exhaled when his father's face appeared through the gap, smiling at him with a look of parental concern.

'Your mother asked me to come in to see how you were.'

'Better, thank you,' Tanner replied, returning to his galactic battle of good versus evil.

'Can we get you anything?'

'I'm good.'

'Something to eat, perhaps?'

'No thanks.'

'Do you think you still have a temperature?'

Without a clue whether he did or not, he simply shrugged, leaving his father to come traipsing over.

Perched on the side of the bed, he swept Tanner's hair from his eyes to place a warm, calloused hand on his forehead.

'You could really do with a haircut,' he commented, removing his hand to press it onto Tanner's chest.

'Do I still have a temperature?' Tanner asked, keen to get back to his battle.

'It seems to have passed – which is good news, as it means you'll be able to go to school tomorrow.'

'Why can't I go today?'

'Because it's Sunday.'

'But – I thought it was Wednesday,' Tanner said, frowning.

'Which means we have a whole day to discuss what we were talking about yesterday.'

Unable to remember anything about the day

before, Tanner tried to sit up, only for his father to push him back down.

'I think you need to stay where you are for a moment,' he said, his rugged features shifting in the shadows. 'At least until we've finished our discussion.'

'But – I can't remember what we were talking about,' Tanner replied, watching his father's face change before his very eyes.

'You accused me of murder, remember?'

With growing alarm, Tanner tried to sit up again – only to be forced back down.

'Don't tell me you've forgotten already,' the man continued, fixing his eyes with an unsettling frown.

'Who – who are you?' Tanner demanded, his voice trembling with fear.

'You know who I am,' the man sneered, leaning closer until his face was an inch from Tanner's.

Pressing down on Tanner's chest, the stranger clasped his other hand around Tanner's neck.

'I'm the man who's going to kill you.'

Gasping for air, Tanner sat bolt upright in bed, staring wildly about.

'Are you alright?' came Christine's voice, from somewhere near the door.

'Yes – fine,' he managed, bringing a hand up to his neck.

'Another one of those dreams of yours?' she asked, stepping inside to lift Samantha from her cot.

'Something like that,' Tanner replied, still catching his breath. 'I thought I was in bed at home – as in, the one I grew up in. My dad came in to see if I was OK, only it wasn't him, it was someone else. Then he said I knew who he was,' Tanner continued, his eyes drifting away as he desperately tried to hold onto the dream that was already slipping away, 'and I did – it just took me a while to place him.'

'Anyone I know?'

'Only by name.'

'And who's that?'

'Your favourite MP – the Right Honourable Mr George Elliston.'

'I never said he was my favourite MP.'

'And I never said he was either right, or honourable – especially as he proceeded to strangle me to death.'

Resting the still-sleeping Samantha against her chest, Christine looked down at him with motherly concern. 'I don't suppose you've given any more thought to seeing a psychologist?'

'Not since the subject last came up.'

'You mean – after you had that dream about the girl being murdered?'

Ignoring her, Tanner swung his legs out of bed to stare down at the carpet.

'Listen, John,' Christine said, softly. 'You can't keep having nightmares every night.'

'I don't have them every night.'

'Every other night, then.'

'And that's where you're wrong, my dear,' he said, using the bedside table to push himself up. 'Evidently, I *can* have nightmares every other night.'

'I meant that you don't have to keep putting up with them all the time.'

'OK, well, we'll see,' came Tanner's non-committal response.

As his attention returned to finding his socks, he jumped to the sound of his mobile phone.

'That's not good,' he muttered, glancing at his

watch before picking it up.

Seeing it was the office, he wondered if he could delay answering it – at least until he'd had a coffee – before deciding to just get it over with.

'Tanner speaking,' he said, as unenthusiastically as possible.

'Good morning, sir, it's Constable Witherspoon.'

'Yes, Constable Witherspoon,' Tanner replied, pleased to hear someone call him *sir* instead of *boss*, for a change. 'How can I help?'

'Sorry to call so early, but Detective Inspector Gilbert asked me to get hold of you.'

'You've succeeded in your main objective. Well done!'

'Er... right. Thank you, sir.'

'Was that it, or can I get back to making myself some breakfast?'

'I've already made your breakfast,' Christine called from behind him.

Batting her away with the phone, he returned to the call. 'Sorry, Witherspoon – I didn't catch that?'

'I was just saying that a call's come in.'

'Yes, well, it does happen,' Tanner replied, spying his socks under the bed.

'Two bodies have been found at the old Longmeadow Estate.'

'And where's that when it's at home?' Tanner asked, rubbing his eyes with weary irritation.

'It's not a home, sir – at least not anymore. It used to be a block of flats, but it's about to be demolished to be replaced by some fancy commercial development.'

Sighing down the line, Tanner stood slowly up. 'Alright. Send me the address, then tell Vicky – I mean DI Gilbert – that I'll be there as soon as I can.'

'Actually, sir, she said you don't have to go. She

just wanted me to let you know that she's on her way.'

'Has she informed our medical examiner?'

'Er, no sir, but I did, just before calling you.'

'I bet he was happy.'

'Delirious, sir.'

Tanner thought for a moment, before saying, 'You may as well send me the address anyway. And if you hear from DI Gilbert again, tell her that I'm on my way.'

- CHAPTER FORTY-SIX -

WITH HIS DREAM leaving him more convinced than ever that Elliston was responsible for the murders of both Tara Lowe and Professor Beaumont – either directly or indirectly – Tanner followed his satnav to the address PC Witherspoon had sent him, wondering how on earth he was supposed to prove it.

By the time he arrived at the security gates, outside what was left of the Longmeadow Estate, he'd made little progress. The only conclusion he'd reached was that it *had* to be him. The fact that Elliston had gone to all the trouble of filing a restraining order against him – for doing nothing more than suggesting he might have been involved – only confirmed it. At least, it did for Tanner. All he could do now was wait until they found some evidence.

Nudging his Triumph up behind Johnstone's boxy old Volvo, he stepped out with a look of dogged determination. With any luck, whoever's bodies had been found would be connected – leading to more clues, and the evidence he so desperately needed.

Spotting Vicky talking to someone from forensics carrying a ladder, he caught her eye to make his way over, as she directed the forensics officer through the security gates.

'I thought I told Witherspoon that you didn't have to come!' she called, the moment he was within earshot.

'He managed to talk me into it,' Tanner replied, with a sheepish shrug.

'He did?'

'Well, no, I managed to persuade myself – but that's nothing against Witherspoon. He seemed like the sort of PC we need around here. Let's just hope he's as good without a spoon. We can't have him carting one around all the time – unless it's very small, and he keeps it in his pocket.'

'I'm sorry, boss,' said Vicky, staring at him with a confused frown, 'but – what are you talking about?'

'I was just saying how much I liked PC Witherspoon, and was hoping he'd continue to impress – even if he happened to leave his spoon at home.'

'Oh, I see. It's a joke.'

'I can't get anything past you, young Vicky – but I suppose that's why you're the Senior Investigating Officer and I'm just a humble detective chief inspector.'

'Have you finished?'

'Er...' Tanner mused, gazing sagaciously up at the cloudless sky. 'I think so.'

'Then perhaps I can brief you on what we've been able to unearth.'

'By all means.'

'Two bodies – both found at the bottom of an elevator shaft.'

'Do we know who they are?'

'Not yet,' she replied. 'It's proving to be a little difficult to gain access, but forensics have managed to find a ladder, so we should be good to go.'

'Then perhaps you can lead the way.'

'I don't suppose you had any more luck gaining access to those CCTV cameras yesterday?' Tanner asked, catching up to her as they made their way through the security gates towards the ashen grey tower block ahead.

'We haven't heard back from the car park's security company, but I've left a note on Henderson's desk to chase them as soon as he gets in.'

'And you didn't manage to find any more witnesses who saw Elliston at the scene?'

'Who – the man you're legally unable to go within a hundred feet of? Unfortunately not.'

With Tanner failing to respond, Vicky glanced around. 'Are you OK?'

'Yes, fine,' he mumbled, his tone both subdued and irritated.

'Sorry, it's just that I was expecting you to come back with some sort of witty repartee.'

'I didn't sleep particularly well,' he admitted, staring absently ahead. 'That's all.'

'Not another dream – I hope?'

'Something like that.'

'The same one you had before?'

'Different.'

'In what way?'

'In that someone tried to murder me, instead of the other way around.'

'That must have made a nice change.'

'Uh-huh,' came Tanner's unamused response.

Reaching the base of the cracked concrete steps leading up to the building's entrance, Vicky stopped to face him. 'Would you like to tell me about it?'

Wondering if it was really a good idea to tell the SIO of an ongoing murder investigation that the

Right Honourable George Elliston had tried to strangle him in his sleep – or that he'd dreamt he had – Tanner shook his head. 'Not really. To be honest, I can barely remember it,' he said, which was true, at least in part.

Vicky's eyes lingered on his for a moment before she nodded. 'Then perhaps we can go inside?'

- CHAPTER FORTY-SEVEN -

NAVIGATING THEIR WAY over a series of small aluminium platforms, laid out across the foyer's uneven surface like futuristic stepping-stones, Tanner followed Vicky towards what he presumed to be the elevator shaft where the bodies had been found, its entrance surrounded by overall-clad forensic officers, peering down into the darkness.

'Where's Dr Johnstone?' Tanner enquired, glancing about.

'He must have gone down already,' Vicky replied, bringing Tanner's attention to the end of the ladder that could be seen resting against the lip of the shaft.

Nodding, Tanner stepped towards the group of forensic officers to clear his throat. 'If you'd excuse me,' he said, smiling around at their mask-covered faces.

Waiting for them to move aside, he lowered himself onto his haunches to lean gingerly forward. 'Dr Johnstone,' he called, squinting down to see a small light flickering about near the bottom, like some sort of oversized firefly. 'Are you down there?'

'Is that Tanner?' came the medical examiner's echoing voice.

'No, it's the Ghost of Christmas Past,' he called back. 'How are you getting on?'

'Well, it's a bit of a squeeze, but I seem to be

managing – just about.'

'Is it too soon to ask what you've got?'

'Two men, both dead – at least I think they are.'

Glancing around to see Vicky standing behind him, Tanner continued. 'I don't suppose you have any idea when they died?'

'At a guess, I'd say the one on top was about three hours ago, and the one underneath more like nine to twelve.'

'How about the cause?'

'It's too early to tell, I'm afraid, but they both appear to have fractured skulls, so it's possible they could have been accidental.'

'Both of them?' came Tanner's dubious response. 'Well, I suppose it's possible. How about identification?'

'One would appear to be someone by the name of Liam Sayers. That's according to his driver's licence.'

'And the other?' asked Tanner, shrugging his shoulders.

'Hold on. Let me see if I can find something.'

Giving him a moment, Tanner climbed to his feet to say quietly to Vicky, 'Do we know who found the bodies?'

'No one,' she replied. 'We had an anonymous tip-off.'

'Who from?'

'Not sure,' came her hesitant response, 'but that's probably because it was anonymous.'

'But we have their number?'

'The caller withheld it.'

'Then I suggest we have it un-held.'

'Yes, of course,' Vicky replied, digging out her notebook. 'Actually, sorry, but – how do we do that again?'

'Have someone back at the office ask our network provider for it. If they put up a fuss, just tell them it's part of a murder investigation.'

'But – we don't know how they died yet.'

'It's suspicious enough for us to warrant knowing who told us about it. If they still say no, then we'll have to get a court order.'

Hearing Johnstone's voice echo up the elevator shaft, Tanner lowered himself back down. 'Any luck?'

'I have another driver's licence, if you're interested.'

'Yes please,' Tanner called back.

'Someone by the name of Simon Balinger.'

Resisting the urge to punch the air, Tanner turned instead to give Vicky a measured look of intrigue.

'Assuming Johnstone is referring to *our* Simon Balinger,' Tanner began, leading Vicky away for Johnstone to continue his work, 'the same Simon Balinger who was listed on Companies House as being in business with Professor Beaumont, Jeremy Southcott, and our very own Mr George Elliston – then I think there's a pattern here that's becoming increasingly difficult to ignore.'

'Which is?' Vicky asked, as they reached the top of the steps.

'That everyone who knew what was really going on at Blackfleet Broad is being silenced, one at a time.'

'But would anyone really murder someone just to stop them talking about a dodgy business deal?'

'Not *anyone*, no,' Tanner replied, looking wistfully away.

'You're thinking about Elliston again.'

'Whatever made you think that?' came Tanner's dry response.

'OK – but we're still going to need evidence to prove his involvement before marching over to arrest him.'

'Yes, of course,' came Tanner's disingenuous reply. 'While we wait, I suggest we try to find out who our so-called anonymous witness was – the one who reportedly found the bodies. You never know, it could just happen to be the same person who pushed them down.'

- CHAPTER FORTY-EIGHT -

AFTER TWISTING THE arm of the network provider to hand over the withheld number, Tanner had to hide his disappointment when they learnt that the caller wasn't his favourite Member of Parliament – nor his other known associate, Mr Jeremy Southcott – but someone neither of them had ever heard of.

'Are you sure this is right?' asked Tanner, stepping up to the door of a small semi-detached house nestled amongst a row of near-identical ones, half a mile from the block of flats where the bodies had been found.

'Why – because it doesn't belong to George Elliston?' Vicky replied, glancing around at him with a reprimanding scowl.

'To be honest – yes!' Tanner shrugged, offering her an impish smile.

As Vicky rang the doorbell for them both to dig out their respective IDs, Tanner muttered beside her, 'I wouldn't be surprised if he doesn't know anything about it, and that someone – who will remain nameless – stole his phone yesterday.'

'Will you shut up,' Vicky hissed, as the sound of approaching footsteps could be heard from the other side of the door.

'Mr Daniel Carter?' Vicky enquired, the moment a weather-beaten face appeared through the gap to peer cautiously out at them.

'I might be,' the man replied, eyeing Vicky's proffered ID.

'DI Gilbert, and my colleague, DCI Tanner – Norfolk Police. May we come inside?'

'No – why – do you have a warrant?'

'Why would we have a warrant?' came Vicky's curious response.

'Because that's what you'd need if you want to come inside.'

After glancing briefly around at Tanner, Vicky continued. 'Then perhaps we can talk to you out here?'

'Help yourself. It's a free country – or at least it used to be,' he muttered, under his breath.

'We understand you made a phone call this morning?'

Vicky's question had Carter's eyes narrowing. 'I don't remember making a call.'

'It was to the local police station, if that helps to jog your memory.'

'Sorry, luv, but you must have me confused with someone else.'

As Tanner shifted his stance beside her, Vicky took a measured breath. 'So, you're saying you didn't call the police this morning?'

'Why on earth would I have done that?'

'Because you discovered no less than two bodies at the bottom of an elevator shaft, over at the old Longmeadow Estate.'

'I've no idea what you're talking about.'

'We have your phone number, Mr Carter. We know it was you.'

'Unless someone stole your phone?' Tanner prompted, catching the man's eye to give him an encouraging nod.

As Vicky glanced menacingly at Tanner, Carter

blinked a few times before nodding. 'That's right!' he eventually exclaimed. 'Someone *did* take my phone. When I was at work yesterday.'

'So what's that in your hand?' Vicky asked, gesturing to the mobile clutched between his dirt-ingrained fingers.

As Tanner closed his eyes to begin slowly shaking his head, Carter stared down at it in vacant bemusement.

'This is my – er – old phone,' he said eventually. 'I keep it as a spare.'

'So you're saying that if I dial the number that called the police station yesterday, the phone you're holding won't ring?'

It took him a full moment to realise he'd been caught lying.

'I'd like to make an official complaint,' he said, shoving the phone into his pocket.

'Which is?' Vicky prompted.

'Invasion of privacy.'

'And how have we invaded your privacy, Mr Carter?'

'Because I made an anonymous call. I know I did because I made sure to dial 141, so my number would be withheld. And I certainly didn't leave my name.'

'Yes, we know,' said Vicky. 'That's why we had to ask our network provider for the number that made the call.'

'Which they just handed over to you?'

'Well, we did ask nicely,' smiled Vicky.

'Then what's the point of the police going around telling everyone that if you see something suspicious, or know someone dealing drugs, you can feel safe knowing any information will be treated anonymously?'

'It's the Police and Criminal Evidence Act, 1984,'

Tanner replied on Vicky's behalf. 'If we have grounds to believe the call relates to a crime, we're legally entitled to that information.'

'So it's all bollocks then, seeing as the call's obviously going to relate to a crime!'

'I assume that means it *was* you who made the call?' Tanner continued.

'I suppose,' he huffed. 'But I didn't do it. I didn't do nothin'!'

'But you did find them?'

'If you mean my mate Liam, and whoever else that was, then yes, I did – but that don't mean I had anythin' to do with it.'

'If that's true, then why go to such lengths to try and hide your identity?'

'Cus I knew what you'd think.'

'Then you'd better start at the beginning,' said Tanner, 'perhaps with what you were doing there?'

Carter's eyes darted from Vicky to Tanner. 'I'd given Liam a lift there,' he began. 'He said he wanted to pick something up.'

'What was that?'

'I've no idea.'

'You didn't think to ask?'

'It was none of my business.'

'Then perhaps you can remember what time it was?'

'Not a clue.'

'Roughly?'

'Around seven?' he shrugged.

'Are you sure it wasn't a little earlier? It's just that our medical examiner seemed to think your friend had been lying there for at least two hours – maybe three. That was at eight o'clock – which would make your visit closer to five.'

'Does it matter?'

'It does if it helps us to establish a time of death.'

'Well, as I said, I don't know.'

'Can you at least tell us how your friend ended up at the bottom of a disused elevator shaft?'

'Honestly, I've no idea. I dropped him off outside the gates to watch him walk into the building. When he didn't come out again, I went in to find him. That's when I saw he'd fallen down the elevator shaft – and someone else was down there with him.'

'That's when you called the police?'

'Uh-huh.'

'Not an ambulance?'

Carter stopped to stare at Tanner with his mouth hanging open.

'It's just that I'd have thought most people would call an ambulance before calling the police,' said Tanner, 'being that your friend had just accidentally fallen down an elevator shaft, and everything.'

'I've already told you – I didn't do it!'

'So why didn't you call an ambulance?'

'B-because,' stuttered Carter, a sheen of sweat appearing on his brow, 'it was obvious he was dead.'

'Or perhaps you were just hoping he was?'

'Why would I be hoping he was?'

'I was merely suggesting that it might've been awkward for you if he'd been found alive, given what the two of you were up to.'

'I've already told you – I weren't doing nuffin'!'

'But your mate clearly was – and as you were there, helping him, that's aiding and abetting, I'm afraid.'

Carter clamped his mouth shut, glaring at Tanner before jutting out his chin. 'Whatever you fink I was doing there, you can't prove it.'

'To be honest, Carter, I really don't give a shit what you were doing there. All I want to know is what happened to your chum, and the man he was found with – more importantly, whether you saw anyone else there at the time.'

Carter eyed him with wary suspicion. 'It was too dark to see much of anything,' he eventually said. 'Liam went inside the building to get whatever it was. He must've either tripped and fallen down the shaft, or heard something that made him look down there. All I know is that when I went to see where he'd got to, I found him lying there with what looked like a broken neck. When I saw another body underneath him, I freaked out. I should've called an ambulance – I know I should – but to be honest, I wasn't thinking straight.'

'You didn't see anyone else?'

Carter shook his head.

'What about a car – or a van?'

'I'm sorry,' he replied. 'As far as I could tell, we were the only two people there.'

- CHAPTER FORTY-NINE -

ORDERING CLARK TO present himself to the duty officer at Wroxham Police Station to have his fingerprints and DNA collected, Tanner led Vicky back to his car. When he reached the door, he jammed the key into the lock to mutter, 'That was a complete waste of bloody time.'

'Are you sure you don't want to have him arrested for aiding and abetting?' proposed Vicky, from the other side of the car.

'Aiding and abetting what?' questioned Tanner. 'Nicking stuff from a building site, lying to the police, or for failing to call an ambulance?'

'How about all three?'

Tanner glanced back at the house to see one of the net curtains twitch. 'To be honest, I can't be arsed – but don't let me stop you.'

Following his gaze, Vicky thought for a moment before looking away. 'Actually, boss, I think I'm with you on that one.'

Hearing her phone ring, she dug it out to glance at the screen, before eventually saying, 'Excuse me for a minute, will you?'

Watching her give him a cheeky smile before turning away, Tanner climbed into his car to mutter, 'It had better be work.'

Pulling out his own phone to check for messages – only to find nothing but the usual onslaught of emails

– he put it away again, just as Vicky climbed in beside him.

'Who was that?' he casually asked.

'Sally.'

'And what did Sally have to say for herself?'

'Do you want the good news or the bad?'

Tanner let out a despondent sigh. 'I suppose we'd better start with the bad.'

'She's broken up with Townsend.'

'And that's bad news, is it?'

'It was for Townsend.'

'Actually, I'm not sure it's even news – given that they'll probably be back together before...' Tanner glanced down at his watch, '...what time is it now?'

'Would you like the good news, now?'

'They're not back together already, are they?'

'A preliminary report's come in for the office where Professor Beaumont's body was discovered.'

'Go on.'

'Elliston's fingerprints weren't only found on the door, and the desk, but on the body, as well!'

'It's a start, I suppose, but I know what his lawyer's going to say – that he'd had a meeting with the professor the week before.'

'We've also been able to access the CCTV cameras from outside the university,' Vicky added, swiping eagerly at her phone's screen.

Tanner watched her with a look of hopeful expectation. 'Anything?'

Vicky held up her phone to show Tanner a video playing on a loop. 'He was captured entering the building at the time in question.'

As a devious smile crept across Tanner's face, he continued to watch the video while listening to

Vicky add, 'I don't think there can be any doubt that it's him, do you?'

'I think the time has come for you to give Forrester a call.'

'Er – yes, boss, but – why me?'

'Because you're the SIO, remember?'

'I know – but I thought we had an agreement.'

'True, but unfortunately, I don't think he's talking to me, so I'm not sure we have much of a choice.'

'Right then,' said Vicky, taking a breath to poise her thumbs over her phone. 'What do you want me to say?'

'Just tell him what we've found out in relation to Elliston – and that we'd like his permission to bring him in for questioning.'

'Anything else?'

'I think that'll do for now.'

As she dialled his number, Tanner thought to add, 'And put it on speakerphone, so I can hear what he says.'

Vicky nodded back, just as Forrester's voice came barking through the tiny speaker.

'Forrester speaking!'

'Superintendent Forrester, sir, it's DI Gilbert calling.'

'Yes, Vicky. How can I help?'

'We – I mean – I have some news regarding the investigation into the bodies found at Blackfleet Broad. The one at Norfolk University, as well.'

'Are you including the two that have just been discovered at the bottom of a disused elevator shaft – the ones nobody's bothered to tell me about?'

'Er...' Vicky began, glancing nervously at Tanner. 'Possibly, sir, yes.'

'Then you'd better continue.'

'We had a witness report from one of Professor

Beaumont's colleagues who saw him talking to someone in his office, shortly before he was thought to have been killed. She said he was a well-dressed man wearing a dark grey suit and a red tie.'

'Sorry, Vicky, is this leading somewhere? Only I have a meeting I need to get ready for.'

'We – I mean – I believe that person might be Mr George Elliston, sir.'

As the phone fell into a sullen silence, Vicky swallowed nervously.

'Is that idiot Tanner with you, by any chance?' Forrester suddenly demanded.

'Er...' Vicky began, glancing sideways at the man in question.

Tanner shook his head at her with some considerable vigour.

'No, sir,' she eventually replied. 'It's just me. I'm on my own – in my car – the one that belongs to me.'

Tanner leant his head back against the headrest to roll his eyes, leaving Vicky cringing at her own words.

As they both held their breath, they sighed in unison when they heard Forrester move the conversation along. 'I assume you've heard about that restraining order Elliston filed against him?'

'Someone did mention something about it.'

'And Tanner didn't put you up to this?'

'Not at all, sir.'

'Do you have any evidence?'

'Yes, sir.'

'By evidence, I mean something that actually proves Elliston was there – not just your DCI assuming he must have been because someone saw an individual there who may have looked a bit like him.'

'Forensics found his fingerprints and DNA on the door leading into the professor's office, on the desk inside, and on the body as well. We also have CCTV footage of him entering the university building at around the time he was killed.'

More silence followed, leaving Vicky to press stubbornly on. 'With Elliston's business connection to the professor, and Tara Lowe's alleged story about their intended development of Blackfleet Broad...'

Seeing Tanner scrawl a name on a scrap of paper before handing it over, she nodded back at him with a smile. '...plus the fact that we believe one of the bodies found in the lift shaft is another of their business associates, a Mr Simon Balinger – who we know had dealings with Tara Lowe during the Bluebell Wood investigation – then I think there's more than enough to at least bring him in for questioning.'

'Very well,' Forrester eventually said. 'But he has to be treated with the utmost respect.'

'Yes, sir,' said Vicky, sitting up in her seat.

'And with that bloody restraining order against him, it goes without saying that Tanner can't be involved. Is that clear?'

'Crystal clear, sir,' she confirmed, fixing Tanner's eyes with an admonishing glare.

- CHAPTER FIFTY -

'WELL, THAT'S NOT going to happen,' huffed Tanner, leaning forward to start the engine.

'What's not going to happen?'

'Me – not taking part in Elliston's interview!'

'Er – I'm sorry, boss, but I don't think you have much choice in the matter.'

'And that's where you're wrong, young Vicky. I do have a choice. I can choose to take part in his interview, or I can choose not to.'

'Not in the eyes of the law, you can't. Besides, his lawyer wouldn't let you.'

'Then how am I going to interview him?'

'I think that's the idea – that you're not.'

'Then who is?'

'Who do you think?' she replied, looking down at herself.

'I meant – apart from you.'

'No you didn't!'

'No, you're right – I didn't. But seriously, I'm going to have to have some sort of input.'

'You don't trust me to interview a suspect?'

'It's not that.'

'Then what is it?'

'I know where Elliston's bodies are buried,' Tanner replied. 'Well, some of them at least.'

'You know,' began Vicky, folding her arms,

'you've never explained to me why you dislike Elliston so much.'

'I have my reasons,' Tanner muttered, as he recalled the moment Elliston confessed to having stabbed a local paedophile to death outside Swanton Morley church – and the orchestrated dispatch of several others.

'It's not because you're jealous of him, is it?'

'Jealous?' Tanner laughed. 'Why on earth would I be jealous?'

'I've no idea, but he is rather handsome. Charming, as well.'

'You're saying I'm not?' asked Tanner, presenting Vicky with a look of wounded disappointment.

'He's also an MP,' Vicky added, deliberately sidestepping the question, 'which makes him one of the most powerful men in Norfolk. To be honest, I'd be surprised if you weren't jealous of him.'

'Well, I can assure you that I'm not! I'd also like to add that I've often been described as both handsome *and* charming. Admittedly, both times by my first wife, before we were married, so I'm not sure it counted. I'm also fairly sure she was being sarcastic at the time, being that we were in the middle of an argument – something about me chatting up a waitress in front of her, which I'm sure I didn't. Even if I did, it wasn't my fault, as I'd only just consumed an entire bottle of wine and could barely read the menu.'

'I don't suppose there's any chance we can move the subject away from an argument you had with your first wife, before you were even married – back to the matter at hand?'

'Yes, of course,' Tanner mumbled. 'Which was...? '

'Me, interviewing Elliston, without you.'

'Right, yes. So anyway,' Tanner continued, 'if I

can't be in the interview room, then we're going to have to devise some way of communicating – preferably without either Elliston or his solicitor finding out.'

'Is that really necessary?'

'Most definitely!'

'OK, so – what did you have in mind?'

'I was thinking you could wear an earpiece with a hidden microphone. That way I'd be able to listen in on the conversation while prompting you as to what to say.'

'I'm sorry, boss, but I'm not going to conduct an official police interview of a murder suspect – one who just happens to be a Member of Parliament – with a hidden microphone jammed between my breasts and an earpiece shoved into my ear.'

'Why not?'

'Apart from the fact that it would be both illegal, highly unethical, and rather uncomfortable, I don't particularly fancy having to spend several hours with you breathing down my neck – almost literally!'

'Then what do you suggest?'

'How about you wait in the corridor outside the interview room until it's over?'

'You mean – listening behind the door?'

'No, I meant waiting patiently, until I've finished.'

'But – how would I be able to interject if I can't hear what you're saying?'

'You wouldn't!'

'There must be some way for me to hear what's going on without breaking the law,' Tanner muttered, just as Vicky's phone started to ring once again.

'You're popular,' he remarked, staring down at

his own with a sense of forlorn redundancy.

'Vicky speaking!' he heard her say. 'Yes, Sally, how can I help?'

Giving Vicky a gentle nudge, Tanner whispered, 'Can you put it on speakerphone?'

Shaking her head to bat him away, Tanner was forced to sit there listening to her saying, 'Uh-huh,' a few times, followed by, 'Sounds good, Sally, thank you!'

'What was that about?' he huffed, beginning to feel like a spare wheel that had just been replaced by a puncture repair kit.

'The search warrant has finally come through for Mr Lowe's house.'

'Hadn't we done that already?'

'If you recall, the previous warrant only granted us access to Tara's possessions.'

'Well, it's not him,' Tanner said, in a dismissive tone.

'So Sally suggested sending Haverstock and Townsend down with forensics.'

'Is that really necessary?'

'He's still a suspect, isn't he?'

'I suppose that depends on how long it takes us to beat – I mean – lawfully extract a full confession out of Elliston.'

Putting her phone away, Vicky turned in her seat to face him. 'May I be so bold as to offer you some professional advice?'

'You don't need to be bold to offer me advice, young Vicky, but if you really feel it necessary to shave your head first, that's up to you.'

'My advice is to stop putting all your eggs in one basket all the time.'

'I don't have to put all my eggs into one basket,' Tanner replied. 'Do you know why?'

'I've no idea,' came Vicky's uninterested response, as she flipped the sun visor down to find the mirror behind it.

'Because I've only got one egg. *Ipso facto*, I only need one basket!'

Vicky spent a moment reapplying her lipstick before glancing back at him. 'I see your Latin's improving.'

'I've been taking lessons.'

'Money well spent. Shall we go?'

'Go where?'

'Back to the station.'

'I thought we were going to bring Elliston in for questioning?'

'Er – no. *I'm* going to bring Elliston in for questioning. You're going to sit quietly in your office.'

'And what am I going to do there?'

'As long as you don't come out until Elliston has been formally processed and is safely tucked away inside one of the interview rooms, I'm really not sure that I care!'

- CHAPTER FIFTY-ONE -

A LITTLE OVER an hour later, Vicky heaved open Wroxham Police Station's heavy glass door to glance back at the disgruntled face of George Elliston, standing with his hands shoved into his pockets immediately behind her.

'Would you like to come inside?' she invited, smiling as she did.

'Not particularly,' came Elliston's unhelpful response.

Glancing up at the two burly police constables standing at a respectful distance behind him, she returned her eyes to his. 'I can always ask one of my colleagues to give you a gentle shove, if that would help – although, I'm not sure how that would play out with the journalists lining the road behind you. I'm sure they're already wondering what you're doing here, and perhaps more importantly, what they're going to write for tomorrow's headlines.'

Sneering back, Elliston lifted his chin to step reluctantly inside.

Following him in, Vicky looked over to see the face of someone she instantly recognised. Unable to remember her name, she watched her lever herself out of the plastic reception seat she'd been wedged into to begin marching determinedly over.

After a brief exchange with Elliston, the woman turned to smile at Vicky.

'I understand you're my client's arresting officer?'

'That's correct, Mrs...?'

'Ms Heatherington,' she replied. 'I'll be representing Mr Elliston, but first, I'd like to hear the evidence you have against him.'

'Excuse me,' they heard Elliston say, 'but what's *he* doing here?'

Following his gaze, Vicky rolled her eyes when she saw Tanner's head appear through the doors leading out to the main office.

'Sorry to bother you,' he said, smiling amicably around at them all. 'I was just making myself a coffee, so I thought I'd pop out to see if anyone wanted one?'

'You do know that I've filed a restraining order against you?' snapped Elliston, fixing Tanner with a murderous glare.

'Really?' Tanner replied. 'I'd no idea!'

'My colleague presented the document to you himself,' commented Ms Heatherington. 'Whether or not you chose to read it is your problem.'

'Oh – *that* restraining order! Sorry, I'm handed so many, it's difficult to keep track.'

'If you're admitting to being aware of its existence,' the solicitor continued, 'may I ask what you're doing here?'

'Offering to get you a coffee. Sorry, I thought I said.'

'Unfortunately, the document clearly states that the defendant – i.e. you – must not contact the protected person – that being my client – directly or indirectly, either by phone, text, email, social media, or through a third party.'

'Does that include asking if he'd like a coffee?'

'You're also not permitted to come within a

hundred feet of my client's home or place of work.'

'OK, well, for a start, this is *my* place of work, not his,' Tanner argued. 'But what I think is more pertinent is the fact that your client is the one who came here. If he doesn't want to be within a hundred feet of me, I'm not sure why he'd have chosen to do so.'

'My client was arrested, Mr Tanner, which typically means he wasn't given much of a choice.'

'And that's my fault because...?'

'The bottom line, Mr Tanner,' the solicitor continued, 'is that if you don't remove yourself from the presence of my client, then I'm going to ask that *you're* the one who's arrested!'

'And who exactly do you think is going to do that, being that you're standing in the middle of a police station, and I'm the highest-ranking officer here?'

'Is it really necessary to remind you that there are officers who rank higher than you? Superintendent Forrester, for example.'

'I'm sure DCI Tanner was only offering to make us all some coffee,' Vicky interjected. 'After that, he'll be more than happy to return to his office. Isn't that right?' she added, glaring at Tanner with a look of demanding intent.

'Absolutely!' he replied, offering them all a congenial smile. 'Now,' he continued, clasping his hands together, 'who takes milk?'

- CHAPTER FIFTY-TWO -

'I THOUGHT I told you to stay in your office!' Vicky exclaimed, the moment Elliston had been led away with his solicitor trailing after.

'Yes, I know, but then I started reading the restraining order, and realised there were a couple of rather obvious loopholes.'

'I sincerely hope you're not thinking about trying to use one in order to barge your way into the interview?'

'I wouldn't dream of it – although, I may not have much of a choice, given that I'm making everyone a coffee. By the way, we're getting low on milk. Are you OK without?'

'I'm being serious, John!'

'You don't think I am? Coffee without milk is like drinking tea without water!'

As if shaking her head clear of the image of someone with a dried-up teabag hanging out of their mouth, Vicky turned back to Tanner with a look of imploring desperation. 'Please, John, can you just let me get on with my job? I mean, you were the one who gave it to me.'

'I'm aware of that, thank you, Vicky – but what I didn't know at the time was that my old friend, Mr George Elliston, was going to end up being the prime suspect.'

'Then perhaps you should have thought twice before sneaking off to accuse him of murder, without consulting me first.'

Tanner looked a little crestfallen, before his expression visibly brightened. 'Anyway, I've been doing a little research, and I think I've come up with rather a good idea.'

'About the investigation?'

'More about how I'd be able to take part in Elliston's interview – without actually being there.'

'Unbelievable,' Vicky muttered, glancing briefly away. 'Dare I ask what you have in mind?'

'Well...' began Tanner, like an over-excited schoolboy. 'I thought you could video call me on WhatsApp, once you've started the interview. That way I'd be able to hear what was being said while at the same time being able to send you messages.'

With Vicky scowling at him in brooding silence, Tanner was left to ask, 'So – what do you think?'

'I think that's just about the dumbest idea I've ever heard in my entire life.'

'But it would work, though,' Tanner continued, her scathing criticism having done little to dampen his enthusiasm, 'wouldn't it?'

Shaking her head, Vicky replied, 'Probably. But if we get caught, we're both going to be in serious trouble.'

'How could we get caught?'

'Oh, I don't know – the solicitor taking a look at my computer screen to find your distorted face staring back at her?'

'But why would she do that?'

'I've no idea, but with my admittedly limited experience of dealing with them, solicitors don't seem to be the most trusting of species. If she suspects we're up to something, I can easily imagine her doing so.'

'Then we'll just have to play it cool.'

'You mean *I'll* have to play it cool – seeing as you'll be in a room on the opposite side of the building.'

'Look, don't worry. If we get caught, I'll take full responsibility.'

'And how are you going to do that, being that we'd be on a video call together?'

'By saying it was my idea – and that I was the one who called you.'

'It wouldn't be exactly difficult for them to prove it was the other way around.'

'But it wasn't your idea.'

'I meant that, for it to work, I'd have to call you – otherwise they'd hear my computer making strange ringing noises, which might be a bit of a giveaway.'

'Tell you what. How about I call you before you go in, then you can just keep me on the line during the interview.'

Vicky mulled that over for a moment, before eventually saying, 'Very well,' with a capitulating sigh. 'But don't forget to mute your microphone. I think the game will be up if they hear you cursing under your breath while bashing at indiscriminate keys on your computer keyboard.'

- CHAPTER FIFTY-THREE -

WITH ELLISTON HAVING been formally processed, Vicky followed Haverstock into Interview Room One to find the suspect glaring at her from across the table, arms locked across his chest, while his solicitor – Ms Heatherington – pulled various items out of a large black leather handbag.

'Do you mind if I use my – er – laptop, to make some notes?' asked Vicky, trying to sound as casual as possible.

As the solicitor glanced suspiciously up, then down at the laptop she was holding in her trembling arms, Vicky swallowed with nervous anxiety. When the woman finally said, 'Be my guest,' before opening her own, more traditional notepad, she took a relieved breath.

Sitting down opposite Elliston, she positioned her laptop in front of her to open it fully – only to flinch at the sight of Tanner's expectant face, filling virtually the entire screen.

Minimising the window as quickly as she could, she glanced up at first Elliston, then Heatherington, half-expecting them to have seen him too. But thankfully, Elliston was now staring at his hands, clasped together on top of the table, while Heatherington was scrawling something in her notepad.

Taking a calming breath, Vicky scowled down at Tanner's now miniature face, only to hear Heatherington say, 'Shall we begin?'

'Yes, of course,' Vicky replied, clearing her throat.

Leaning over to start the digital recording device fixed to the wall, she sped through the formalities, making sure to introduce her colleague, DI Haverstock, before resting her elbows on the table.

'Perhaps we can begin with the night we believe Ms Tara Lowe was drowned in the middle of Blackfleet Broad?'

'Perhaps we can begin with the evidence you have against my client!' demanded Heatherington, her pen poised above her notepad.

Seeing something move on her screen, Vicky glanced down to see Tanner had typed: *Don't let her push you around.*

Shaking her head, she quickly typed: *I know that, ffs!*

'Do we have your attention, Detective Inspector?' the solicitor enquired.

'Sorry – yes, of course,' Vicky replied, looking up. 'I was just taking some notes.'

'But we haven't said anything – at least nothing of importance.'

'I was asking about your client's whereabouts at the time of Ms Lowe's murder – or at least I was about to.'

'And I was asking for the evidence you have against my client. All the arrest report says is that he's been brought in for the suspected murder of no less than...' She paused to count with her fingers. '...four people, with no mention of a single shred of evidence.'

Vicky glanced down to see Tanner had typed: *Tell her she can't count – there are only three victims. We don't believe the fourth has anything to do with it.*

Resisting the urge to type *Please shut up*, Vicky pressed on.

'We'll be presenting the evidence we have against your client during the course of the proceedings, but for now I'd like to ask where he was on the night we believe the first victim, Ms Tara Lowe, was killed.'

'I understand,' the solicitor replied, 'however, as you haven't even told us when that was yet, it may be a little difficult for my client to answer.'

'Sorry, yes, of course,' Vicky said, reaching for her handwritten notes.

Seeing Tanner type *Don't apologise!* she shoved the laptop to one side. 'Ms Lowe's body was found on Monday morning. Our medical examiner believes she'd been dead for three days. She'd last been seen by her mother on Friday at around seven o'clock in the evening, which means we need to know where your client was from between then and – say – the morning of the following day?'

With Vicky now looking expectantly at Elliston, he frowned back to ask, 'Sorry, but who's Tara Lowe?'

Seeing Tanner type *And don't let him change the subject*, she snapped the laptop closed to stare directly at Elliston. 'I wasn't asking if you know her or not,' Vicky replied. 'I was attempting to determine your whereabouts at the time of her death.'

'I'd have to check my diary.'

'Be my guest.'

Vicky spent an impatient moment watching him pull out his phone to begin swiping at the screen.

After conferring with his solicitor, he eventually said, 'I was attending a bilateral conference with my European counterpart as part of my official parliamentary duties.'

'And where, may I ask, was that?'

'Brussels!' Elliston exclaimed, giving her a look of triumphant disdain.

Shit, Vicky cursed to herself, as Elliston smiled back at her to ask, 'May I go now?'

'If you don't mind, we have just a few more questions.'

'Surprisingly, I do mind,' Elliston replied, 'but I suppose I don't have much choice.'

Beginning to wish Tanner was there, Vicky wracked her brain for what to ask next.

Glancing over at Haverstock, only to see him shrug uselessly back, she heard the solicitor say, 'If you don't have any more questions for my client, then I'd like to request his release – along with a written apology for both his public humiliation and for wasting his time.'

'Earlier, your client said he didn't know the victim,' Vicky continued. 'Is that still the case?'

'I can honestly say that I've never knowingly heard of her before,' came Elliston's measured response.

'But you do know Blackfleet Broad?'

'Doesn't everyone?'

'And you were aware that it was going to be drained as part of an archaeological dig?'

'I wasn't, no – but it certainly sounds fascinating. Do tell me more.'

'The dig was being led by a local historian, Professor Albert Beaumont, from Norfolk University. Perhaps you've heard of him?'

'I must admit, the name does ring a bell, but only because your colleague, Mr Tanner, brought it up with me earlier.'

'Perhaps this will help to jog your memory,'

Vicky continued, presenting him with a document from Companies House.

After taking a moment to study it, Elliston looked up with a questioning frown. 'It would appear that I'm in business with him. So what?'

'Are you honestly trying to tell me that you're unable to remember the name of someone you're in business with?'

'Unfortunately, yes – but in my defence, as the document clearly states, the company was founded in 2002. I can barely remember what I had for dinner yesterday, let alone who I happened to start a business with nearly a quarter of a century ago.'

Furious with herself for having failed to check the company's incorporation date, Vicky did her best to recover: 'Which makes it even more likely that you'd remember him – being as you said yourself – you'd been in business with him for the best part of twenty-five years.'

'Had that been the only business I'd been involved in during that time, then perhaps. But it isn't. Furthermore, it's an investment company – meaning very little business is actually done. We simply use it to pool resources. I can't remember the last time we were in the same room together. Furthermore, he wasn't a professor when we first met, and nobody's ever used his surname. Everyone just calls him Alfie.'

Snatching the document out of his hands, Vicky did her best to control her temper. 'How about the others?' she demanded. 'Simon Balinger and Jeremy Southcott? I suppose you don't know them, either.'

'Not at all. I know exactly who they are. Simon owns a construction company, and Jeremy is the Chairman of Norfolk Council's Planning and Housing Committee. Actually, I had a meeting with him and his committee only yesterday.'

'May I ask what that meeting was about?'

'I would normally be able to answer,' Elliston smiled, 'however, on that particular occasion, my concentration was interrupted by your colleague, Mr Tanner, dragging me out by the scruff of my neck to accuse me of murder.'

'No doubt he had his reasons,' said Vicky, smiling back.

'Which brings us back to the subject of evidence,' interjected the solicitor, 'or should I say the distinct lack of it.'

'If I may, I'd like to first ask where your client was yesterday evening between five and six?'

With a shrug, the solicitor looked to her client. 'You're free to answer, if you wish.'

'I'd be more than happy to,' Elliston replied. 'I was attending a meeting at Norfolk University.'

'So, you admit it then!' Vicky exclaimed, her voice rising with dramatic flair.

'Sorry – I admit what?'

'To meeting Professor Beaumont, inside his office!'

'Sadly not. If I had been inside his office, it was only to have a look around.'

'To have look around?' Vicky repeated, in an incredulous tone.

'The university has applied for a grant to have an extension built,' Elliston continued, 'so I thought I'd better see the place for myself before giving my approval.'

'You're lying, Mr Elliston.'

'I am?'

'And we have the evidence to prove it.'

'It's about time you mentioned the word "evidence",' muttered the solicitor. 'Would you like to tell us what it is?'

Removing another document from the file, Vicky pushed it over the table. 'Your client's fingerprints and DNA weren't only found in Mr Beaumont's study, but on his body as well!'

Leaving the solicitor to study the report, Vicky caught Elliston's eye. 'While Ms Heatherington is checking our findings, perhaps we can chat about another of your business associates – one whose name has already come up.'

'Which one is that?'

'Mr Simon Balinger.'

'Yes, OK. What about him?'

'I don't suppose you can remember when you saw him last?'

'Why – what's happened to him?'

'It wouldn't have been last night, by any chance?'

Looking uncharacteristically nervous, Elliston blinked rapidly before saying, 'No – I – I was at a friend's house for dinner.'

'Would you be able to provide us with the name of this so-called "friend"?'

'Yes, of course. It will be in my diary,' Elliston continued, returning to his phone. 'Actually, there were quite a few of us. I'm sure they'll be able to vouch for me.'

'What time did you leave?'

'It was late – I remember that much – but you still haven't told me what's happened to Simon?'

'We believe he was murdered, Mr Elliston – just like Tara Lowe and Professor Beaumont. But instead of being drowned in the middle of Blackfleet Broad, or stabbed through the eye with a silver letter opener, he was shoved down an empty elevator shaft at the old Longmeadow Estate.'

- CHAPTER FIFTY-FOUR -

WITH AN EMAIL containing the contact details of the people Elliston had allegedly been dining with on the night in question, Vicky suspended the interview to ask Haverstock to give them a call – only to find Tanner, lurking in the corridor outside.

'How's it been going?' he asked, nodding at Haverstock as he passed.

Making sure the interview room door was closed, Vicky whispered towards him in an accusatory tone, 'Have you been listening at the door?'

'As you ended our video call – rather abruptly, I might add – you didn't leave me with much of a choice.'

'Then you don't need me to tell you what happened, as you would have heard for yourself.'

'Well, I would have done, but the room's remarkably soundproof. On top of that, one of my ears is blocked.'

Shaking her head in disbelief, Vicky barged past him to march away, leaving Tanner trailing in her wake.

Reaching the door at the end, Tanner eventually asked, 'Aren't you going to update me?'

'I need a coffee first,' came her curt reply.

'Just the highlights will do,' Tanner grumbled,

forced to follow her out.

Arriving at the kitchen, Vicky finally stopped to fill the kettle – only to hear Tanner immediately behind her.

'And...?'

Switching the kettle on, she pulled some instant coffee out from the cupboard above. 'Do you want one?'

'Er... no thanks,' Tanner replied. 'You were saying...?'

With nothing to do until the kettle had boiled, she turned reluctantly around to face him. 'He has an alibi for both Tara's murder and Simon Balinger's.'

'Which was?'

'He was at a friend's house for dinner last night. He's given us the names of those in attendance, so I've asked Haverstock to give them a call.'

'And for when Tara was killed?'

'Brussels,' she replied.

'What do you mean – Brussels?'

'That's where he was – attending some sort of bilateral conference with his European counterpart.'

'And we know that for a fact – do we?'

'Not yet, but it won't be difficult to find out.'

'Shit,' muttered Tanner, under his breath.

'My thoughts exactly.'

'What about Professor Beaumont?' asked Tanner, lifting his voice above the noise of the boiling kettle.

'Oh, he fully admitted to being at Norfolk University at the time.'

'That's something, I suppose.'

'But he said he'd dropped by for an impromptu visit. Apparently, they'd just applied for a grant to have an extension built, so he thought he'd better check the place over before giving his approval.'

'Well, that's bollocks, for a start!'

'But it doesn't help much with our cause.'

'It does when we have both his fingerprints and DNA on the professor's body.'

'Maybe so,' replied Vicky, 'but I know what his solicitor's going to say – that they could have found their way there at any time – even by bumping into each other in the street.'

'Rather unlikely,' huffed Tanner, as the kettle clicked itself off.

'But still possible,' countered Vicky, pouring its contents into a cup.

Hearing someone clear their throat, they glanced around to see DC Henderson's goat-like face staring at them.

'Sorry, Henderson,' said Tanner. 'Do you want to make yourself a drink?'

'No, boss,' he replied, shaking his head. 'I've just taken a call from Townsend. He's over at Mr Lowe's house.'

'Let me guess – he won't let them inside?'

'Well, apparently, he did put up a bit of a fuss, but that's not what they were calling about.'

'Are you going to tell me, Henderson, or am I going to have to beat it out of you with a cricket bat?'

'They've found what they think is Tara Lowe's laptop. It was hidden under some files on her father's desk, inside which was a printout of that newspaper article we were looking for – the one about Blackfleet Broad, and the plans to have it turned into a commercial development.'

'Sounds like we need to have another word with him,' commented Vicky, taking a ruminative sip of her coffee.

'But it doesn't prove anything, though, does it,' said Tanner, glancing over at her. 'At least, not really.'

'It proves he was lying about not knowing where her laptop was – and that he didn't know anything about the article she'd written.'

'Maybe so, but for all we know, Tara may have simply left it there – or he placed it there by accident when he was tidying up.'

'Both possible,' countered Vicky, 'but so was Elliston's excuse for being seen lurking around Norfolk University at the time Professor Beaumont was killed.'

'You think it's worth having another word with him?'

'I think it would be remiss if we didn't – if for no other reason than to ask where he was at the time Professor Beaumont, and now Simon Balinger, were killed.'

Tanner let out a petulant sigh. 'OK, fine – but I want Elliston to remain exactly where he is until we get back.'

'Sorry, but what do you mean – until *we* get back?'

'You want me to go with you, don't you?'

'Yes, of course!' came Vicky's rather disingenuous response. 'I just thought you'd have more important things to be getting on with – like a crossword, for example, or maybe an exciting game of Battleships.'

- CHAPTER FIFTY-FIVE -

ARRIVING BACK AT Mr Lowe's house about half an hour later to find the drive cluttered with squad cars and forensics vans, Tanner climbed out of his car to hear Vicky ask behind him, 'I assume you're happy for me to do all the talking?'

Tanner turned to see her climbing out. 'You can do some of the talking, Vicky, but you can't do all of it.'

'As long as you can trust me enough to lead,' she added, smiling briefly over the car's black felt roof at him, 'then I'm sure that will be fine.'

'Of course I trust you,' Tanner replied, leading the way to the front door. 'I wouldn't have made you the SIO if I didn't.'

'Sorry, boss, but it doesn't always feel that way – like when I'm forced to have you on the end of a clandestine video call during a suspect's interview, for example.'

'I didn't force you. Besides, that was what I'd describe as being a special circumstance.'

'Because the suspect had filed a restraining order against you, making it rather challenging for you to attend in person?'

'Because I have a unique insight into what makes Elliston tick – and it's not a Duracell battery.'

'Should I include that in my notes?'

'That I have a unique insight into Elliston's devious, psychotic little mind?'

'That he isn't rechargeable,' she smiled.

Reaching the door, Tanner turned to face her. 'I think you need to take this a little more seriously, young Vicky.'

'You're the one who wants to go off and play mini-golf all the time,' she replied, reaching forward to press the bell.

'That was ages ago – and besides, I wasn't being serious.'

'I rest my case,' she mumbled, standing back to the sound of approaching footsteps.

When the door opened, Vicky held out her ID to the face of Mr Lowe, staring out at them from the shadows beyond.

'Sorry to bother you again,' she began, smiling at what little of his face she could see. 'DI Gilbert and DCI Tanner. Would you mind if we had another word?'

'Great,' he sighed. 'Just what I need – more bloody policemen.'

'We can do it outside, if it's easier?'

'Well, you can't do it inside. I'm not sure there's enough room!'

Leaving the front door open, he stepped out into the daylight to join them.

'OK – what is it?' he eventually demanded, glaring around at them both.

'We need to ask you some questions about something that was found on top of your desk this morning,' Vicky began.

'I don't suppose it was a stapler? I've been looking for the damned thing for ages.'

'It was a laptop. Your daughter's, to be precise.'

'Yes – and...?'

'If you remember, we were asking about it when we were last here. You said it must have been stolen, when you told us that your house had been broken into.'

'And so you've found it. Well done!'

'We were just curious to know what it was doing there?'

'I've no idea,' he replied, with an exaggerated shrug. 'Backstroke?'

'You didn't put it there?'

'Why would I have done that?'

'The only reason I can think of is that you wanted to hide it from us.'

'You think I left it on my desk to hide it from you?'

'That is what's being suggested.'

'For what possible reason would I do such a thing?'

'Because you didn't want us to find out what was on it,' Vicky proposed, fixing Lowe's eyes with a steady gaze.

'If that was the case, wouldn't it have made more sense for me to have simply thrown it away?'

'Maybe you were trying to gain access to it first – just in case she'd uploaded something to one of her online providers.'

Shaking his head, Lowe shoved his hands down into his pockets. 'If you've come to arrest me for the heinous crime of hiding my daughter's laptop, then I suggest you'd better get on with it.'

After a furtive glance at Tanner, Vicky continued. 'Were you aware of what was found tucked inside?'

'As I didn't know it was there, how would I know what was inside it?'

'It was an article your daughter had been writing about Blackfleet Broad, and a dodgy building development she thought was to take place there.'

'I'm sorry, but what's that got to do with me?'

'Because when we were here last, you denied knowing anything about either the laptop, or the story.'

'A position I continue to maintain.'

'If you don't know anything about it, then how did it end up on your desk?'

'As I've already told you – I've no idea! Perhaps Tara put it there for safekeeping – or maybe I put it there by accident, when I was tidying up. Either way, I wasn't lying to you before, and I'm not lying to you now.'

'The problem is, Mr Lowe,' Vicky continued, 'having to listen to you stand there, telling us that you didn't know anything about something we later found to be within your possession, could be considered suspicious.'

'It wasn't in my possession – it was on my desk!'

'OK, but if either your fingerprints or DNA are found on the laptop, or the article discovered inside it, it won't be difficult to convince a jury that you did know it was there – and that you had also seen the story.'

'And – so what if I had?'

'Because it would provide you with a motive.'

'You're suggesting that I killed my own daughter because she'd written a newspaper article about some dodgy building development?'

'We're not here about what happened to your daughter, Mr Lowe.'

'I'm sorry – now I'm really confused. If you're not here about her, then why are you?'

'May we ask if you've heard of someone by the

name of Alfred Beaumont?' Vicky continued. 'He's a History professor at Norfolk University.'

'Why should I have?'

'Because his name is mentioned in your daughter's article.'

'As I've told you – numerous times now – I haven't read my daughter's article!'

'And because his body was found inside his office yesterday,' Vicky continued.

'I still don't see what that has to do with me.'

'How about Simon Balinger?'

'Simon who?'

'He's the owner of a local construction company. His name is also mentioned in your daughter's story.'

'Well, it certainly sounds like a riveting read.'

'More pertinently, his body has also been found – this time at the bottom of a disused elevator shaft.'

'Yes, I see – but you still haven't answered my question.'

'Which was?'

'Just what the hell any of this has to do with me?'

'It gives you motive, Mr Lowe,' interjected Tanner, risking a dirty look from Vicky.

'What gives me motive?'

'The fact that your daughter named all these people in a newspaper article she was trying to get published – the same one that was found on your desk.'

'I'm sorry, I'm clearly not reading enough crime fiction to connect all the dots.'

'If you had read her article, then it would have been logical for you to assume that the person – or persons – responsible for her death could well have been those she'd mentioned in it – being that they had the most to lose if she'd been able to publish it.'

'You're seriously suggesting that I've been going around murdering random people in order to avenge my daughter's death?'

With Tanner looking at Vicky, as if passing the question on to her, she pulled in a breath.

'Mr Lowe, may we ask where you were yesterday, between five and six in the afternoon?'

'I was here,' he replied, in a matter-of-fact tone.

'And between nine and twelve later that evening?'

'Here again – but you know that, surely?'

'I'm sorry, Mr Lowe, but how should we have known that?'

'Because I've been under what is effectively house arrest ever since you first came to see me. I haven't even been allowed out to buy some bloody milk!'

- CHAPTER FIFTY-SIX -

HEARING SOMEONE'S PHONE ring, Tanner glanced around to see Vicky digging hers out from the depths of her handbag.

'May I go back inside my own house now?' he heard Lowe huff, as Vicky turned away to take the call.

'If you can wait there for just a minute,' said Tanner, watching the side of Vicky's face tighten as she ambled away.

Hearing Lowe curse loudly under his breath, Tanner excused himself to join her.

'Are they sure?' he soon heard her say, lifting her head to stare briefly at him before looking away.

Deciding to give her some space, Tanner stepped aside to take in the house – and Mr Lowe, now pacing up and down in front of it.

Hearing Vicky say, 'Then perhaps you can email it over to me,' before ending the call, Tanner was about to ask who it was when the crack of a branch made him turn sharply around.

Unable to see anything but an overgrown tangle of shrubs and weeds, spilling out onto the driveway ahead, he was about to look away when he caught the briefest flicker of a woman's pale, enigmatic face, staring at him from the shadows with wide, unblinking eyes.

'That was Sally,' came Vicky's voice behind him.

'Huh?' he replied, glancing around.

'On the phone,' she added.

Looking back to see nothing but the ghostly head of a graceful lily, its delicate petals stark against the surrounding weeds, he shook his head in confused apprehension.

'Forensics' final report has come through.'

'For what?' he asked, taking one more look at the flower before turning away.

'Professor Beaumont's office. She's emailing it to me now.'

'Had she read it?'

'Uh-huh.'

'And...?'

'You can see for yourself,' she replied, holding her phone out for him.

Taking it from her, he began scanning through a paragraph from what must have been the forensic report, relating specifically to collected samples of DNA.

'Are they sure about this?' he soon found himself asking, glancing up at her with a dubious frown.

'That's what it says,' she replied. 'I'm not sure why they'd make something like that up.'

Tanner turned to look over his shoulder at Lowe, still pacing up and down, but now with his hands buried inside his pockets.

'OK, so – what do you want to do?' he eventually asked.

'I don't think we have much of a choice,' she replied, following his gaze.

'You do know that his motive for murdering the professor and Mr Balinger is tentative at best.'

'You've always told me to follow the evidence.'

'I have?'

'And if his DNA has been found at one of the crime scenes, that would make him a prime suspect.'

'What about his alibi, which, to be fair, is rather convincing – being that we've had a squad car parked outside his house for the past two days?'

'Well, yes, but that doesn't mean he couldn't have slipped out.'

'In what would have had to have been the middle of the day, without anyone noticing?'

'I must admit,' continued Vicky, 'it doesn't seem very likely – but neither is the idea that Elliston could have killed Mr Lowe's daughter, when he was supposedly attending a bilateral parliamentary conference in Brussels.'

- CHAPTER FIFTY-SEVEN -

WITH A DISTINCTLY belligerent Mr Lowe shoved into the back seat of one of the squad cars, Tanner led the way back to the station, arriving some twenty minutes later to watch him being hauled unceremoniously out.

'You'd better take him in for formal processing,' he said to the squad car's driver, before glancing over at all the reporters, already taking an interest. 'Perhaps you should take his handcuffs off, as well. I don't want to fan the flames of intrigue any more than we already have.'

With Vicky apparently struggling to open his car's passenger door, he scooted around to the other side to offer her a hand, only for it to fly suddenly open, its leading edge jamming straight into his unprotected groin.

Creasing over in pain, Vicky peered out at him to say, 'Sorry, boss – the door was jammed.'

Seeing his predicament, she leaned forward to ask, 'Are you all right?'

'Quite all right, thank you,' he lied, as the sound of subdued laughter could be heard drifting towards them from where the journalists stood, closely followed by the unwelcome clatter of cameras.

'Then would you mind holding onto my handbag for a sec?' Vicky continued, passing it out to him. 'Just while I climb out.'

Knowing that half the nation's press must be watching, unsure he had much of a choice, he took hold of the oversized bag to throw over his shoulder in a masculine, carefree manner – only for his lower back to give way under its enormous weight.

'Ow – fuck,' he groaned, finding himself unable to move.

'Actually, if you could stay there for a minute,' he heard Vicky say, 'that way, hopefully the press won't be able to take a picture of me trying to climb out of this stupid bloody car of yours.'

'That shouldn't be a problem,' Tanner grimaced. 'Maybe you could then give me a hand to get inside?'

'Why – what's wrong with you?' Vicky queried, climbing out to slam the door.

Holding his breath to watch the car rock from side to side, its suspension creaking under its burgeoning weight, Tanner remained there for a moment, ready to catch anything that might fall off.

Not seeing anything, he dared to breathe whilst gazing up at Vicky. 'Would you mind not doing that?'

'Would I mind not doing what?'

'Slamming my car door like that.'

'Oh – sorry,' she replied, glancing around, 'but you have to give it a bit of a shove, or it doesn't close properly.'

'Perhaps you could be a little more careful when you open it, as well,' Tanner added, tentatively removing a hand from his groin.

'Oh – right. Did I do that?'

'And this handbag of yours,' he continued, struggling to remove it from his shoulder. 'Do you have a licence for it?'

'What sort of licence?'

'How about a dangerous handbag licence – or at least something to warn people about how much the damned thing weighs?'

'It's not *that* heavy!'

'Well, I don't seem to be able to remove it from my shoulder, so it must be.'

'Don't be such a wuss,' she replied, helping him to lever it off before smiling at him. 'Shall we go in?'

'After you,' came Tanner's terse response, as he wondered if he'd be able to walk.

- CHAPTER FIFTY-EIGHT -

WITH THE PAIN in his groin beginning to ease, and doing his best to keep his back straight, Tanner inched forward through the door – only to find Elliston's formidable solicitor, Ms Heatherington, seemingly waiting for him in one of the plastic chairs.

'Mr Tanner!' she exclaimed, jumping up. 'May I have a word?'

'As long as it's only one,' he groaned, somewhat reluctantly.

'I couldn't help but notice that you've brought another suspect in for questioning.'

'How very astute of you.'

'Does it have anything to do with the murder inquiry my client is being held for?'

Unsure if he should tell her, Tanner glanced around for Vicky, hoping she'd be able to come to his rescue.

'If it does,' he heard the solicitor continue, 'and you've managed to find a more suitable suspect, then I'd like to request that my client is released.'

'I'm sorry, Ms Heatherington, but until we've had a chance to have a chat with our new suspect, we won't be making any decisions regarding Mr Elliston.'

'Have you at least been able to confirm my client's alibis for the times in question?'

'My colleagues are working on that as we speak.'

'To save everyone a little time,' she continued, digging out her phone, 'whilst you've been gallivanting around the Norfolk Broads in search of seemingly random suspects, I've been doing a little digging of my own.'

'That's nice,' Tanner replied, finally seeing Vicky, lurking inside the main office. 'If you'll excuse me, I just need to have a very quick word with my colleague.'

'I have copies of the aeroplane tickets he used to travel to Brussels on one of the days in question,' she went on. 'I also have the flight manifest confirming he was on board. His passport, as well, stamped by customs officials on entry. I've also spoken to everyone who attended his dinner party on the other date in question. They've all confirmed his presence. Interestingly enough, one of his guests was none other than one of your superior officers, Chief Superintendent Thornton. He's even offered to come in to provide a formal statement.'

'For fuck's sake,' Tanner moaned, under his breath.

'Assuming he's as good as his word,' the solicitor continued, glancing at her watch, 'he should be here any minute.'

Hearing the entrance door open behind him, Tanner turned to see none other than Chief Superintendent Thornton stepping inside to begin peering about.

'Right on time!' the solicitor exclaimed, lifting her hand to draw his attention. 'You're very lucky to have such a punctual boss,' she continued to Tanner. 'Mine always seems to end up being late.'

'He's not my boss,' Tanner muttered, doing his best to avoid Thorton's pivoting glare – only to catch the eye of the man marching into reception immediately behind him.

'You must be fucking joking,' he said – out loud that time – as the man who *was* his boss – Superintendent Forrester – pointed his chin at him to come marching over.

Nodding briefly at the solicitor, Forrester sidled up to Tanner to whisper, 'I need a quiet word with you, Tanner.'

'I'm not sure there's any need,' Tanner sighed. 'Ms Heatherington here has already told me what the problem is.'

'It's not a problem, Tanner – it's a fucking catastrophe!'

'Oh – I wouldn't go that far.'

'Have you released him yet?'

'Have I released who?'

'Elliston, you muppet-brained moron!'

'Oh – sorry. Er... no. Not yet.'

'Why the hell not?'

'Well, firstly, I've only just been told that Chief Superintendent Thornton was having dinner with Mr Elliston on one of the nights in question, and secondly, I thought I'd better ask your permission first.'

'My permission? Why do you need my permission?'

'If you remember, sir, you gave me permission to arrest him, so I thought it only fair if you granted me permission to have him unarrested, as well.'

'There's no such word as unarrested, Tanner!'

'Forgive me, sir, but I'm fairly sure there is.'

Forrester turned to face Tanner directly. 'I sincerely hope you're not trying to wind me up?'

'I wouldn't dream of it,' Tanner protested,

returning to him an innocent smile. 'Tell you what – let me look the word up now,' he continued, pulling out his phone. 'At least then we'd know.'

'If you're not very careful,' Forrester seethed, 'you'll be spending the remainder of your career directing traffic on the M1 – without the use of a high-vis jacket.'

'Wouldn't that be dangerous, sir?'

'I'm warning you, Tanner!'

With Forrester's glare suggesting he may have meant it, Tanner put his phone away to look around for the duty sergeant.

Seeing him propped up behind the reception desk, he lifted a hand to call out, 'Sergeant Taylor! Would you mind having Mr George Elliston released, at your earliest convenience? Thank you!'

Seeing him nod, Tanner turned back to find Forrester was continuing to glare at him like a bull in search of a china shop. 'Was there anything else?' he gently enquired, sincerely hoping there wasn't.

'Yes, Tanner – there was one more thing.'

'Fire away!'

'I'm curious to know why you never bother to reply to my emails.'

'Ah, well, sir, that's because I've been having trouble with my email account. For some reason, it seems to keep placing all your emails into what they call a "spam file". At first I thought it was somewhere to keep my spam sandwiches, but when Vicky told me it was for the storage of malicious emails, I had yours immediately redirected into my inbox, where they should be.'

Forrester continued to glare at him for a moment longer, before finally taking a breath. 'Does that mean you'll be replying to a few more in the future?'

'Absolutely, sir. Especially the ones marked

urgent.'

Hearing someone clear their throat behind him, Tanner glanced around to see Sergeant Taylor, waiting to speak to him.

Grateful for the interruption, Tanner turned away from Forrester to face him. 'Yes, Taylor – what is it?'

'I just thought you'd like to know that Mr Elliston's solicitor is bringing him out now, boss.'

'So I can see,' Tanner replied, as the door leading down to the interview rooms opened for Ms Heatherington to appear, closely followed by the man he still considered to be his prime suspect.

'Before he leaves,' Forrester murmured beside him, 'perhaps you could offer him an apology.'

'It would be my pleasure,' Tanner replied, nudging past.

Catching Elliston's eye, Tanner lurched forward with his hand extended. 'I just wanted to say how truly sorry I am for any inconvenience we may have caused you – your family and your illustrious group of friends as well. If there's anything I can do to make it up to you, please don't hesitate to ask.'

'Don't worry,' Elliston sneered back, staring inhospitably down at Tanner's still outstretched hand, 'you'll be hearing from my lawyer.'

'Oh, right!' Tanner exclaimed, glancing around at Ms Heatherington. 'You mean this one?'

'I have more than one, Mr Tanner.'

'Of course. I'm sure a man with your moral inclination can never have enough. In the meantime, if you do need anything – anything at all – my cell door is always open.'

Watching Elliston force a smile back at him, Tanner ground his teeth as he was forced to watch the man's solicitor open the entrance door to beckon him graciously through.

'If you do get the chance to look up the word "unarrest",' Forrester grumbled behind him, 'perhaps you could also look up the definition of "apologise", because whatever that was, it missed the mark by a very long way.'

'I'm sorry, sir,' Tanner replied, 'but under the circumstances, I honestly think it was the best I could do.'

- CHAPTER FIFTY-NINE -

SEEING VICKY FINISH a discussion with Sergeant Taylor to beckon for his attention, he seized the excuse to extract himself from Forrester's overbearing presence to step quickly over.

'Mr Lowe is ready to be interviewed,' she said, the moment he was in ear shot. 'I was just wondering if you'd like to join me?'

'I'm happy enough to leave you to it. Besides, it would appear that I have a rather large number of Forrester's urgent emails to reply to.'

'I don't suppose they can wait?' she asked, pursing her lips into a smile.

'Oh, I see. *Now* you want me!'

'I would have welcomed your company before, but if you remember, you had that restraining order.'

Tanner thought about it for a moment before eventually saying, 'OK. Let me grab myself a decent cup of coffee, and I'll see you in there.'

Heading through the doors into the main office, Tanner dived into his own to glance furtively out of the window.

Seeing Elliston and his solicitor, deep in conversation behind a gleaming black Mercedes, he made a note of the number plate before bursting back out the way he'd come.

Spying Townsend on one side of a desk, and Henderson on the other, he launched over to present Townsend with the scrawled out number plate.

'I've got a little job for you,' he began, his gaze shifting between the two of them. 'There's a black Mercedes in the car park that I want you to follow – more specifically, the man you should find inside. But you'd better be quick; it looks like it's about to leave.'

As the junior detectives jumped out of their respective chairs, Townsend plucked his suit jacket off the back of his.

'Who are we following, boss?'

'George Elliston.'

'You mean – the MP, George Elliston?'

'That's the one. Right – that's the car's number plate,' added Tanner, pressing the note into his hand, 'just in case you lose sight of it. And report back every half hour or so, to let us know what he's up to.'

'Who should we call – you or Vicky?'

'Good question,' said Tanner, allowing his eyes to drift up to the ceiling. 'It's probably best if you call me. I think Vicky's got enough on her plate as it is.'

'But – she does know about it, right?'

'Of course she knows about it!' Tanner exclaimed, presenting Townsend with a disapproving frown. 'It was her idea to have him followed!'

- CHAPTER SIXTY -

UNSURE IF THEY'D believed him, Tanner headed back to his office to wait by the window. The moment he saw Townsend and Henderson emerge to jump into Townsend's car – just as the Mercedes reversed sedately out – he congratulated himself on a job well done by pouring himself a coffee. With that in hand, together with a Chocolate Hobnob, he hurried over to join Vicky in Interview Room One.

Bursting in to find her waiting for him, with Mr Lowe sitting in the same chair Elliston had been only minutes before, deep in discussion with an elderly gentleman Tanner presumed to be his solicitor, he smiled amicably around at them all to say, 'Sorry I'm late.'

'We were just about to get started,' said Vicky, offering him the seat next to hers.

'Right then,' he replied, making himself comfortable. 'Do carry on.'

Sipping quietly at his coffee while Vicky whistled through the interview's formalities, he glanced down at his tie to realise it was covered in crumbs from the biscuit he'd devoured on the way over.

Brushing them discreetly away, he glanced up at the sound of his name – only to find nobody was looking at him.

'Sorry,' he interrupted, looking at Vicky, 'but did someone mention my name?'

'Only to say that you were present,' she replied, before sitting up straight to smile at the suspect.

'Mr Lowe, perhaps we can start by asking you –'

Hearing a phone ring, Tanner glanced curiously around the table, only to realise it was his own.

'Sorry,' he said, fumbling around for it. 'I must have forgotten to turn it off.'

Glancing down at the screen to see it was Townsend calling, he pushed himself up to whisper to Vicky, 'I'd better take this.'

As she rolled her eyes, he ducked out into the hall, making sure to close the door behind him.

'Yes, Townsend,' he eventually said. 'Do you have some news?'

'Mr Elliston's been dropped off at his house, but he hasn't gone inside.'

'Then what's he doing?'

'He's just waiting on the doorstep, fumbling with his keys. I think he might be waiting for his solicitor to go.'

'Is she still there?'

'She's just driving off now.'

Tanner waited a moment, before asking, 'What's he doing now?'

The phone remained silent for a while, before Townsend's voice came back on the line. 'He spent a few moments admiring his car, but now he's getting in.'

'OK, keep following him – but don't let him see you.'

'Don't worry, boss. We won't.'

'And call me again the moment he's got to wherever it is that he's going.'

'Right you are.'

Ending the call, Tanner re-entered the interview room to find Lowe and his solicitor glowering at him from the other side of the table, with Vicky looking equally perturbed.

'Sorry about that. Now – where were we?'

'I was about to ask Mr Lowe about yesterday,' began Vicky, returning her gaze to the suspect, 'in particular your whereabouts between five and six in the afternoon.'

'I've already told you,' Lowe replied, leaning back in his chair. 'I was at home, surrounded by either your fellow police officer chums, or their forensic counterparts.'

'Yes, of course. The problem is,' Vicky continued, 'that the aforementioned forensics unit found your DNA inside an office within Norfolk University's main building – where the body of a certain Professor Alfred Beaumont had been discovered the following day – the same Professor Beaumont mentioned in a newspaper article written by your daughter, Tara Lowe.'

'Forgive me,' interjected the suspect's solicitor, scratching his bald grey head, 'but if my client was inside his house at the time, surrounded by either your fellow police officers, or their forensic counterparts, then how could he also have been at Norfolk University, murdering one of their staff members with what's described as being a silver letter opener?'

'That's what we're here to find out,' said Vicky, her eyes remaining focused on the suspect.

'And another thing,' the solicitor continued, 'and forgive me if I'm being a little obtuse, but why on earth would he?'

'We believe his motive is linked to what happened to his daughter. As you may be aware, her body was recently found in Blackfleet Broad. It's our belief that your client found the article she'd written, naming Professor Beaumont – together with various others – in a scheme to acquire planning permission for what had the potential to be a highly profitable commercial development project.'

'I'm sorry, but I still don't see the connection,' the solicitor replied, leafing through the report.

'Our theory is that he put two and two together – what happened to his daughter, and the people she'd named in her article.'

'You're suggesting my client murdered this Professor Beaumont character out of vengeance for what happened to his daughter?'

'That's correct,' Vicky confirmed.

'Well – it's a little tenuous – but do carry on.'

Glancing down at her notes, Vicky took a breath to continue, only to hear Tanner's phone ring once again.

'Shit,' he muttered, under his breath, as he began scrambling around for it, much as he'd done before.

'I'm really sorry,' he eventually said, staring down at the screen, 'but I'm going to have to take this.'

As he stood up to make his way out, he turned to Vicky to whisper, 'Actually, it might be better if you carried on without me.'

- CHAPTER SIXTY-ONE -

'YES, TOWNSEND?' SAID Tanner, the moment he'd closed the door. 'What's happening?'

'He's just pulled up outside a block of flats.'

'Whereabouts?'

'On the outskirts of Ludham.'

'OK – what's he doing now?'

'Just sitting there. I think he's on the phone to someone.'

'There's no way you can overhear what he's saying?'

'Not unless we go over there, knock on his window, and ask if we can climb into the back.'

'Was that a no?'

'I'm afraid so, boss.'

There was a momentary silence, before Tanner impatiently asked, 'What's happening now?'

'Er... nothing. He's just sitting there, talking on his phone.'

'Do you think he might be there to meet someone?'

'It's certainly a possibility, but there's no one here now – no one apart from us, of course.'

'Where was this place again?' Tanner asked, glancing down at his watch.

'It's at the end of Sycamore Grove, just outside Ludham.'

'And you said it was a block of flats?'

'I think it's going to be, but at the moment it looks more like a building site.'

'Does it have any signage – or advertising?'

'Uh-huh,' said Townsend.

'What's the name of the construction company?'

'Hold on. I can't quite see from here. I'll edge the car forward a little.'

Hearing Townsend start the engine, Tanner waited restlessly before his detective inspector's voice came back over the line.

'It's SKB Holdings, boss. Simon Balinger's company. And Mr Elliston has just stepped out. Looks like he's heading inside.'

'OK, stay where you are. I'll be over just as soon as I can.'

- CHAPTER SIXTY-TWO -

AS TANNER'S CONSPICUOUS bright yellow Triumph Stag pulled up alongside Townsend's more discreet dark grey Audi A3, he wound the passenger window down to lean his head towards him.

'Has anything happened?'

Townsend shook his head. 'Not since we last spoke.'

'You haven't seen anyone else going in, or coming out?'

'Not a soul, boss,' he shrugged.

'Then I think I'd better go inside to take a look.'

'Would you like us to come with you?'

'You're all right. I'm only going to see what he's doing. I'm not going to confront him, or anything.'

'But – er – you do know that you don't have a search warrant?'

'I'm looking, Townsend, not searching.'

'And there's a difference?'

'Obviously!'

'Right you are, boss,' Townsend replied, retreating into his seat to wind the window up.

Leaving his car in front of Townsend's, Tanner climbed out to cross the road.

Taking a quick look inside Elliston's

ostentatious Bentley Continental, he raised a hand at Townsend and Henderson before making his way towards an advertising façade, and the entrance door that had been sawn into it.

Undoing a bolt, he levered the door open to find himself inside a seemingly deserted building site, littered with dismantled scaffolding, scattered roof tiles, and piles of bricks – all being swallowed by an impenetrable tangle of grass and weeds.

Hearing a magpie's distant chatter, he stared up at the half-finished building, its windowless walls standing stark against the cloudless sky above. When he heard what sounded like glass breaking, somewhere near the top, he edged forward, picking his way through the detritus until reaching the building's doorless entrance.

With a bare concrete staircase to the side, he placed a tentative foot on the first step to peer cautiously up the shadow-filled stairwell, all the way to the roof's exposed timber frame.

Unable to either see or hear anyone, he crept slowly up, pausing each time the staircase opened onto an empty floor. Only when he reached the top did he finally hear something – a movement from somewhere amid the dozens of unclad brick walls, spreading out like a maze before him.

Unsure which way to go, he crept slowly along an empty corridor. When he reached the low brick wall of a balcony at the end, he dared to peer over the side to see Townsend, climbing out of his car to stare vacantly up.

About to wave silently down, Tanner heard the distinctive sound of something being dragged along a floor, not too far from where he was standing.

Holding his breath, he turned towards where he thought it was coming from – the other side of the wall ahead.

Seeing an empty doorframe a few feet away, he inched towards it to peer cautiously through. There, near the middle of the otherwise empty room, was George Elliston, dragging the body of a man back towards where the floor disappeared into a gaping chasm.

Struggling to believe what he was seeing, Tanner held his breath to take a step back, only for his shoe to clip the edge of the doorframe.

Wincing as he listened to the sound echo around the bare-bricked walls, he glanced up to find Elliston staring straight at him – his blood-stained hands still holding onto the body's ankles.

For a full moment they stood in silence, before Elliston eventually opened his mouth.

'It's not what it looks like.'

Taking a breath, Tanner glanced down at the body, and the gash that could be seen running the length of the man's blood-soaked head.

'Well, it looks like you're dragging the body of a smartly dressed middle-aged man across the top floor of a half-built block of flats. Am I missing something?'

'I meant – it's not what it looks like as in I didn't kill him. I actually tried to save him!'

'You're saying that you just happened to find him here, with blood pouring out of his head, and instead of calling an ambulance, you thought you'd try to stop the bleeding by dragging him around by his ankles, in the vague hope that it might make him feel better?'

Letting go of the body's legs for the victim's shoes to thud against the dusty floor, Elliston pulled himself up straight.

'As unlikely as that may seem,' he said, 'that is

correct.'

Stepping cautiously into the room, Tanner continued to hold Elliston's gaze. 'If you'd just happened to find him here, may I ask why you were moving him?'

'Because I thought it would be easier to hide the body than to spend another twenty-four hours being interrogated about it,' Elliston replied, taking a backwards step, 'especially given my relationship to him – not to mention the others you've chalked me up as having killed.'

'May I ask who he is?'

'Don't you know?'

'If I had to guess,' Tanner replied, gazing down at the man's ashen grey face, 'I'd go with Jeremy Southcott, Chairman of Norfolk's Planning and Housing Committee – being that he was the last person left alive from that list of names in Tara Lowe's newspaper article – the last person apart from you, of course.'

'Then you can see why I thought it would be more sensible to dispose of the body instead of calling an ambulance?'

'Well, yes, I suppose I can – but that doesn't tell me what you were doing here, if not to hit him over the head with some sort of heavy blunt instrument.'

'We'd arranged to meet to go over some planning issues to do with the building's roof, but thanks to you, I was late.'

'Or maybe you were right on time,' Tanner proposed, 'you just didn't expect me to be here to watch you dispose of the body.'

'OK – it's a fair cop. You've caught me moving the body of some dead guy. But what possible motive would I have for killing him?'

'The same one you had for murdering Tara Lowe,

Professor Beaumont, and Simon Balinger. Now that I think about it, it's the same one you had for killing those other people, a year or so ago. Good old-fashioned greed!'

'Those "other people" you so aptly mentioned,' muttered Elliston, inching further away, 'gang-raped my thirteen-year-old daughter, leading her to take her own life. As I've told you before – they fully deserved what happened to them.'

'What about Sir Charles Fletcher?' Tanner demanded.

'If you remember,' Elliston continued, glancing over his shoulder as he edged further back, 'I wasn't the one who killed him. That was you!'

'You were the one trying to frame him for murder – which is how he ended up falling off the back of a ferry!'

'You're the one who couldn't hold onto him long enough to stop him from going over!'

Taking a breath to control his temper, Tanner took a deliberate step forward. 'Either way, Mr Elliston, you're going to have to come with me.'

'You're not going to arrest me again, are you?' he questioned, with a nervous laugh. 'I'm not sure what your boss would have to say about that.'

'When my superiors hear that you've been caught red-handed – literally – I think they'll understand.'

As Elliston continued backwards, now staring at his blood-covered hands, Tanner realised he was inching ever closer to the missing section of floor, the same one he'd been dragging the body towards.

Briefly entertaining the idea of remaining silent, in the hope that he might inadvertently step back over the edge, Tanner shook the thought from his mind. 'If you are going to come with me,' he said at last, 'then it may be wise to look where you're going.'

As Elliston edged further back, his feet drawing ever closer to the missing floor, he looked up from his hands to stare at Tanner in confused bewilderment.

'For Christ's sake, man!' Tanner shouted, lurching suddenly forward. 'Behind you!'

As if waking from some distant dream, Elliston turned at last – just in time to see himself step back into what was nothing but a waiting void.

As if destiny itself had been holding its breath for this very moment, Tanner stared in muted silence as his body vanished like a shadow fleeing from the rising sun.

Throwing himself forward to teeter on the edge, Tanner stared helplessly down to watch in abject horror as Elliston continued to fall – his face turned towards Tanner's in questioning silence.

Only when Tanner dropped to his knees to hold out a desperate hand did Elliston finally cry out – a scream that was forever silenced a heartbeat later.

- CHAPTER SIXTY-THREE -

MORE THAN TWO hours later, with his ears still ringing from the sound of wailing sirens, Tanner arrived back at Wroxham Police Station to find the car park virtually empty, and the rooms inside in a serene state of tranquil silence.

With Vicky being one of the few people still behind their desks, he stepped quietly up to her.

'Hi, Vicky,' he began, his voice strained and tired. 'How's everything been going?'

'Yes, fine,' she replied, pushing herself away from her desk to offer him an apathetic smile. 'How are you?'

'I've been better,' came his honest reply. 'Any news on Lowe?'

'I was – er – going to call, but I thought it could wait until you got back.'

'Why – what's happened?'

Swallowing hard, she lifted her chin to meet his gaze. 'I decided to release him.'

'You did what?' Tanner demanded, his eyes boring into hers.

'I asked Forrester's advice before doing so,' she continued, 'and we both agreed that it was the right thing to do.'

'But – why?'

'Because we didn't have enough evidence to

hold him – not when half our forensics department were able to provide him with an alibi, that being he was in his house at the time of the murders.'

Tanner held her gaze for a moment longer before letting out a reticent sigh. 'Fair enough, I suppose – but in the future, I'd appreciate it if you could ask me first.'

'Yes, boss, of course.'

Glancing around at the empty desks, Tanner turned to look towards his office, and the car park he could see through the window beyond.

'I assume everyone's out dealing with Elliston?'

'I believe so.'

'Any news on anything else?'

'Nothing of importance.'

'Right then,' he sighed once again. 'I suppose I'd better get back to my desk.'

As he turned to shuffle listlessly away, Vicky called after him. 'Before you go, I should tell you that Forrester wants a word.'

'No surprises there,' he muttered to himself.

'He wants to know what happened – from the horse's mouth, so to speak.'

Stopping where he was, Tanner turned slowly back. 'Then he's just going to have to wait for my report, like everyone else.'

Staring at Vicky for a moment longer, as if daring her to say something else, he turned back to enter his office and close the door.

With his hand still on the handle, he paused for a moment to drink in the calm, blissful peace.

Making himself a coffee, he sat behind his desk to switch on his computer. As he listened to the hard drive whirr into life, he took a sip from his drink to stare out of the window, and the journalists still lining the road outside.

'Bloody reporters,' he sighed. 'Haven't they got anything better to do?'

As the screen flicked on, he took hold of the mouse to open his dreaded email.

Shaking his head at the sight of another dozen or so that had come through since he'd last looked, he saw one from Forrester – the subject line reading *GEORGE ELLISTON* in full caps.

'Well – I'm not opening that,' he muttered, dragging it into his favourite spam file.

Wondering if he could rename the label to something more appropriate, like *Forrester's Extra Special Case File*, he hovered the cursor over it when another email appeared.

'For fuck's sake,' he moaned, before realising it was from forensics – more specifically, an interim report relating to the two bodies found at the Longmeadow Estate.

With the vague hope that they'd found Elliston's fingerprints or DNA, preferably on the body of Simon Balinger, he opened it to begin scrolling through.

Reaching the relevant section, he held his breath, scanning the paragraphs for the late MP's name.

Unable to see it, he went back to the beginning to start again, this time reading the document more thoroughly. When his eyes glanced off a name that was instantly recognisable, he checked the heading above before sitting slowly back.

Taking a gulp from his coffee, he checked his watch before launching himself over to the door.

Flinging it open, he stared out at Vicky.

'What time did you release Mr Lowe?'

'What?' she asked, glancing up in confusion.

'Mr Lowe,' Tanner repeated. 'What time did you

release him?'

'I – I don't know,' she stammered, glancing down at her watch. 'Is it important?'

'His fingerprints and DNA have been found on Simon Balinger's body – the one shoved down that abandoned elevator shaft!'

- CHAPTER SIXTY-FOUR -

WITH VICKY SITTING beside him, Tanner turned into the drive of Mr Lowe's house, half-expecting to see the same number of vans and squad cars that had been there before. Instead, the only car there was the silver-grey Saab 900 belonging to Mr Lowe, parked immediately outside the front door – just as it had been when they'd first arrived.

With the house looming up behind it, its windows closed and curtains drawn, Tanner parked alongside the Saab to climb slowly out, half-expecting to be met by the tranquil silence the scene seemed to suggest. But instead of the undulating notes of distant birds drifting effortlessly through the evening air, came the muffled sounds of a domestic dispute, one that appeared to be in full, unfettered swing.

'Someone's having a bad day,' he mused, raising an intrigued eyebrow at Vicky.

'His wife?' she suggested, gazing up at the house.

Tanner glanced curiously around the drive. 'Well, her car's not here, but I suppose he could have picked her up.'

'Or she could have taken a taxi.'

With a shrug, Tanner invited Vicky forward. 'Shall we take a look?'

'After you,' came her wary response.

'You mean – you don't want to do all the talking?'

With the argument reaching new heights of heated animosity, Vicky cast her eyes over at him. 'Even if I did, I'm not sure anyone would be able to hear me.'

Smiling back, Tanner stepped up to the door to ring the bell, only to hear the altercation inside instantly dissipate – leaving the barely audible sound of what he could have sworn was a man sobbing.

When that, too, came snivelling to a halt, the house fell into an unnatural silence.

After waiting for a few moments for someone to come to the door, Tanner exchanged an apprehensive glance with Vicky before ringing the bell again.

Listening to the sound echo through what now appeared to be an empty house, Vicky looked up at the windows.

'Everything's gone rather quiet,' she said, stepping slowly back.

'Too quiet,' Tanner replied, crouching down to peer through the letterbox.

Unable to see anything but a shadow-filled hallway, he lifted his mouth to call, 'Hello! Is anyone there?'

Hearing nothing but the rhythmic tick of a clock, echoing from somewhere inside, he climbed back to his feet.

With Vicky cupping her hands to peer through a window beside the door, Tanner called, 'Can you see anything?'

'Not much,' she replied. 'It doesn't exactly help that the curtains are drawn.'

'Which is strange in itself,' Tanner muttered.

Taking the window on the other side, he tried to do the same. 'This curtain's only been partially drawn,' he quietly said.

Lifting himself onto the balls of his feet, he tried to see over something that had been nudged up against the window from the other side.

'How're you getting on?' asked Vicky, stepping over to join him.

'About as well as you, I'm afraid.'

He was about to give up when a flicker of light caught the corner of his eye.

'Hold on,' he said, pressing his face against the glass. 'I think there's a mirror on the wall.'

'Are you saying you can see yourself?' asked Vicky, in a curious tone.

'Not me, no, but I think –'

His voice trailed away as he stepped back from the window to begin searching the ground.

'What are you looking for?' asked Vicky, following his erratic gaze.

'I need something to stand on.'

'Well, I would offer my services, but I'm already feeling repressed. I'd hate to imagine how I'd feel if people started using me as a footstool.'

'This'll do,' Tanner replied, reaching for a large, weed-filled terracotta flowerpot.

Dragging it towards the base of the window, he flipped it over to hoist himself up.

As he peered through the glass, he heard Vicky ask behind him, 'Anything?'

'It's just a reflection of the kitchen.'

About to look away, he thought he saw something within the reflection move. Looking more closely, he found himself staring at what appeared to be a deflating orange balloon, hovering just above a kitchen chair.

Blinking hard, he looked again – only this time, the balloon began to inflate.

'Jesus fucking Christ,' he suddenly snapped,

jumping down from the pot to stare wildly about.

'What is it?' Vicky demanded, stepping back. 'What did you see?'

'We need to get inside,' came Tanner's breathless response, throwing himself at the window to try wrenching it open. 'Have a go at the front door,' he added, unable to lift it. 'Failing that, try another window!'

'But – you haven't said why?'

Staring down at the upturned pot, he said, 'Fuck it,' before reaching down to haul it up.

With Vicky staring at him as if he'd completely lost his mind, he hurled it at the window – the pot striking the pane with a hard, hollow crack to send a storm of glass spiralling into the darkness beyond.

- CHAPTER SIXTY-FIVE -

LAUNCHING HIMSELF THROUGH the jagged hole, Tanner landed on the broken glass to stare madly about. Seeing a half-open door in the corner, he continued on, bursting through to find himself inside a kitchen, in the middle of which was a man tied to a chair, a plastic bag pulled tight over his head.

As Tanner watched it being sucked deep into the man's mouth, Tanner lunged forward to rip the bag off, only to come stumbling to a halt at the sight of a stainless-steel kitchen knife, held up against the victim's swollen neck.

'That's as close as you're going to get,' came the shrill sound of a woman's voice, from somewhere behind the deflating bag.

As the victim's body twitched violently in the chair, a young woman's face gradually appeared, her hand wrapped around the knife's worn wooden handle.

With the sickening feeling that he was staring into the eyes of a ghost, Tanner opened his mouth to say a name, before realising his mistake. 'Sasha?' he eventually asked, if his eyes were still playing tricks on him. 'What are you doing?'

'Forcing the confession out of my father – the one you seemed unable to get.'

'Confession?' Tanner asked, his forehead

creasing with confusion. 'For doing what?'

'For murdering my sister!' she spat, drawing the blade against the man's pulsating neck.

Watching her father's hands spasm as he began to suffocate under her deadly grip, Tanner stared back into Sasha's demonic gaze. 'If you don't take that bag off his head, you're going to kill him!'

'Oh, I'm sure he's fine,' she grinned. 'Besides, it's no more than he used to do to me, whilst raping me from behind, I may add. Tara as well, no doubt – which is probably how he ended up killing her.'

'OK, listen, Sasha,' Tanner continued, as her father's entire body began to twitch, 'we can talk about that later, but for now, you have to let him breathe!'

'Why the hell should I?'

'If you don't, then he's going to die. If he does, he'll never be able to confess.'

Relaxing her grip on the knife, Sasha seemed to think about that for a moment, before drawing it back. 'I reckon he's got another minute.'

'Another minute?' came Tanner's incredulous response.

'Or maybe two,' she added.

'OK, look – why don't you take the bag off, then we can talk about what you think he's done.'

'I don't need to. I already know.'

'But – you want him to confess, don't you?'

'I was expecting you to have made him do that for me.'

'But – we didn't arrest him for your sister's murder.'

'Which is why I had to work so hard to persuade you otherwise.'

'That your father murdered your sister?' Tanner asked, struggling to understand what she was saying.

'I thought you were going to arrest him,' she eventually continued. 'I mean, it was so fucking obvious. But instead you became fixated on the idea that it must have been someone from the article she'd been writing. So I was left with little choice but to persuade you otherwise.'

'And how did you try to do that?'

'By killing two birds with one stone – at least I killed two with a stone. The other I was forced to use a letter opener.'

'You're telling me it was you? You're the one who killed all those people?'

'The word "killed" seems a little strong,' she mused. '"Dispatched" is probably more suitable.'

'But – why?'

'You mean – apart from who they all were, and how they'd made Tara's life a living hell with their sordid notes and perverted death threats, ever since that day her friend was found hanging in Bluebell Wood?'

With Tanner struggling to grasp what she was saying, Sasha returned to him a breezy smile. 'Besides that,' she continued, 'I was trying to refocus your attention on my father. If you weren't prepared to arrest him for Tara's murder, then I thought the least you could do would be to charge him for the murder of the other men who'd made her life so miserable.'

'You killed all those people just to make your father look guilty?'

'Finally!' she exclaimed. 'And now that you're here, you can listen to him confess to how he sexually abused me, then my sister, before finally taking his twisted sex games too far to end up leaving her body tied to a mud weight at the bottom of Blackfleet Broad.'

Snatching the plastic bag off her father's head, she wrenched his chin back to stare down at his face. 'Did you hear that, Daddy? You're going to tell the nice little policeman here what you did to Tara.'

With her father gazing up at her through a pair of unseeing eyes, she pressed the knife against his neck. 'Tell him, Daddy, or swear to God I'm going to cut your throat!'

As a single tear rolled down the man's otherwise lifeless face, Sasha's head jolted back. 'Stop mucking about. Tell me what you did or I'm going to do it – just you watch me!'

Taking in the purple hue to the man's otherwise ashen grey face, Tanner pulled in a reluctant breath. 'It's too late, Sasha,' he quietly said. 'He's already dead.'

'He can't be,' she replied, still holding onto the knife. 'He's passed out, that's all.'

Taking his mouth between her hand, she glared down into his eyes. 'Wake up!' she screamed, digging her fingernails into his skin. 'I said wake up, you sick fucking bastard!'

Ripping her fingers away from his skin, she lifted her hand to slap him hard across the face, only for his head to fall first to the side before rolling steadily forward.

As Tanner saw Vicky step up behind him, he turned back to look at Sasha, gazing down at her father's lifeless corpse with a look of bewildered horror.

'I think you'd better come with us,' he eventually said, taking a step towards her.

'No – wait,' she breathed, her tear-filled eyes lifting to meet with his. 'He's going to be alright. He just needs time to recover.'

'He's dead, Sasha. You killed him,' said Tanner, in

a dispassionate tone.

'He's not dead – he – he can't be.'

'I'm sorry, but the colour of his skin is a bit of a giveaway. That, and the fact that he's not breathing.'

Hearing the sound of a distant siren, Tanner stepped forward once again.

'You're not taking me away!' Sasha cried, blinking tears from her eyes to stare dementedly at him. 'He's the one who killed Tara – not me!'

'We're not arresting you for Tara's murder.'

'What happened to the others is your fault – not mine!'

'But we didn't kill them, though, did we?'

'You left me with no choice!'

'We all have a choice, Sasha,' Tanner said, inching ever closer. 'Unfortunately, the ones you've made have led us to where we are now.'

Resting her eyes gently down onto her father's face, as if whispering to him an unspoken farewell, she lifted her gaze to Tanner once more. 'I'm sorry, Mr Tanner, but I'm not going to prison for something that wasn't my fault.'

'Unfortunately, I don't see that you have much of a choice.'

'You just told me that we all have a choice.'

'Not in this instance, I'm afraid.'

'I beg to differ,' she replied, holding the knife towards Tanner as she crept steadily forward.

Hearing at least two more sirens join the one growing steadily louder, Tanner held his ground. 'I really don't think that's a good idea.'

'Well, no, but you would say that, wouldn't you?' she replied, her mouth becoming a feral snarl.

'Apart from the fact that you'd have to kill me –

and my colleague as well – you wouldn't get very far, not with half of Norfolk's police about to land on the doorstep.'

As if hearing the sirens for the first time, Sasha gazed wistfully towards them.

'They'll be here any minute,' Tanner continued, trying to catch her eye, 'so I suggest you put the knife down and place your hands on top of your head.'

'There is one more option that has yet to be considered,' she said, still staring into space.

'We're not letting you go, if that's what you mean.'

'No, of course,' she replied, 'but that wasn't the option I was thinking of.'

With an unsettling feeling in the pit of his stomach, Tanner watched her lower the knife to her side before pulling herself up straight to face him.

Bringing his shoulders back, Tanner held her gaze. 'Drop the knife, Sasha. It's the only way.'

'As you said yourself, Mr Tanner,' she replied, the knife trembling in her delicate hand, 'we all have a choice. This one just happens to be mine.'

Within the blink of an eye, she lifted the knife to her throat.

'No – wait!' Tanner screamed, throwing himself at her only to watch in agonised horror as she drew the blade from one side to the other in a single, fatal move.

- EPILOGUE -

THREE DAYS LATER, Tanner was slumped behind his desk, staring at an unopened email from Forrester – one that had arrived a few minutes before. He didn't need to open it to know what it was about; the subject made it clear enough.

As his mind turned to Christine, then Samantha, he let out a weary sigh.

Pushing himself up to make yet another coffee, he heard a knock at the door.

'Go away,' he mumbled, only to see Vicky's head appear.

'Forgive me, Vicky,' he said, staring at her with belligerent foreboding, 'but I thought I told you to go away?'

'Sorry, boss. I thought you said, "Come in".'

'Since when did "Go away" sound like "Come in"?'

'When you're in one office, and I'm in another.'

'Well, you're here now. What is it?' he asked, returning his attention to his coffee machine.

'Actually, boss, I just thought I'd come in to see how you're doing?'

'Really well, thank you,' he replied, in a heavily sarcastic tone. 'At least, I will be when I can go home.'

'Did you hear any more from Forrester?'

'What about?'

'You know what about.'

'You mean – whether or not he's going to recommend that I'm kicked off the force for allowing his favourite Member of Parliament to fall through a hole in the top floor of an unfinished block of flats – after I'd caught him trying to dispose of the body of one of his colleagues, one who he hadn't murdered after all?'

'Something like that,' Vicky mused, closing the door behind her.

'Yes and no,' came his curt response.

'Yes *and* no?' Vicky repeated.

'Yes, as in there's an email from him about it that came in five minutes ago; and no, as in I haven't opened it yet.'

'Are you going to?'

'I wasn't planning on.'

'Then how are you going to find out what his decision is?'

'No doubt someone will tell me – probably when I turn up to work to find my replacement sitting here with his feet on my desk.'

As Tanner sat down to do just that, Vicky pulled out a chair for herself.

'I really think you should open it,' she said, making herself comfortable. 'For all you know, he's reached the conclusion that it wasn't your fault – being that you were just doing your job.'

'My job was to find the person responsible, not to allow an innocent man to plummet to his death – and not for the first time – either.'

'You can't win them all,' she replied, offering him a casual shrug.

'Maybe not all, but I should at least be able to win one occasionally.'

'I thought you did?'

'I'd hardly describe identifying Tara Lowe's murderer, only to watch him be suffocated to death at the hands of his eldest daughter – who then decides to kill herself right in front of our eyes – as a win. Would you?'

'Perhaps "win" isn't the right word,' Vicky replied, glancing absently around. 'We also didn't know she'd been receiving treatment for depression, or that she'd been diagnosed as a clinical sociopath. But putting that to one side for a moment – you said it was your job to find the person responsible.'

'Yes – and?'

'Well, it wasn't your job. It was mine – being that I was the SIO. If anyone's to be kicked off the force, it should be me.'

'But you weren't the one who chased Elliston off the top of a block of flats.'

'The report said he stepped back of his own accord.'

'The report that *you* wrote.'

'It was my report to write,' she replied, offering Tanner just the hint of a smile. 'That *was* what happened, wasn't it?'

'I suppose,' Tanner shrugged.

'There's one thing that is surprising me,' Vicky continued, leaning back in her chair.

'Which is?'

'Considering how much you disliked the man, that you're not a little more upbeat about the whole thing.'

'I wanted him to spend a lifetime behind bars, not a few bemused seconds plummeting to an instant death.'

A moment of silence followed, broken by Vicky,

shifting in her seat.

'You know,' she said, 'you never did tell me why you disliked him so much.'

'Another time,' Tanner muttered, reaching for his mouse to open Forrester's email – only to hear another knock at the door.

'GO AWAY!' they shouted in unison, leaving them smiling around at each other.

'Sorry to bother you, boss,' came Townsend's voice, his face appearing from the other side of the door, 'but there's someone in reception to see you.'

'Can't you deal with it?'

'She's asking specifically to speak to you, boss.'

'She's not some crazed axe-wielding maniac, I hope?'

'I don't think so. Although, saying that, she does have rather a large handbag. There *could* be an axe in it. Do you want me to check?'

'Is the handbag larger than Vicky's?'

'Er – no, boss. I don't think anyone has a handbag larger than Vicky's.'

'I'm right here!' Vicky exclaimed, sitting up in her chair to stare around at them. 'You do know that?'

'Remind me why that was again?' Tanner asked, raising a curious eyebrow at her.

'You know what – for the life of me, I can't remember,' she replied, pushing herself up to make her way out.

With Townsend still hovering in the doorway, Tanner looked at him to say, 'You're still here?'

'The lady? In reception?'

'If you really don't think you can deal with her, then I suppose you'd better show her in.'

Watching Townsend leave, Tanner waited for the

mysterious woman.

Deciding to leave Forrester's email till later, he closed the account to check how his online game of Battleships had been going. When he saw he'd lost yet another, he thought for a moment before launching his next missile.

A moment later, his unknown opponent sent one flying back in return, sending his flagship aircraft carrier to the bottom of an imaginary ocean.

Shaking his head in annoyance, he was about to retaliate when there was a knock at the door.

Refraining from shouting 'Go away!', he instead adjusted his tie to call out, 'Come in!'

'Miss Chloe Bennett to see you, boss,' said Townsend, stepping to one side to allow a petite, timid-looking young woman inside, dressed in a pair of tight-fitting jeans and a baggy T-shirt.

With her hovering by the door, Tanner stood up. 'Won't you come in?'

'Thank you,' she replied, glancing nervously at Townsend before stepping inside.

'Do take a seat,' Tanner continued, offering her the chair opposite.

With Townsend loitering by the door, Tanner shot him a look. 'Was there anything else, Detective Constable?'

'Er... no, boss,' came his reluctant reply, leaving him stepping gracefully away to close the door.

As the young woman made herself comfortable, Tanner offered her a drink.

'I'm all right, thank you,' she said, hoisting a large carpet bag onto her lap.

'How may I help?'

'You are Mr Tanner – I mean, Detective Chief Inspector Tanner?'

'On a good day,' he smiled.

'Then I have something I think you should see.'

Tanner raised an intrigued eyebrow as she began rummaging around inside her bag.

'I've only just found it,' she continued, still searching, 'else I'd have brought it in sooner. She'd left it inside a book I'd been reading – but it's been a while since I picked it up.'

Becoming increasingly curious, Tanner leaned over his desk to watch her finally pull out an envelope with a letter inside.

'It's from someone I think you know,' she said, holding it out for him.

Seeing tears pooling at the corners of her eyes, Tanner graciously took the envelope to lean back in his chair. As he removed the letter to begin to read, he heard her add quietly, 'She was always very good with words.'

'Is this from Tara Lowe?' he asked, glancing up.

'We were going out together,' said Chloe in a relieved tone, as if revealing a long-hidden secret. 'Before she... before she...'

'You're saying this is a suicide note?' Tanner enquired, as he continued to read.

'I think it's fairly obvious what it is,' Chloe replied, wiping at an escaping tear. 'Don't you?'

Tanner read the letter twice before setting it down, its weight far greater than the single page it filled. When he eventually looked up, he found Chloe, watching him with a look of desolate fragility.

'I'm sorry,' he eventually said. 'I honestly had no idea.'

'She'd been struggling for a long time. I'm just sorry it took me so long to find.'

'That's not your fault,' said Tanner, gazing wistfully away.

As he remembered what Forrester had told him to make sure of, shortly after Tara's body had been found, he knew exactly whose fault it was – and that meant only one thing. *He* was responsible for everything that had happened since: Sasha murdering all those people to make her father look guilty for something he hadn't done, only to end up taking her own life – and for what?

'Anyway,' said Chloe, climbing to her feet. 'I'd better be getting on.'

Seeing her look expectantly down at the letter, Tanner caught her eye. 'Is it alright if I keep this – for our records, I mean?'

Chloe hesitated for a moment, before saying, 'But – I will be able to have it back?'

'Yes – of course,' Tanner replied, folding it to place back into its envelope. 'Just a soon as the investigation has been officially closed.'

DCI John Tanner will return in The Watch House

- ABOUT THE AUTHOR -

David Blake is a No. 1 International Bestselling Author who lives in North London. At time of going to print he has written twenty-seven books, along with a collection of short stories. When not writing, David likes to spend his time mucking about in boats, often in the Norfolk Broads, where his crime fiction books are based.